Coram Boy

'Full of music, tension and colour, this enthralling story
brings vivid life to a hidden side of the eighteenth century'
Jenny Uglow

'*Coram Boy* is a glorious web of changing fortunes and subtle
intrigues. There is tragedy and corruption, hope and evil . . .
the genre of historical fiction has rarely been this good'
Amazon

'The different strands of the novel . . . come together in a
thrillingly satisfying conclusion'
Sunday Telegraph

'A rich and almost gothic drama unfolds, full of dastardly
villains, cold-hearted aristocrats, devoted friends and passionate
lovers, and set against a background of cruelty, music, murder
and the neglect of children. The story sweeps along with
great exuberance'
Philip Pullman, *Guardian*

'A powerful family saga . . . a stunning new novel'
Books for Keeps

Also by Jamila Gavin

The Blood Stone
The Singing Bowls
The Wormholers
From Out of the Shadows
Three Indian Princesses
Three Indian Goddesses

THE SURYA TRILOGY
The Wheel of Surya
The Eye of the Horse
The Track of the Wind

For younger readers

Danger by Moonlight
Fine Feathered Friend
Grandpa Chatterji
Grandpa's Indian Summer

Coram Boy

JAMILA GAVIN

EGMONT

For Sarianne,
who gave me the tools of the trade.

First published in Great Britain in 2000
Reissued 2004
by Egmont UK Limited, 239 Kensington High Street, London W8 6SA

Text copyright © 2000 Jamila Gavin

The moral right of the author has been asserted.

ISBN 978 1 4052 1282 3

7 9 10 8 6

A CIP catalogue record for this title is available
from the British Library

Typeset by Avon Dataset Ltd, Bidford on Avon
Printed and bound in Great Britain by the CPI Group

Contents

PART TWO – 1750

Foreword

I t was a passing remark which triggered the story – as is so often the way with writers. A friend murmured something about 'the Coram man' in the eighteenth century: someone who collected abandoned children, ostensibly to deliver them to the newly founded Coram Hospital for the Maintenance and Education of Exposed and Deserted Children. But the Hospital had never employed such a man, and any so-called Coram man was acting on his own, and most likely in his own interests without any regard for either the abandoned children or the miserable women who had entrusted their pathetic offspring into his safe-keeping. Indeed, the highways and by-ways of England were littered with the bones of little children. Children in the eighteenth century were routinely brutalised, whether it was at home or at Eton College, whether it was in the parish orphanages, which were no more than dying houses, or in the cathedral choir schools. It was often entirely a matter of luck if a child was kindly and lovingly reared, and it was to redress this that Captain Thomas Coram opened his hospital in 1741. It was people like him who gradually changed the whole perception of child care and who touched the conscience of the nation.

When I heard this, it was as if my brain became a stage. The story seemed to have been there all along, and my characters made their appearances fully formed and demanding my attention. I think I have loved these characters almost more than any I have ever created, and I still find myself grieving for those who were not so lucky as the Coram boy.

Once I let it be known that I was writing a book set in the eighteenth century, so many friends and acquaintances fed me with historical facts and details, some trivial, some important – but all of which were of invaluable help to me as I tried to immerse myself in the period. I must thank Peter Patten from whom, over fifteen years ago, I actually first heard the name Coram and who sowed the first seed of the story; Robert Eagle, who thought there was a terrific story to be told; Vivien Richmond, Marlyn Leese, Robin Lunn, Rajan Chet Singh and John Irving, who went beyond the call of friendship in providing me with information and inspiration; Lowinger Madison, librarian at Gloucester Cathedral; and Jenny Uglow, for her encouragement and for taking the precious time off to read the manuscript. Most of all, I must thank my editors: Miriam Hodgson, who never wavered in her patient support through all the doubts and fears as I trod new ground, and Cally Poplak who, with her meticulous eye and rigorous attention to detail, constantly kept me on my mettle.

The Coram Foundation exists today in Coram Fields. A manuscript of the *Messiah* is held in their archives (the *Messiah* was performed at the hospital in May, but for the purpose of my story I have moved it to December) and the portrait by Hogarth of Sir Thomas Coram still hangs there. The foundation's work on behalf of children goes on.

The following books were of invaluable help to me in my research: *Coram's Children* by Ruth McClure, *Hogarth* by Jenny Uglow, *A History of England in the Eighteenth Century* by Roy Porter and *The Singing Game* by Iona and Peter Opie, from which I adapted a number of rhymes.

Jamila Gavin
September 2000

Prologue

'A fine lady went to Stowe Fair. She was pregnant for the first time and, keen to know what the future held for her, she consulted an old gypsy woman.

' "Why, my dear, I do believe you will have seven babies," said the gypsy woman studying her hand. The fine lady went away and thought no more about it.

'When the time came for her child to be born, a midwife was summoned to attend the labour. "What have we here?" she exclaimed as she delivered first one baby, then another and another.

' "Oh no!" cried the young wife, remembering the gypsy's prophecy. "That can't be so!" She wept. But sure enough, one by one, seven little baby girls were born and laid into a basket.

'The fine lady was upset fit to die. "I don't care what the gypsy prophesied; I will only keep one baby. Take the other six away," she begged the midwife. "Drown them in the river, but whatever you do, don't tell my husband," and she pressed a purse of silver into her hand.

'So the midwife took the basket of six babies down to the river. But on the way she met the husband, a fine gentleman. He heard little squealings and noises. "Pray, what have you in that basket?" he asked.

' "Oh it's nothing but six little kittens I am going to drown in the river," quoth she.

' "I'm going that way myself," said he. "Give them to me. I shall deal with them." Whereupon, he took the basket and rode down to the river.

'When the husband got to the riverbank and opened the basket, what did he see, but six little newborn girls. He frowned a dark, dreadful frown, then closing the basket took it away to a secret place.

'Seven years passed. The gentleman and his fine lady prepared to celebrate their daughter's birthday and to give thanks to God for preserving her through infancy. First they would go to church for a special service, then afterwards throw a party to which the whole village was invited.

' "And what shall our daughter wear for this special day?" the husband asked his wife.

' "Because she was born in October, I shall stitch her a dress of autumn colours," the fine lady told him.

'The little girl's birthday dawned and she was all decked out in nut-brown velvet trimmed in red. The gentleman and his fine lady set off for the church with their pretty little daughter between them.

'They sat in the front pew and said their prayers. The organ played, the choir sang. The minister raised his hand to give the blessing and make the sign of the cross, but he was interrupted. The east door of the church swung open. Everyone turned to see who had arrived so late. There standing in the threshold were six little girls, all dressed in nut-brown velvet trimmed in red. All were identical to the fine lady's daughter.

'At the sight of them, the fine lady gave one dreadful scream and fell down dead.'

The children clustered round the nursemaid were silent as she ended.

'That's a sad story,' one whispered at last.

'It's a sad world out there,' agreed the nursemaid. 'Now come on, Nanny says it's time for bed.'

There came six maids on their knee.
When do they come?
They come by night as well as by day,
To take your little child away.

My little child is yet too young,
To stay away from his mam.
Whether he's old or whether he's young
We'll take him as he am.

Part One – 1741

Chapter One

★

The Coram man

'Oi! Meshak! Wake up, you lazy dolt!' The sound of the rough voice set the dogs barking. 'Can't you see one of the panniers is slipping on that mule there! Not that one, you nincompoop,' as the boy leapt guiltily from the wagon and darted in an agitated way among the overloaded animals, 'that one – there – fifth one back! Yes. Fool of a boy. Why was I so cursed with a son like you? I don't have to have eyes in the back of my head to know that one of the mules had his load slipping. What goes on inside that addled brain of yours?'

A man and his boy were coming out of the forest with a wagon and a train of six mules. They were heading for the ferry at Framilodes Passage, which would take them across the River Severn and on to the city of Gloucester.

'Why I don't ditch you is more than I can say. Thank your lucky stars that blood is thicker than water. Tighten him up properly. Don't want no hold ups now. We can just catch the ferry before nightfall if we hurry!'

Otis Gardiner, pots man, Jack-of-all-trades and smooth-tongued entrepreneur, ranted non-stop. It was a side of Otis that not everyone saw; he could be so attractive, so charming, so sweetly spoken. A young man still, he had wide, appealing, brown eyes and shoulder-length red-brown hair drawn back to show off his broad, handsome brow. He could barter the hind leg off a donkey – especially if the donkey was a lady. By flirting with the wives, bantering with the gentlemen, demonstrating magic tricks to little children, he could persuade a customer to part with twice as much money as they should, all the while making them think they had themselves a bargain.

Meshak tightened the straps round the mule's belly. He ignored the faint kitten-like wails which came from the sacks and tried not to look at the sneering face of the man he called his father. From his driving seat Otis peered round the covered wagon and flicked his whip at him. Jester, the brown scraggy lurcher, shadowed Meshak among the mules as the boy tried to compensate for his negligence by meticulously checking all the panniers. The other dogs, tied to the wagon by bits of string, barked their heads off and leapt and twisted in a frenzied bid to pull free. They didn't calm down till Meshak and Jester were back on the wagon.

Meshak was an awkward lad. At fourteen he was taller than his father and growing. But he looked as if he had been put together all wrong; his body was all over the place, his head too large, his ears too sticking out, his lips never quite closing. There seemed always to be a sleeve at his runny nose. His arms and legs dangled from his body, uncoordinated and clumsy; he dropped things, tripped over things, fumbled and stumbled. All this meant that people – especially his father – shouted at him, cuffed him, jeered and sneered at him, so his whole look was that of a cowering dog. If he had had a tail, it would have always been between his legs, as he slunk by waiting for the next kick. He had a vulnerable, infantile look, with his pale-freckled face beneath a stack of wild red hair, and his large, watery, blue eyes, which often stared round at the world with incomprehension. But no one ever saw him cry or laugh. People called him a simpleton – a loon – and wondered why his father hadn't abandoned him years ago. People assumed that he was nothing but an empty vessel, lacking in all substance, feeling or emotion; neither able to love nor in need of being loved.

How could Meshak speak of his terrors? There was no one to tell except Jester. He saw trolls and witches; evil creatures crouching in shadows, lingering round trees, hanging in the sky; demons with hairless heads and glinting teeth. He never knew when they would come to poke and prod him, to torment his sleep and rampage through his head. Even now, the darkness of the forest they had just left behind seemed to be creeping down the road after them, gobbling up their tracks, soon to consume them too.

His father was mean with the lamps and only kept one up in front for the road ahead, so Meshak hated being out on the highway at night. He was afraid of the dark. It was not just the spirit world which frightened him, but the real world of robbers and highwaymen, especially near the forest. And then there were the wild animals. He hated the green eyes which glimmered in the dense undergrowth, and the scufflings and gruntings of unseen creatures stalking among the trees.

Most of all he hated the pathetic squeals which came from the sacks bumping against the scraggy flanks of the mules, and the task Otis and he often performed at night in some bleak lonely place. He never told anyone of the frightful nightmares he had, and how he had learnt to smother his gasping whimpers lest he woke his father. He never told anyone of the faces and voices and clutching fingers of all those children, who drifted like lost spirits through his dreams.

He glimpsed the tall towers of Gloucester Cathedral in a distant smoky haze, and his heart leapt. He loved churches because there were angels there, sometimes within gleaming stained-glass windows or out in the graveyards; stone angels with gentle hands and loving faces. He would go to the cathedral as soon as he could and find his favourite angel. His father would usually abandon him in the city and go off for days on end, making his deals, meeting his contacts, disappearing into the pubs and taverns to indulge in gambling, dog-baiting, womanising and furthering his career. Meshak knew his ambition was boundless. He would not stay a pots man. Meshak, meanwhile, would live and sleep in the wagon. With the few pence he was given, he could fend for himself, especially as he always had Jester.

'Get on up front, boy!' A yell from his father indicated that he had spotted someone on the roadside. Otis liked to have his 'idiot' son up next to him during certain transactions. It gave him the air of being a devoted and caring father; a man you could trust and entrust with secrets. Meshak dutifully climbed up next to him.

With a shock of pleasure he saw the vast shining back of the river, so close now. The first tremulous lights of the fires and torches were being lit along the riverbank as dusk deepened into evening. Great hulks of ships brooded at anchor, and small craft scuttered like insects to and fro across the surface. Silhouetted tall and stiff as a scarecrow was the ferryman standing on his punt with pole in hand, about to embark with a full load of passengers, sheep and mules and baskets of goods. Corgis barked and scuttled in and out of the other animals' legs to keep them from bunching together.

Otis and Meshak were in a queue of at least three drovers' trains ahead of them, each with their thirty or so head of cattle, so they would be lucky to get across before nightfall.

'Pots, pots, pans and pots, griddles and ladles, kettles and skillets, mugs and jugs, knives, forks and spoons, farming tools, all Cornish tin and Newcastle iron,' Otis sang out in his trader's patter.

'The charity man's here!' A murmur went round. Word had gone on ahead that he was coming and some had waited for him.

In recent times, Meshak had got used to his father being called a 'charity man', though it had puzzled him. A wayfaring minister to whom they had once given a lift told him that in the Bible the word 'charity' meant 'love'. It was true that a lucrative part of his father's business as a travelling man was to collect abandoned, orphaned and unwanted children – many from local churches and poorhouses – and take them to the ever increasing number of mills that were springing up throughout the country. Otis always called the children 'brats' – as if, like rats, they were really vermin – but he made money out of them. Older boys, he handed over to regiments and naval ships, which were always on the lookout for soldiers and sailors to fight whatever wars were going on with the Prussians or the French abroad or the Jacobites up in the north. Down at the docks of London, Liverpool, Bristol and Gloucester, he made deals with ships who took both girls and boys to North Africa, the Indies or the Americas, along with their cargoes of slaves, cloth, timber and metal.

That may have been considered by some to be an act of charity, but Meshak wasn't at all sure that it was love. He only had a vague idea about what love was. He thought he had been loved by his mother, though he could hardly remember her. She used to hug him and kiss him; she had played with him and told him stories. Then one day she had died and was gone for ever, and no one ever hugged or kissed him again, except for Jester – if you count face-licking, tail-wagging and jumping up a dog's way of hugging and kissing. Meshak knew he loved his dog and that Jester loved him, but he would never have called that charity.

The children whom his father picked up on the open road or in small villages, towns and cities, and took into his wagon as an act of charity, never looked happy or grateful. They were usually handed over roughly, received roughly, fed little, beaten often. All in all, Meshak couldn't say that either they, or indeed himself, were loved. If this was love, it was also business. Money changed hands, sometimes a lot of it.

But Meshak accepted that his father was a good and Christian man because everyone said he was. He was admired for this most Christian virtue, charity.

The sky was darkening not just with evening, but with a cloud bank of dark, purple rain expanding across the sky. A spiral of gulls circle-danced across the surface of the river; the evening light turned their white underbellies to silver. A few foresters and farming people converged eagerly on their wagon, bearing tools which needed sharpening, mending or exchanging.

Meshak knew what to do. He pulled back the flaps of the wagon and lifted out the pots and pans, knife-sharpeners, meat hooks, scissors, graters, mincers, goblets, griddles, knives and axes, as well as knick-knacks like combs and beads, bobbins and cottons, balls of string, trinkets and baubles. He spread out a large piece of sail cloth in a clearing by the side of the road and laid everything out so they could finger and question and calculate their terms for bargaining.

Meshak was up to dealing with simple transactions so, while he bartered, his father moved away in deep conversation with a well-dressed man, who led him into the cottage. He was not a wigged gentleman but a parish man with his hair drawn back under a broad-brimmed hat and wearing brown wool breeches and leather boots.

The skies darkened further and the first plops of rain thudded to earth. The queue for the ferry had shortened to just one wagon in front now, and Meshak had already repacked the wagon by the time Otis reappeared.

'Get these brats in,' he muttered. He referred to five solemn, poorly clad children in tow: a girl and a boy as young as three and five, who clutched each other's hand tightly, and the rest – all boys – aged eight and nine years old. The children were silent, as though they had been born learning to stifle their fears. They allowed Meshak to herd them into the back of the wagon.

When the children were in place, tucked round the sides, still mute, still staring, Meshak and Otis began to separate the train of mules from the wagon. The ferryman was impatient now, looking anxiously at the stormy sky and the low sun, and urged them to hurry.

Otis tugged the reins down over the wagon mule's ears and roughly cajoled it on to the ferry. The nervous animal resisted, unwilling to step on to the rocking craft, until a sharp stroke of the whip made it leap aboard with a clatter of hooves. Otis pulled a sack over the animal's head to blinker it from the heaving water. He had just about cajoled a fourth mule on to the ferry when a woman's voice called out softly, 'Are you the Coram man?'

Meshak turned to see. He was surprised that his father reacted instinctively, as if that had always been his name. Meshak had never heard it before. Otis tossed Meshak the reins. 'The boy will see them on,' he yelled to the ferryman, and as Meshak took the reins and soothed the frightened mule, his father had already leapt ashore.

It was no housemaid or potato picker, like so many others who had hailed him, but a gentlewoman who, though trying to look modest and inconspicuous, was unmistakably a lady. Even had her refined voice not given her away, the cut and cloth of her cloak betrayed her. Her head was lowered into a basket, which she hugged tightly to herself, and she hung back in the shadows of the trees on the riverbank, trying not to be seen or identified.

The transaction was rapid. A heavy purse of money went into Otis's pouch and he took the basket with a great show of reverence and concern, as if he would protect it with his life. Meshak heard the lady give one short, pitiful shriek of grief, quickly stifled. Otis leapt back on to the wagon and thrust the bundle into Meshak's arms. 'Look caring,' he muttered, 'till we're on the other side.'

The ferry pulled away, but the woman continued to stand stiffly at the water's edge, watching them. Meshak felt her eyes fixed on them all the way across. She was still standing there when they disembarked.

Chapter Two

★

The Black Dog

The rain came down with a vengeance. The wind swished through the trees, making them bend and sway. The road turned to mire, and they still had two or three miles before they reached Gloucester city centre. The mules bowed their heads into the driving rain. The squeaks and mewlings in the sacks ceased. The wooden wheels ground along the deep, water-logged ruts, heavy with wet, sticky, clinging mud which sent out a spray with every turn and coated the dogs outside. Their legs kept running incessantly, also sending out muddy sprays; running, running, because they had no choice but to keep their legs moving, tied as they were to the axle. Jester was lucky; as Meshak's dog he was allowed in the wagon.

Meshak pulled the flaps tightly shut to keep out the damp cold. The brats all looked at him with long, doleful glances as he snuggled up to Jester for warmth. He shut his eyes so as not to witness their despair. He felt hungry. They felt hungry. They were starving, probably hadn't eaten since dawn. He didn't want to know. Didn't want to think about it. He had an apple in his pocket. He took it out with his eyes still closed and began to munch. He knew they were staring at him, their eyes huge with longing. He ate it as quickly as he could and fed the core to Jester. There was a shudder of repressed envy from the brats. They would have fallen eagerly on it and eaten every scrap if they could. Jester swallowed the core in a gulp.

It was dark now. The rain still beat down on the canvas covering and, for a while, they were mesmerised by the rhythmic swish and sway of the wagon and the hollow slurpy plod of the animals' hooves. There was a stir of surprise and a quiver of anxiety among the children when the creaking of the wheels stopped and they came to a halt. Apart from the sound of the rain and the snorting of mules, blowing away the rain from their nostrils, there was no other sound.

They were not yet within earshot of the city. Meshak sat up, his arms still clasped round Jester. The brats' eyes gleamed in the darkness. They seemed not to have moved a muscle since he had climbed inside to get out of the rain half an hour ago. He heard Otis jump down. The light of his lantern swung a yellow shaft across the canvas. Then the flap opened and his dark drenched face looked in. Rain was spangled through his thick, straggly hair, reflecting in the light like so many diamonds. He nodded curtly to Meshak. 'Get the spade. There's a good ditch just here. We'll dig them in,' he jerked his head in the direction of the panniers strapped to the train of mules. 'I don't want to take them into Gloucester.' Meshak jumped out and had to tie the flap to keep Jester in, so he then set up a continuous barking. Meshak knew from many, many times before that they couldn't have Jester digging anything up.

It was a hurried affair in all that wind and rain and darkness and the swinging light from the storm lantern, which Otis hung on a branch directly over the ditch. Otis plunged in his spade. Nothing too deep or careful. There was a lot of water. Just dig a hole deep enough to submerge the bundles. Foxes would do the rest. He wouldn't have bothered burying them had he not taken money for them and given undertakings. Otis dug and Meshak went from mule to mule, extricating one bundle after another from the panniers to hand to his father, who dropped them like seeds into the ditch. Meshak stared wonderingly as they sank into the mud and vanished even before his father had shovelled a few spadefuls of earth over them. What was it like to be dead? Meshak tried to imagine. What did they see under the mud? Would they find angels there; angels like the ones he saw in church windows?

They came to the last one – the one the lady had given them on the other side. Meshak hesitated. 'Come on, lad – drop it in!' rasped Otis.

'Moving. Still alive,' stammered Meshak. Usually, if they

weren't dead, they at least tried to sell them off first.

'Not worth it. Drop it in, I say.'

Meshak let go the feebly moving bundle. He heard it splosh into the ditch. He backed away whimpering. He never did like burying the live ones. He felt the apple he had just eaten rise with the bile up his gullet. He vomited against a tree, leaning his head into the bark so that it left its imprint on his brow.

'Don't go lily-livered on me,' snarled Otis, grabbing his coat and herding his son back to the wagon. Jester was still barking. 'Go on, get in. Mrs Peebles is expecting us tonight at the Black Dog.' Jester stopped barking.

Meshak didn't need eyes to know they had entered Gloucester. Despite the constant thud of rain on to the canvas covering, he heard the swell of sound. It came towards them like a distant wave and then crashed over them; an overwhelming cacophony of babble, all the stuff of humans and their animals and their livelihoods. He had been dozing, lying with his face still partly buried in Jester's fur, relishing the sounds of the city while not yet ready to face it. He didn't even open the flap when he heard the wagon and the mules' hooves clattering over cobblestones; nor when he smelt the stench of open sewers and foraging pigs, and the manure of horses and mules, and wet straw intermingled with women's perfume and polished leather and charcoal fires and grilled fish. He knew without looking, by the heavy smell of beer and the raucous sounds of fiddling and singing, that they had entered the courtyard of the Black Dog inn.

No good getting too excited yet. There were jobs to be done: the wagon unhitched, the mules unloaded, water pumped, hay gathered, stable space negotiated . . .

'I want to piss,' whimpered a child.

Oh yes, and the brats seen to. He would have to rope them all together so they wouldn't run away, and lead them out of the far gate to relieve themselves in all that rain and mud, and then go to the kitchen and get them some gruel. It reminded him of how hungry he was.

It was still raining. Girls in bonnets and shawls slopped across the yard to and from the kitchen, fetching and carrying water for the cook, or chickens for the slaughter, and buckets of swill and scrapings for the animals. Young lads, eager to make a few pennies, rushed forward to grab the bridles and lead the mules to the barns, clamouring to offer their services. Otis selected three of them, yelled out orders, and then made for the door of the inn. 'See to things. I'll be inside,' he yelled, leaving Meshak squelching about in the yard, ankle-deep in mud and manure.

Meshak 'saw to things' as he always did, but began to feel his stomach tightening with hunger, especially with a smell of roast beef coming from the kitchen. He was almost tempted to eat the gruel dolloped out from the kitchen for the brats, though just looking at it made him want to puke. He was sure even the pigs wouldn't eat it. But the brats fell upon it. He took the wagon and children into a barn to stay for the night. As he closed the huge wooden doors, one of the brats called out plaintively, 'Can't we have a light, mister?' Meshak didn't bother to answer and, pulling the doors to, dropped the great latch and locked them into the pitch, rat-scuttling darkness.

He went to look for Otis and pushed his way into the dark inn with Jester at his heels. The atmosphere was choking with smoke and stuffiness. In a corner by the roaring fire, red-faced musicians and sailors, entwined with young women, jigged and sang, glad to be on dry land after months at sea. Others played cards and, in a further room, serious gambling was going on.

Meshak squinted through the haze and at last discovered his father deep in conversation with a naval man. These days, Otis made more from selling boys on to the ships than anything else. They would sell the three older boys he had just brought in.

Meshak managed to squeeze himself on to the bench next to Otis, who grabbed a passing barmaid. 'Hey, darling!' He pulled her down on his knee, causing ale to splash out of the four tankards she was carrying, two in each hand.

'Now look what you've made me do,' she giggled. As it was Otis, she wasn't cross. 'Good to see you, Otis,' she purred.

He burrowed into her neck and then murmured, 'Is Mrs Peebles in her parlour?'

The barmaid tut-tutted with exaggerated disappointment and wriggled off his knee. 'Why is it you always fancy her more than me?' she pouted.

' 'Cos she's prettier!' He slapped her bottom and they both laughed.

'She's back there. Shall I tell her you're here?'

'Do that, my sweet, and while you're about it bring me and the boy some ale and meat.'

'Hello, Meshak,' she purred, tweaking his chin before weaving her way through the crowd and disappearing into the kitchen.

It was an hour later, after Meshak and Otis had drunk several pints of ale and consumed a full plate of meat and potatoes and dumplings, when the barmaid came and said Mrs Peebles could see him. Otis got to his feet and, like shadows, Meshak and Jester followed him through the dense crowd and out of a far door which led into a dark narrow passageway at the back. It was instantly chillier and Meshak shivered. He knew Mrs Peebles' parlour. Whenever they passed through Gloucester, Otis always called in.

Otis reached her door and was about to knock when it opened. A woman holding a flickering taper stood in the doorway taking her leave. Meshak gawped up at her. She was not young and the bright colours of her clothes, her body squeezed in at the waist and bodice, her flounced-up hair and rouged face, were all part of an effort to knock a decade off her age. 'Ah yes . . . Lady Philomena,' she spoke in a heavy confidential way, 'now that young woman is one to watch, Mrs Peebles, you mark my words. There's powerful talk of goings on up at the house with the tutor. A German, you know and–' The woman stopped abruptly. 'What you staring at, you insolent pup?' she said sharply, pushing Meshak away, but then she saw Otis standing there, a slight smile on his face. She held her taper up as if to see him better. The shadows wavered around them, encircling the flame. 'Oh! It's you,' she simpered. 'The boy's got bigger. I didn't recognise him. I think you have a visitor, Mrs Peebles,' she called over her shoulder. 'Good to see you, Otis. I hope you're keeping in good health. Will you be coming up to Ashbrook this time? We could do with our knives sharpening and a few new pots, perhaps?' The woman in the doorway tipped her head flirtatiously.

'Nothing would keep me away, Mrs Lynch.'

'Goodnight, Mrs Peebles,' Mrs Lynch called out, without taking her eyes off Otis. 'See you in the morning.' As she sidled past, Meshak shrank back in case he received another blow and watched her go, looping her skirts over her free arm as she climbed the narrow winding stairs to the bedrooms above the inn.

'Sleep well, Mrs Lynch,' answered Mrs Peebles from within.

'Mrs Peebles!' Otis greeted her from the doorway, leaning nonchalantly, one arm up against the lintel as if he held it up.

Meshak peered beneath his father's arm into the parlour beyond, where a lady draped in a veil sat at a round table. No one crossed Mrs Peebles. She had been born nothing but a bargee's daughter; no education, no position. But she had such intelligence, such a snake-like ability to target a person's weaknesses, such an ear for gossip, scandal and innuendo, that people feared her. It was said she had been employed as a spy in her youth – when she was beautiful, and able to mix with any company, especially the foreigners who came through the city – and was clever enough to entrap or compromise anyone targeted by her paymasters. Now she wasn't beautiful; although she was old enough to be Meshak's grandmother, it wasn't age which had spoilt her looks, but smallpox. He sensed his father wince and drop his eyes as she pulled her veil across her ravaged, pitted face.

Pushing Meshak into a corner to sit and wait, Otis strode towards her, smiling that restrained half-smile which usually did more to soften the hearts of women than the effusive lace-handkerchief-sweeping charm of so many men trying too hard to please. He knew she despised them anyway, for if it's one thing a woman with such a disability can cut through with a knife, it's cant and false flattery.

He kissed her hand. She waved him to sit down opposite her.

The double candlestick with its broad flapping flame favoured him, while leaving her in a kinder shadow from which she could scrutinise her visitor without effort.

Meshak settled on the floor with his arms clasped round Jester. The ale had made him sleepy.

'What about him?' Mrs Peebles indicated Meshak.

'No need to trouble yourself. His body's got bigger, but his brain is still soft as it always was. He won't say nothing.'

Meshak knew that his father and Mrs Peebles had been doing business together since before he was born. Otis had just been a lad when she spotted him. He was born a wheeler-dealer, already knowing how to make himself useful, dependable and indispensable. She took him on as a boy and liked to think she turned him into a man – the kind of man she could use and control. She liked to gather young men around her – those she felt she could groom and manipulate and trust to get involved in her various enterprises.

'I hear they've given you a new name,' she said, pouring out some gin from a large earthenware jug.

'Pots man, charity man – even Mrs P's man – so? What's in a name?' He shrugged.

'They are calling you a Coram man. What's that?'

Meshak looked up. How did she know? He himself had only heard it for the first time today by the river.

Otis shrugged.

'Come on, Otis, don't play coy with me. What does it mean?' demanded Mrs Peebles. Her eyes gleamed at him with intense curiosity. 'What have you been up to that I don't know about?'

'Nothing that you don't know about, Mrs P.' Otis leant back, still smiling. 'It's the same old business: brats. Just another angle. Haven't you heard of Coram?'

'I know of a Thomas Coram, the sea captain. I thought he was in America. Came this way sometimes. Didn't have anything on him though. Clean as a whistle. Do you mean him?'

'Look, Mrs P,' said Otis, leaning forward conspiratorially. 'I think I may have hit on something good, something which can benefit us both, if we cooperate.'

'*You* have always cooperated with *me* in the past,' muttered Mrs Peebles. 'Are you asking *me* to cooperate with *you?*' She cackled scornfully.

'Suit yourself. Yes, it is Captain Coram. He's in London now. Given up seafaring and turned to good works. He's something of a *benefactor!*' There was derision in his tone as Otis said, 'Wants to save the poor children of England. He's set up a hospital, an institution for foundlings. But I tell you something, it's not just the poor children he's saving but the brats of the rich. Word has spread about the thousands of pounds being poured into his enterprise to feed, clothe and educate bastards – thousands, Mrs P. Money coming from the wealthy to salve their consciences and purchase their respectability. I saw it for myself. I was in London last year. I saw the rich carriages, the fine weeping ladies hiding their faces behind Spanish lace veils, leaving their illegitimate babies in satin-lined baskets with a pouch of gold coins tucked under their pillows. "Otis," I said to myself, "if there's not something to be gained in all this for me, I'll eat my hat." '

'So? And have you turned this to your advantage?' enquired Mrs Peebles softly. 'Blackmail?'

'That – and other sidelines.' He took another swig of gin straight from the jug. 'You know things develop for themselves if you let them. I've been developing my sidelines.'

Mrs Peebles leant forward into the light. 'Tell me more.'

Meshak's head lolled as he drifted into sleep. He thought about Captain Thomas Coram, a charity man like his father. Loves little children. His brain filled with images; dreams overwhelmed him. He saw angels and children soaring among the stars, but he was drowning and, as he drowned, he called out, 'Save me, save me!' But no one heard him.

Then there came a great galleon with billowing sails, tossed in an ocean of sky and clouds. Meshak could see the outline of a captain at its helm. 'Save me, save me!' he yelled, but his voice was lost in a chorus of singing angels and children, their voices mingling with the gulls as he sank down, down beneath the waves.

He awoke suddenly, just when he thought he had drowned. Jester had jumped to his feet, his body taut, his fur raised, his ears pricked, and he whined softly between bared teeth. Meshak looked around. The room was empty, the candle almost out. His father and Mrs Peebles had gone. In the pre-dawn darkness, when most of the city was finally silent, even the people of the night were subdued. The gambling had ceased, the drunkards were asleep, the servants, lackeys, labourers and traders had all surrendered their limbs and brains to the secret world of the unconscious. Only sailors watching for the dawn tide were up, and the nightwatchmen, huddled near fires in between doing their rounds. They could be heard whistling at regular intervals all over the city or calling out the time on the hour to reassure their employers that they were still alert and that all was well.

One of the inn dogs started to bark frantically. It set off the other dogs, including Jester. His fur bristled all along his spine. 'Hush, boy, hush!' Meshak clamped a hand over his muzzle. Wide awake now. Keeping his hand over the dog's mouth, Meshak staggered to his feet. He should check the mules and the wagon. He peered out into the yard. The wind buffeted a lantern hanging from a hook, causing shadows to swing like a ship tossing at sea.

Then from an upstairs window he saw another light, a steady
flame which lit up the pale face of Mrs Lynch peering out into the
night. Meshak thought she would close her window and return to
bed, but she didn't. She seemed to be observing something going
on in the lane, which only she could see from upstairs. Curious,
Meshak wandered across the yard with Jester padding silently
beside him.

He pushed open a door in the wall and stepped into a side
lane. In the clouded moonlight, he dimly perceived a small
carriage harnessed to a single white horse. He glanced up and saw
that Mrs Lynch was watching it too.

The cathedral clock had just tolled four. Someone moved
out of the shadows carrying a low light; it was the cloaked
figure of a woman. Could it be Mrs Peebles? He edged closer.
Certainly it was roughly her height. The carriage door opened
and the woman went forward. Meshak couldn't see who was
inside. All he saw by the light of the lantern was a basket being
passed out. The hands that gave the basket stayed outstretched
– the empty fingers seeming unsure – then, abruptly, they were
withdrawn and the carriage door was slammed shut, and
Meshak glimpsed the coat of arms of a leaping deer entwined in
letters he couldn't read. The figure turned away with the basket
as the carriage moved off swiftly. Meshak pressed himself hard
up against the wall, hugging Jester into silence as Mrs Peebles

hurried past him. Then the tavern dogs stopped barking and the lane was empty again. The transaction lasted a minute.

Meshak looked up again at the window but it was closed. He tapped his thigh softly, 'Come on, Jester,' and went back to finish the night in the stables.

Meshak had been dead asleep when he was woken by a fierce kick.

'Get up, damn you,' snarled Otis. He looked red eyed and short of sleep himself. 'We've got to get rid of these brats before we take on any more. Get 'em up.'

Meshak got the children up, snivelling and sniffing with anxiety, afraid of what was going to happen to them. He took them into the yard. Otis had already got the mule harnessed up to the wagon. 'Get 'em inside,' he snarled.

Meshak bundled them in and Jester too, then went over to the pump to drink and splash his face. As he did, Mrs Peebles and Mrs Lynch passed each other in the yard.

'What the deuce was all that about in the lane last night? It was you, wasn't it?' he heard Mrs Lynch say. 'Out there in the lane last night?'

Mrs Peebles stopped short, looked hard at Mrs Lynch, paused for a split second and said without batting an eyelid: 'Not me, dearie. I was tucked up and dead to the world all night.'

Meshak saw that brief pause and thought, She's lying, I wonder why?

Mrs Lynch saw it too, but decided she would bide her time. If there was anything important to learn, she would find it out.

Chapter Three

*

Meshak's angel

'Come on!' roared Otis, and flicked his whip across Meshak's back to hurry him up. Meshak clambered into the wagon and they rumbled out into the street, heading for the dockside.

Down at the docks, Otis found a press gang and, for a fee, handed the three older boys over to the navy. What a palaver that was. One of the little ones – a younger sister – had screamed and clung to her brother, and would not be prised off until Otis struck her such a blow, she had fallen unconscious. As Meshak carried her away, he could hear the boys hollering and fighting and kicking, and they had to be carted off and tossed down a ship's hold to cool off. They would be well down river now, heading out to sea and then North Africa.

Otis came back, grumbling and snarling. Meshak knew to stay well out of arm's length when his father was in this mood. If it weren't for the fact that there was money to be earned in this area, Otis wouldn't have touched snivelling brats with a barge pole. But there was money – much money – especially if he could tap into those wealthy families who would pay any amount to protect their respectability. Having dealt with the older boys, there were the little ones to see to. Once more the wagon rolled on, this time into the city. Mrs Peebles had told him of a weaver and a milliner both requiring small children to work for them.

Later, Meshak wandered away from the docks among the pedlars and traders, often pausing wide-eyed to gawp at a street entertainer, a dancing bear or a tinker juggling with a dozen plates while yelling out his prices. He headed for the cathedral and at last arrived at the south door. He picked his way through the hordes of homeless children who congregated at evening, like the starlings, to look for the most sheltered niche into which they could huddle for the night.

It was a late rehearsal after evensong. Boys' voices drifted through the deep shadows among the massive stone pillars and pinnacles which lined the nave. The sound lapped round the walls, translucent and as cool as water. The cathedral was dark, except for the soft fall of candlelight gleaming in the alcoves.

He stepped inside. 'Look, Jester.' He knelt down to be level with his dog and gazed up at the huge stained-glass windows, awesome in the dark night, their brilliant colours almost absorbed into black. The faces of saints and martyrs bent down to him in their suffering and ecstasy; they reached to clasp his outstretched hands. They drew him through their windows into the throng of all the spirits of the dead, who rose up from beneath the stones and stepped out from their entombment within the walls. But it was the angels he loved, with their huge curving wings and gentle smiles. They were his friends. Sometimes, they leapt out of their lead-encased glass windows and swooped round him, enveloping him in feathers and gentle hands and caressing fingers, and they would fly with him up into the stars above the towers and steeples of the city. 'Why can't I stay with you for ever?' he would cry.

There was one angel in particular, with blue eyes, auburn hair and a face of the utmost beauty, who, whenever he stood before her, seemed to look directly into his eyes. Often, he would talk to her in whispers. 'You are my angel. I would die for you,' and he would lie down on the hard cold flagstones of the aisle so he could see her better and think himself dead. He was always doing that, ever since his mother died, though Meshak wasn't always sure about the difference between being alive and being dead; wasn't sure which was best.

He often looked at dead people – old people, poor people, babies and abandoned children. He sometimes saw them huddled in ditches or crouched in the forest trying to find shelter. They had died from cold or illness, or such strength-sapping poverty that they had lost the will to try to live. And then he would think about his mother and wonder whether she liked being dead. When he was awake, he couldn't always remember her face, though he had an impression that it had been sad. But in his dreams, she would sometimes come, stroking his head, showering him with kisses, and her face would be smiling. She seemed so happy that he would wake up crying, 'If being dead makes you so happy, should I not be dead too?'

When Meshak had 'dead' days he would lie for hours, stiff as a board, with open eyes but not seeing anything in this world. Otis gave him such a beating for his 'stupidity', but nothing would rouse him, even when his father kicked him and tried to beat him into activity. Gradually, even Otis had to accept that Meshak had dead days and leave him to it, especially when Mrs Peebles told him his boy had fits and that he should leave well alone. What no one knew was that Meshak stepped out of his body and into a paradise where he would meet his Gloucester angel. She would lead him through beautiful gardens of lawns and flowers and playing fountains, and sometimes show him his mother. Somehow, he was never able to touch her or talk to her, but he would see her from a distance, smiling and being happy. Once she waved at him with such sweetness, and he called out, 'Why can't I be with you?' and she said, 'Because you're not dead.' He would have tried to be dead then and there, but the Gloucester angel would lead him away and say, 'Not yet, Meshak.'

Today, as he looked at his angel, he didn't lie dead. The choir was rehearsing and he always loved hearing the singing. He edged further down the nave, wanting to be closer. Beyond the wooden carved Kent screen, in the chancel, men and boys stood in their stalls. He peered round, catching glimpses of their faces in the flickering candlelight as they concentrated on bits of paper held in their hands, with wriggly symbols which they translated into music. Tears welled in his great sloppy eyes. Music always affected him. He wished he could sing as they did. He opened his mouth. A frightful squawk came out. Some boys looked up and giggled.

'Hey, you! Go on, get out of here and take that hound with you!' A cleric came flapping down the aisle like some clumsy bird, waving his hands at them. He was always on the lookout for vagrants, who would endeavour to sneak into the church out of the cold rain for the night. Meshak and Jester ran out, little as ants beneath the huge flying buttresses and stone walls rising high as the walls of a canyon. They scuttled away across the great paved entrance and out into the mud and mire and filth of the city streets.

Chapter Four

✭

Thomas and
Alexander

The cathedral bells chimed. 'Home, home, tomorrow we go home,' the boy choristers murmured excitedly.

Thomas and Alexander shuffled in their stalls in line with the other boy trebles. They nudged and pushed and exchanged boyish insults, while the lay clerks, older men – the tenors and basses – cuffed their ears and told them to mind themselves.

'Ummum, now boysum . . . we'llum sing through psalmum 48 . . . Sssh . . .' Dr Smith, the choirmaster, rapped the lectern fiercely with his baton. The great organ boomed out the opening chords of an anthem by their old organist, William Hines. The boys, with eyes fixed on the choirmaster, opened wide their mouths and sang with piercing sweetness.

Treble voices rang round the great cavernous cathedral. The candles flickered softly in the evening light, which barely penetrated the cathedral. They had been up since five, working to earn their keep by scrubbing floors, digging vegetables, feeding the livestock and cleaning out the sheds and stables in the cathedral close. Now they were yawning but excited, wanting to sleep so that the next day came quicker.

Alexander's voice soared above the others as he took the solo – always causing a shiver of wonder at its purity. When he hit the very highest note, it cracked slightly. Thomas felt his friend shudder beside him, though Alexander didn't falter and continued strongly to the end. Everyone knew that, no matter how glorious the treble voice, the time would come when it would break. And no one – but no one – could prophesy which boy could make the transition and become an equally good tenor or bass.

Alexander's face was pale as he concentrated on producing a clear sound.

He had already begun to confide his fears to Thomas. 'Once my voice has broken, that will be the end of my musical life,' he had said with anguish.

'But that's not possible,' Thomas had exclaimed. 'Surely, you will play and compose. You're not just a singer, you are a musician!' Thomas glanced up at Alexander who, at fourteen, was tall now – almost manly. He wasn't handsome in the normal way; he had thick, dark-brown, curly hair which fell round a broad-boned face, heavy lips, a protruding brow and eyes which, though blue, could look almost black and gave him a dazed, inverted look, as if he lived more inside himself than outside. Thomas noted the faintest shadow round his jaw and above his lip, and knew that his friend would not sing as a treble much beyond Christmas. But Thomas couldn't understand how that would be the end of his life in the cathedral. Surely the cathedral wouldn't want to lose him, and Alexander would teach, conduct and continue to compose as other gifted pupils had done when their voices broke?

But Alexander was gloomy and just said, 'My father forbids it.'

'Home, home, home.' It sounded like the low buzz of honey bees. It was August and for a whole month there would only be 'said' service instead of 'sung' so that the boys could go back to their farms and help with the reaping and hay-making. Not since they became choristers had the boys been at home for Easter or Christmas Day, because that was when their music was most needed.

Alexander nudged Thomas in the ribs. 'At last you're coming to Ashbrook. At last you'll see my dog Bessie and my new wolfhound pup Zanzibar – well not a pup any more. Isobel writes to say he's nearly full size and very naughty. I hope he'll know me and react to my commands . . . We'll go shooting with him – yes?'

'Ummum now, boysum . . . we'llum sing through psalmum 48 again.'

Thomas was saved from having to try to look enthusiastic when inside he was uneasy about his forthcoming visit to Alexander's house. It would be the first time that he had ever left the city of Gloucester. Most of the other boys came from all corners of the county, one as far away as Dursley and others from Wotton-under-Edge, Bibury, Minchinhampton or Cirencester. Thomas had been born near Gloucester docks, and the first time he had ever been away from home was when he became a chorister and came to live in the cathedral. With the cathedral being barely a stone's throw away from the docks, it hardly felt like leaving home, for Thomas was often able to escape to see his mother and father and all his brothers and sisters. So he was full of apprehension at the prospect of leaving the city for the very first time. But more than that, he was nervous about going to the home of a boy the others called a 'gentleman'. He wasn't sure that he had ever met a gentleman, although he could recognise a gentleman if he saw him on the street by the cut of his clothes and the deference with which he was treated. They were people far removed from him, who rode round in carriages and lived in remote big houses which he had only heard about, but never seen. He knew that the clergy at the cathedral were gentlemen but, somehow, enveloped in their clerical robes that was different.

What would it be like to go to the home of a gentleman, be under the same roof as a gentleman – especially someone like Alexander?

It was five years now since he joined as a new chorister aged eight. Alexander had already been a scholar for a year. Only slightly older, it was Alexander who had been put in charge of him and ordered to show him the ropes. A dour and unsmiling boy, he had dutifully led Thomas round the cathedral precincts, showing him the schoolroom and the song room where they learnt their music, and Miller's Green, the schoolmaster's house. He told him where he could and could not go, where they practised, where they worked, ate, slept and studied, the times of the services and practices. But once the tour was over and they were back in the schoolroom with the other boys, Alexander seemed to relinquish his responsibility for him.

It was in the schoolroom that they slept, on thin mattresses on the floor and lining the walls, and Thomas would never forget that first night. The boys had jumped on him. Not Alexander – he had disappeared – but the others. Then had followed a few hours when he was sure he was going to die. They had held his legs and tipped him head first out of the window; they had dunked his head in the piss pot; they bundled him out of the room and into areas of the cathedral he had never been; they had pushed him up steep spiral steps till they reached the tower, and there they made him stand, blindfolded on the parapet, knowing that one false step could cause him to plunge to his death. The next night and the next, there were more trials and tribulations. Where was Alexander, his supposed protector? he wondered bitterly. He was never around during this torture, either to take part or intercede for him.

Thomas was so miserable that it was almost in his mind to run away back home. After all, it hadn't been his idea to be a chorister. He would have been quite content to follow his father's trade as a ship's carpenter. He was only there because someone heard him singing in a tavern and urged his father to let the boy try for a scholarship as a chorister at the cathedral. But then he thought of all the high hopes his mother had placed on him, and how humiliated his father would be if he got to hear that his own son couldn't put up with the tauntings of a bunch of choir boys. So somehow he got through each day and each night, having no notion of when it would end and who, in the end, would be his friend or his enemy.

It all changed suddenly. One night, Thomas was hanging by a rope, upside down from the beam, when he became aware of Alexander watching from a corner. He lounged against one of the wooden posts as if he were carved out of it, half in shadow, his face chiselled into a mask. Only his eyes glimmered darkly. He did nothing while two, three times, the boys twisted the rope then let it go, so that he spun fiercely like a top, helpless, dizzy, sick, while the boys laughed uproariously. Alexander's movement was unexpected. Even his torturers paused and turned. As if to show he was one of the lads, Alexander came forward. He grabbed Thomas's wrist and roughly tied one of the knots but, while doing so, he whispered in his ear, 'Make them laugh. If you can make them laugh, they'll never trouble you again.'

Thomas spiralled slowly from the beam as Alexander retreated to the shadows once more. 'Make them laugh!' They were the first words that had been spoken in kindness to him since he arrived. Another boy stepped forward. He was about to start the twisting of the rope all over again, when Thomas mimicked:

'Err . . . rrum . . . now then . . . errum . . . boys . . . errum . . . let usum turn . . . errum to psalmumm 48 . . . errum . . .' he said from upside down in a voice exactly like Dr Smith, the choirmaster.

The boy stopped short. The others looked at each other in amazement, and even checked to be sure it wasn't in fact Dr Smith, and then they burst out laughing. 'More, more!' they demanded. Despite being swung and prodded and spun round and round, still dangling from the beam, Thomas managed to scramble through his repertoire of jokes and rhymes and imitations.

As Alexander predicted, they cut him down, still laughing. But his ordeal wasn't quite over – perhaps they were having too much fun. They stood him on top of the bookcase and told him to sing. So Thomas sang; he sang all the songs he had ever sung in taverns and inns to make extra pennies for the family; the sea shanties, the mummers' and morris songs, and foreign songs he'd picked up from sailors and travellers in the inns round the docks, imitating the characters and their accents, which had the boys splitting their sides. Finally, when he felt he had got them sufficiently on his side, he leapt down from the bookcase and went into a dance, accompanying himself with foot-tapping and thigh-slapping. And he even found a pair of spoons which he then played with incredible skill, to everyone's amazement. Soon all the boys were also foot-tapping and thigh-slapping and making such a rumpus that Mrs Renshaw, the matron, came hurrying in to put a stop to it.

Later, lying on their mattresses side by side in the darkness, instead of dropping wet toads on his face or inserting wriggling spiders into his bed, the boys begged him for more imitations of Dr Smith and the Bishop. He duly obliged, and added Mrs Renshaw to the list, which had everybody giggling and sniggering in the darkness until, gradually, all but Thomas himself subsided into sleep. He lay long into the night, staring into the darkness, wondering if at last his troubles were at an end. They were as far as teasing was concerned; from then on, Thomas was not only accepted but he became the most popular of boys, at least with all except Alexander.

Alexander was a loner and didn't seem to want any close friends. He often disappeared for hours at a time, and if discovered it was usually at the schoolroom virginals with his nose in a musical score or scribbling on a page of manuscript, much to the scorn of the other boys. In the school it wasn't always good to be different. Most boys, wearing as they did their uniform jacket and tails and mortar board in school, or the black cassock and white ruffs for cathedral services, managed to seem like a single organism. They conformed to a group mind and a group purpose – except Alexander. He didn't care. He didn't try to conform or attempt to be one of them. Where they spoke with the same soft, broad, Gloucestershire dialect, he spoke like a gentleman; where the other boys got up to larks and laughed at the same jokes, he would be standing apart, watching but not joining in; and though they slept side by side, ate together, practised together and studied together, he was never quite one of them, and they referred to him as 'Gentleman Alex'.

It was not just because he seemed a gentleman that made Alexander different. Although the boys joked about him, they never laid a finger on him and Thomas soon realised they respected him after all, for no one doubted that Alexander had the finest voice of them all and, more than that, was the most musically gifted. Even the bishop treated him with awe and called him 'our little genius'. Not only did Alexander have the voice of an angel, but he played the harpsichord and virginals precociously well and had composed obsessively from the age of six. His anthems and choral pieces were often sung at services and concerts.

At first, Thomas was disappointed to find himself ordered to sit next to this surly, uncommunicative boy in the schoolroom. Strange that Alexander, who had advised Thomas to make the boys laugh, seemed impervious to jokes and wise-cracking. When Thomas tried to get even a smile out of his companion, his attempt was received with a blank uncomprehending stare. But Thomas was gifted at algebra, and when he saw Alexander drifting helplessly over a calculation, he offered to help him. Alexander grudgingly accepted his assistance and, in due course, reciprocated by helping Thomas with Latin, Greek and French. Then, when Thomas took up the violin, he soon showed himself to be such a skilful performer, Alexander began writing pieces for him. Without realising it, they had become friends.

It was a strange friendship. No two boys were more unlike each other: Alexander introverted and gloomy, Thomas popular and sociable; Alexander able to enchant people with his voice, Thomas to make them laugh. But the difference which troubled

Thomas the most was their difference in class and status and when, with each summer, Alexander began to invite Thomas to spend the holidays with him, Thomas always found excuses. Until now. Perhaps it was because Alexander was so sunk in the depths of depression as August approached, so certain that the life he loved was coming to an end, that Thomas agreed to spend the summer at Ashbrook.

The vaulting rang with the sounds of the opening chords of an anthem. The great sound of the organ resonated among the vaultings. The choirmaster's raised hand demanded attention and, at his stroke, the choristers' voices burst into song like a dawn chorus.

'Tommy!' a voice hissed from behind the pillar. A small bare-footed girl peered round shyly, carrying a bundle in her apron. 'Our mam's sent some clothes for you. Wants for you to look like a gentleman.' She giggled at the thought.

Thomas peeled away from the choir, embarrassed. He pulled his little sister out of sight. 'What are you doing here, Lizzie?' he asked roughly.

'Mam wanted you to be dressed proper for going away. She sent you these.' Lizzie thrust a bundle into his arms, wrapped in a piece of sail cloth.

Thomas wondered how his mother could possibly afford to send anything decent that he could wear. He had intended going in the clothes provided by the cathedral: his choir school breeches, stockings and tailed jacket.

He prised open a corner and peeped inside. There was a jacket and breeches made of sturdy broadcloth, a shirt of not too coarse a cotton and a woven waistcoat. He looked up, puzzled. 'How did she come by these?'

Lizzie giggled again. 'They were our uncle Martin's clothes. You don't mind, do you? Mam thought you would fit them now – being as how you're the same age he was when he died.'

'Thanks, Liz,' he dropped a kiss on her bonneted head. 'Thank Ma for me, and tell her I'll take care of the clothes. Now, go – or you'll get me into trouble.'

'Tommy – are you going to be a gentleman?' teased Lizzie. 'You will come home and tell us all about it, won't you? You'll never be too grand for us, will you?'

'Shoo – you silly little goose,' laughed Thomas, and pushed her off. 'And don't forget to give our mam a big kiss from me,' he called after her.

'Mother has promised us a feast to make up for Christmas and Easter,' Alexander told Thomas. 'We will eat duck, roast lamb and Easter almond and simnel cake. We'll eat ourselves silly to make up for all that eel pie, stewed fish and vegetable broth we get day in day out.' Suddenly the talk was of food as the boys packed their bags and put on their walking boots. Those who didn't live in the city were preparing to walk up to ten or fifteen miles home. Thomas was getting ready to do the same when word came to Alexander that the Ashbrook carriage was here and that John Millman, the head groom, was waiting.

'We're going by carriage?' murmured Thomas with awe. Silently, he followed Alexander out into the close where a two-horse carriage was waiting. The shiny dark green painted body of the carriage had a coat of arms with the letter A in gold, swirling round the symbol of a white swan.

There were warm greetings as the boys emerged. Alexander shook the groom's hand warmly and introduced him to Thomas. 'This fellow, John, is my dearest friend, so I hope you'll look out for him and show him the ropes if he seems lost.' John Millman nodded courteously and opened the carriage door to reveal Mrs Lynch, swathed and bonneted, looking more matronly, and her face quite free of rouge. She smiled ingratiatingly and struggled to get out in deference to the young master.

'Stay, stay, Mrs Lynch. Don't disturb yourself. We'll sit up with John. I hope you don't mind just having our bags for company – oh, and this is my friend Thomas Ledbury. I trust you have prepared his chamber and will make him comfortable.'

'We have been making preparations for his arrival ever since we heard you were coming home with a friend,' replied Mrs

Lynch reassuringly. She nodded briefly in response to Thomas's polite but dream-like bow. In a daze, Thomas followed Alexander, clambering up on to the driver's seat next to John, who flicked the pair of black horses with his whip and set off along the road beyond the city walls towards the hills. Behind them, laughing and chortling and yelling cheerful abuse, several of the choristers chased behind and leapt on to the back bar of the carriage for a lift part of the way. One by one, at different junctures, the boys fell away with shouts of, 'See you in September,' and soon the carriage was out on the open road, lurching through the ruts and ridges and mudpools left by the bad weather of the night before, towards the hills and Ashbrook.

They didn't speak much, though every now and then Thomas couldn't resist calling out, 'Hey, look at that!' Or, 'Did you see that?' The raucous sounds and smells of the city gave way to the more harmonious and gentle tones of the countryside. He listened and watched enchanted: stone-pickers and farm labourers – men, women and children – moved down the furrows of newly ploughed fields, calling to each other and singing together as they tossed in the seed – barley or millet, wheat or rye. Wheatear, chiffchaff and swallows who, in the winter, emigrated to warm lands where oranges grow dived and swooped, as if delighted to see the folds of Cotswold hills rising and falling from valley to valley and upland to high common. Long shadows of beeches streaming with sunlight slatted the wold and ribbons of stone walls, now gold, now silver, meandered through light and shade down the meadows, dividing flocks of snowy sheep from grazing cattle.

Thomas wondered what Alexander was thinking; he sat so silently, not looking round, impervious to the countryside as they rumbled through. Only once did he turn and gaze back intently at the city walls, as if he couldn't bear to leave the cathedral behind him. Then he looked forward again, his head dropping to his chest, humming under his breath, his brain unable to contain all the melodies which flowed from it.

'This will be the first time you'll be meeting Mrs Milcote and her daughter, I take it, Master Alexander?' Mrs Lynch's overly high voice broke through their thoughts as she leant out of the carriage window. 'She's a pretty young thing, and there's no mistaking . . .'

'Who?' retorted Alexander tartly. 'The mother or the daughter?'

'Ooooh, you are become quite a wag, sir, if you don't mind me saying,' tittered Mrs Lynch. 'Why, the young lady, to be sure – *Miss* Milcote. She and your sister have become quite bosom friends.'

'Hmmm . . .' Alexander grunted and glanced at Thomas with a bemused look.

Thomas grinned and shrugged. 'Nowummm . . . ummum . . .

Look here . . . ummum, Alexander me boy . . . ummum . . . about young ladies . . . ummmummmumm . . .'

Alexander laughed. To make him laugh was always a triumph and Thomas laughed too.

They left the soft lowlands and the road began to climb up and up into a dark wilderness of dense woods. Thomas shivered with apprehension as they seemed to leave civilisation behind them. The road became rougher and narrower. The trees loomed over them as if they would swallow them up. No wonder he had heard such stories of wild brigands roaming the hills.

Ahead, a coarse voice swore and cajoled. John reined in the horses. A wagon was half up on the bank trying to get out of a deep rut and a train of pack mules snorted and attempted to munch the hedgerow as they waited. A large, red-headed boy was trying to push the wagon from behind as, in front, a man on foot cursed and shouted and whipped the lead mule impatiently, then ran round and laid the whip across the back of the boy as well.

'Oi, Otis,' John yelled to the man. 'Be that you blocking the way? Shall us give you a hand?'

A stream of expletives preceded Otis shouting, 'We'll abandon the wagon at the Borham barn,' he shouted. 'No good trying to get the darn thing up into the hills till the road's drier. But if you'd be so good as to help my boy with giving it a shove to get us going, I would be greatly indebted.'

John jumped down, followed instantly by Thomas and Alexander. They joined Meshak in putting their shoulders to the wagon, while Mrs Lynch leant out of the carriage window calling out encouragement. The huge wheels crunched into motion, creaking and groaning, and, with a jerk which nearly sent them tumbling face down, was suddenly free.

'We'll not be in your way for long now, John!' shouted Otis, climbing up on to the wagon. 'The barn is just beyond the corner.' Thomas and Alexander stood in the road, brushing themselves down. For a moment, Otis towered over them. With an exaggerated sweeping bow he said mockingly, 'Good day to you, young master, and my thanks for your help.'

Alexander nodded an acknowledgement and climbed back on to the carriage. 'I dislike that man. He's insolent. What's more, he treats his animals abominably and his son not much better,' he muttered. They looked at Meshak running behind now with the mules, as Otis drove the wagon on at speed.

'Otis Gardiner! Otis!' Mrs Lynch called out as the mules and wagon reached the Borham barn. 'Don't forget to call at Ashbrook! I would be most obliged.'

'Rest assured, Mrs Lynch! I'd as soon forget my right hand. I'll be calling by in a day or two,' and Otis turned into the barn, leaving the road free.

John Millman coaxed the carriage onwards. They began to

climb and their pace was slower now. They entered the depths of thick beechwoods, where knotted roots thrust up through the earth. The track became more pitted and rutted and, had there not been two strong horses, the carriage would have got bogged down and abandoned. As it was, the boys, feeling sick with all the swaying and tossing, jumped down and said they would walk.

Alexander guided Thomas to a track. 'I want to show you something,' he said. They climbed and climbed. The path rose, twisting gradually round the edge of the hillside until, suddenly, it levelled out and the woods gradually thinned.

Alexander took Thomas to the edge of a knoll and grasped him by the arm. 'Look down there!' Far, far below, shining amber in the noon sunlight, he saw Gloucester Cathedral gleaming like a jewel. 'Now let me show you something else,' cried Alexander. He left the path and began to scramble almost vertically up the hillside. On hands and knees, they scrambled and slid and sometimes clung to creepers which hung from the branches to haul themselves upwards. Finally, they surfaced like swimmers out of the dark wood into the bright open reaches of a heath. The sky was wildly blue; it surrounded them as though they stood on the rim of the world.

Far below them, in the middle of all that Cotswold wilderness, stretched a landscape of smooth, deforested slopes which extended into cultivated lawns, hedgerows and paved walkways culminating in an artificial lake. In the middle of the lake stood a small Greek temple. Beautiful ornamental gardens were bursting with summer flowers and elegant walks entered shady pergolas and secret bowers. It looked like a hidden kingdom, guarded by the overlapping wooded hills which encircled it. Dominating it all was the finest house Thomas could ever have imagined: a huge honey-stoned mansion of steeply pitched stone-slated roofs, gables and elaborate cornices, of tall ornate chimney stacks and mullioned windows.

'That's a fine house. Who could possibly own that?' murmured Thomas. 'I can't imagine anyone normal living there.'

'Can't you, Thomas?' said Alexander lightly. 'Come, let's get back to the carriage,' and, oblivious of his fine clothes, Alexander led the way, slipping and sliding down through the dense undergrowth till they dropped back on to the track.

In due course, the carriage came lurching and bumping into view with Mrs Lynch walking alongside. 'Oh goodness me,' she wailed when she saw them. 'I swear this must be worse than being at sea. The tracks get more and more impossible.'

'You will find it easier going as from here,' John Millman assured them. Soon the road levelled out and ran evenly between avenues of elm and whitebeam. They entered Ashbrook village with its church and inn, where hordes of bare-footed children and scraggy dogs came bounding towards them, cheering and hollering. The road climbed the gradient once more and they broke the brow of the hill. There, at a crossroads, stood a huge oak tree with the remnants of a gallows rope still tossed over its highest branch. A fifth track passed between two tall stone gates which flanked a long avenue of lime trees. And there, at the end of the avenue, was the house Alexander had shown him from the top of the moor.

'Welcome to Ashbrook House,' exclaimed Alexander.

'Oh!' Thomas gave a small gasp. Then was silent. This was worse than he had imagined. Alexander wasn't just a gentleman, he was more like a prince. Thomas could have leapt from the coach and run away. This was no place for the likes of him – where he was lower born than the servants themselves.

'Am I not normal any more, now that you see where I live?' asked Alexander with a smile.

'You are normal for your kind and I for mine,' answered Thomas warily, not wishing to offend. He couldn't imagine such a place being a home, not home as he knew it: a one-up, one-down, and his mother smoking her herrings, the chickens and hens strutting in and out of the door as if they owned the place, and all his brothers and sisters tumbling around, the big ones in charge of the little ones, each with their tasks, and his father with shirt sleeves rolled above his elbows and bibbed apron, hammering and sawing, and the geese honking demandingly, the pig snuffling in its box out in the yard and a cow tethered in the shed. That was his home.

As the carriage wound round the forecourt to the great porticoed front door, scarlet and gold liveried footmen in white wigs and white gloves were already running down the steps to open the carriage doors and carry in the baggage. Several hounds of various sizes came lolloping out, wagging and barking, not yet aware of who they were greeting.

'Alex, Alex! Alexander is here!' Young voices yelled out joyfully and, as Alexander jumped down, a small boy and girl hurtled out of the house and flung themselves on top of him, followed by a large, black, long-haired dog, determined not to be left out of the welcome. Alexander, half strangled by loving arms, managed to greet them all, kissing and patting child and beast and calling out to Thomas, 'Hey, Tom, Tom – these little horrors are Edward and Alice, and this great shaggy beast of a dog here is Bessie. Dear old Bessie – she's as old as I am, you know, and this – is this Zanzibar? I thought he was a puppy, but look at him!' Alexander gathered up the large wriggling creature and attempted to hug him, but the dog leapt from his arms and went bounding around in excited circles. 'We'll train him up to be the best hunting dog – you'll see. We'll go hunting in Ashbrook Woods . . . and where's Isobel?'

An upright lady in a stiff bonnet and stiffly starched grey

skirts appeared in the doorway. She was accompanied by two young ladies, whose excitement she seemed intent on controlling. She lost the battle with one, who simply flew down the steps, all hooped petticoats and frills and ringlets tossing beneath her cap, and clasped Alexander, little ones and all, in her arms. 'Alex, Alex, welcome home! At last you've come. We expected you *hours* ago.'

Alexander plonked the two little ones down, who hugged his knees and nearly toppled him over, while he embraced the girl.

'Oh, Alex,' she burbled, 'look at the size of you! You've grown as tall as Papa.'

'This is my sister, Isobel,' laughed Alexander introducing her to Thomas, who bowed shyly, his cap clasped in both hands. 'Isobel, meet Thomas. He is the most splendid fellow that ever walked the earth and the funniest!'

Isobel was smiling broadly, and Thomas immediately thought how nice she looked with her laughing face. 'I'm very pleased to meet you. Very pleased indeed, Miss Isobel!' he burst out, bowing over and over again.

The other girl at the top of the steps still hadn't moved. She was very pretty, with a delicately featured face, rich auburn hair and briefly glimpsed eyes, blue as thrushes' eggs, before she lowered them. Thomas wondered if the stiff lady next to her was Lady Ashbrook, for she held herself so proudly.

Alexander, still entangled by excited younger siblings, was dragged up the steps by Isobel. 'Alex, this is Mrs Milcote, our governess. She has been with us some weeks now,' cried Isobel. 'She's Mama's cousin, you know.'

Alexander took the stiff lady's hand and kissed it, bowing low. 'A pleasure, Mrs Milcote.'

'My pleasure, Master Alexander. My pleasure indeed.' Mrs Milcote's clipped accents seemed to have trouble coming out of her tight small mouth, though she took a while to withdraw her hand. 'You have been much spoken of and so highly praised that I have been awaiting your acquaintance with great impatience. My daughter too; please meet Melissa.' She nudged the girl almost imperceptibly, but Thomas noticed. Melissa bobbed shyly as she took Alexander's outstretched hand, but did not lift her eyes.

'Melissa is my dearest friend – my sister,' enthused Isobel, throwing an arm round her shoulders. 'My life has changed since she came. I had been so lonely after you went away.'

'And Thomas is *my* dearest friend,' replied Alexander with quiet warmth. 'Mrs Milcote, Miss Melissa, meet Thomas.'

Mrs Milcote merely nodded politely. She did not look Thomas in the eye nor extend her hand to take his which he had held out, and by keeping her arm firmly linked with Melissa's, prevented her daughter from doing more than giving a slight bob.

Thomas withdrew his hand quickly, feeling a rush of blood seep over his face and neck. He bowed low and stood back. Now he remembered why he had felt anxious about coming to Ashbrook.

Chapter Five

✫

Dawdley Dan

The first day was an ordeal for Thomas. The meeting on the steps of Ashbrook was just the start of it. How he wished he had never come; how he wished that the ground could have opened and swallowed him up. Why, even the servants were better dressed than he, even when he wore his uncle's clothes. Never was he more ashamed than when he saw their eyes scan his heavy jacket and breeches, his hob-nailed boots and cotton shirt – and these were his best clothes. How would he get through four weeks? He was spared meeting Sir William Ashbrook, who had had to go to Bristol to see one of his ships, late in from Barbados.

Lady Ashbrook had been solemnly kind and enquiring and tried to put him at his ease, but it was the bowing and bobbing and intricate details of the pecking order that existed in the household which left him clumsily bewildered. The arrogance of the butler, the superciliousness of the footmen and the whispered jibes of the servants, scullery maids and housemaids made him feel like a piece of clod from the farmyard which should be swept out of this elegant house.

At that first dinner, he could almost sense the sneering laughter at his elbow as he tried to serve himself from the platters, and he was sure that the way he was always a little after everyone else in picking up a piece of cutlery, glancing round first just to ensure that he lifted the correct knife, fork or spoon, did not go unnoticed. But this time, unlike when he first arrived at the cathedral school, he was comforted by the reassuring kick he got from Alexander sitting next to him and Isobel's sympathetic glances.

The food was borne in on silver platters by white-gloved manservants; food he had never even seen before: venison pie, partridge breasts, grilled trout, slivers of ham, trifle with cream and jam, cheese and little biscuits. Too nervous to eat, he had taken tiny portions. But Lady Ashbrook had noticed and said in a kindly way, 'Ah, Thomas dear, don't hold back. You're a thin sort of youth and need building up. Take more, take more.' So he did and, tentatively, began to enjoy it.

That night would be the first of his life that Thomas had ever slept on his own, and in a proper bed rather than a mattress on the floor which had to be cleared away by day. Mrs Morris, the assistant housekeeper, showed him up to his bedroom, leading the way with a candlestick which held three blazing candles. Huge shadows swung round the well of the broad winding staircase as they climbed, and he was aware of being under the gaze of all the family ancestors, whose portraits stared down at him from the walls. They went up and along a broad corridor and then turned right into another, all flickering with candles. He couldn't believe such extravagance. Oh, Mam, he thought to himself, if you could but see the number of candles they use. Why, just a quarter of them would last us a lifetime!

They reached an elegant door with a brass lock. She opened it with one of the keys which hung in a huge bunch dangling from her waist. He entered a room so big he was sure it could have contained him and his mother and father and all of his thirteen brothers and sisters with ease. A log fire was burning in the grate, throwing a warm pink glow round the high walls. A four-poster bed was partly hidden behind thick velvet curtains and made up with pillows and cushions and blankets. There were two oak cabinets and between them was his small cloth bag of clothes.

'Lady Ashbrook said I was to tell you that everything in the cabinets is for your use,' said Mrs Morris. Suddenly, she turned and looked at him in a motherly sort of way. 'They do go in for a number of changes in this household, depending on the time of day, who they have to a meal, what the weather is like, what they intend to do and who they intend to visit. It could be confusing. Hmm?'

'Yes, ma'am,' agreed Thomas miserably.

'You not being a gentleman and all that – if you don't mind me saying, young man – allow me to be of help in advising you what to wear. Hmm?' She tipped her head to one side.

'Yes, ma'am! Indeed. I would be most grateful,' cried Thomas.

She opened the cabinet in which were hung a number of jackets and cloaks; folded neatly on shelves were woollen undershirts, pure white cotton shirts, velvet and brocade waistcoats and broadcloth breeches. She took out a complete day outfit and laid it on the couch. 'I suggest you wear these for breakfast. You can try them on in the morning. If it's to your liking, of course.'

'Yes, ma'am. Thank you, ma'am,' murmured Thomas, awe-struck as he gazed at the gentleman's clothes.

Before she left him, Mrs Morris toured the room, checking to see that everything was in order. 'Here is a nightshirt for your use.' She shook it out and draped it on a chair where the heat of the fire could reach it. She put her hand into the bed. 'Yes, you'll be cosy and dry. Becky has used the warming pan on your sheets.' She peeped under the bed and pulled out the chamber pot to make sure he saw it, then pushed it back again. She went over to a side table on which stood a large china jug and bowl. She noted that the towel was clean, then dipped her fingers into the jug and commented, 'You have warm water. You'll be able to wash.' She poked the fire and threw on an extra log. 'Becky will be here in the morning to build up the fire again, but this will last well into the night, I've no doubt. There's a bell pull there if you need assistance, and one of the servants will attend you. Sleep well, lad.'

'Goodnight, ma'am, and thank you kindly,' replied Thomas gratefully as she closed the door behind her.

Thomas stood for a long time in the middle of the room, just where Mrs Morris had left him, pondering his situation. Then he undressed and put on the nightshirt. 'What would me mam say if she could see me now?' he murmured.

He heard a light but insistent tapping on his door. 'Who is it?' he whispered, pressing his mouth to the wood.

'Me. Alexander. Open up!'

Thomas opened it with a big grin.

There stood Alexander also in his nightshirt. 'Come, come, come. No one will go to sleep until you've done some of your funny imitations and sung us some songs.' He grabbed Thomas's arm and raced him along the corridor. They stopped before a small door which looked like a cupboard, but when he opened it they stared into the pitch darkness of a narrow stairwell. It was the servants' stairway which took them up through the stomach of the house. Alexander didn't hesitate; he dragged Thomas in. Then he opened another door and, suddenly, they were in a fully candlelit corridor, just like the one lower down.

'Here he is!' announced Alexander, throwing open a double door at the end of the corridor. Thomas stood, blinking, on the threshold of a large nursery. There were puzzles and toys and a wooden doll's house, small chairs and tables and a sofa. Before a blazing fire knelt Isobel and Melissa and Edward and Alice all in their night robes, their hair brushed out and gleaming in the firelight. Their eyes shone merrily at the sight of him.

'Oh come in, do! We're so glad you're here!' cried Isobel, jumping to her feet. 'Alexander has told us so much about you and how funny you are.'

'Show us, show us, Thomas!' yelled the little ones, rolling around like puppies.

In an instant, all the shyness and doubt he had had about having come to Ashbrook vanished in front of their eager friendly faces.

'Welllummum . . . now then, Ashbrook ummummumm . . . will you umm kindly lead us in the ummum *introit* . . .'

'Why certainly, sir,' said Alexander solemnly.

Thomas grabbed a drumstick from the toy drum nearby and held it up as a baton. He squinted and blinked, and began waving the stick in the air. 'Da dee dum da di da . . .' he imitated an organ.

'That's Dr Smith! He's exactly like that,' chortled Alexander, and he began to sing.

'No no no no . . . my boy . . .' Thomas rapped the baton like Dr Smith did. 'That's no way to sing to Almighty God. No no nonnno. With love, with feeling, with . . .' he waved his arms around dramatically, 'with . . . rev . . . er . . . ence . . . Remember! You are speaking to God. Almighty God.' He moaned it out in a mournful way.

'That's just how he speaks!' Alexander shook his head in amazement.

'I want to be a choir boy,' shouted Edward, as everyone laughed.

'Me too,' echoed Alice, and they lined up next to Alexander.

Melissa and Isobel looked at each other and both leapt to their feet to stand in line before Thomas.

'Well . . . ummum. Whatumm can you sing, my little onesummm? How about um . . . A frog he wouldum a wooing go ummmmummum.'

'Yes, yes, yes! We know that!' they shouted.

'Oneummmum . . . two . . . mmum . . . er . . . what comes after two, eh ummummum?'

'Three!' shrieked Alice.

'Ummummumer . . . three, four . . .' and Thomas waved the baton and brought them in on the fourth beat.

'*A frog he would a wooing go, Hey ho said Rowley!*'

They sang it rowdily. 'I'm deeeeeply impressed,' commented

Thomas in his Dr Smith voice when it ended.

'I want a story, Thomas. Story now,' demanded Edward once the laughter had died down. 'Alex says you know lots of funny stories.'

'Well,' said Thomas, as they gathered round. 'I could tell you the story of old Dawdley Dan, the peg-leg man.'

'Yes, yes, yes!' The children flopped eagerly to the floor beside the fire, while Thomas stood on one leg and began hopping about.

'I need a crutch,' he said, looking around.

'Will this do?' cried Melissa, leaping up to get the hobby horse which was propped in a corner.

'Just the job!' said Thomas, propping the head of the horse under his armpit. 'Now then see you here, old Dawdley Dan,' began Thomas in his broadest Gloucestershire, ''im was called Dawdley 'cos 'e did dawdle, see? Not surprising what with 'is wooden leg an' all that . . . An' 'im did like 'is rum, yer see . . . and I tell you, a man with a wooden leg wot can't hold 'is liquor is quite somethin' to behold.' Thomas went reeling round the room, while Edward and Alice shrieked with laughter, and Thomas glimpsed Melissa out of the corner of his eye losing all her shyness. She threw back her auburn hair and chuckled like a baby, while Isobel gazed encouragingly at him with the same dark eyes as her brother.

'An' then one day old Dawdley Dan, after 'e'd 'ad quite a lot to drink, 'e says, "When I was a lad an' 'ad two legs, I dived from the bridge an' swam all the way across to Over."

' "You never did," challenged one of 'is equally drunk mates.

' "I could do it now," retorts Dawdley Dan. "I'll show yer–"

' "Not now, you couldn't, Dawdley," says 'is mate, "not with that peg leg of yours an' all that."

' "No? I'll show yer!" roared Dawdley. "Goddamn your eyes, I'll show yer. Come on, let's go to the bridge . . . and then . . ." '

Thomas by this time had hauled himself up on to the table, pretending it was the bridge, and was reeling around, almost falling off.

' 'E slung first his good leg over the side, then 'is peg leg – an' there 'e was, sittin' on the bridge, starin' down into the dark swirlin' waters . . . and–'

'What in heaven's name is going on here?' Mrs Milcote stood in the doorway. Her body was rigid with indignation.

The laughing stopped instantly. Five startled faces turned.

Melissa, who had been laughing the loudest, stopped dead at the sight of her mother and thrust her hand to her mouth to stifle the sound. She pulled her gown round her tightly and stared speechlessly.

Isobel recovered enough to say, 'Oh, Mrs Milcote! Do watch Thomas telling his story about–'

'Miss Ashbrook,' Miss Milcote spoke, her words freezing like icicles as they left her pursed lips, 'I hardly think it is fit for young ladies to be seen in their night-time attire before gentlemen – least of all a . . .' For a moment, Thomas wondered whether she would say it: 'a common working fellow'. But she paused and completed her sentence: 'least of all a vis-it-or.' She stretched out the last word meaningfully. 'I think, sir,' she looked hard at Alexander, 'you'd better accompany your young friend back to his chamber now. It is rather late.'

Alexander raised an eyebrow as if he was going to refuse to be told what to do by a governess, even if she was a distant relative, but Melissa had gone to her mother's side and was looking so humiliated that, for her sake, he swallowed his anger. Instead, he hugged the little ones, Edward and Alice. 'We'll hear the rest of the story in the morning,' he reassured them. 'Now, goodnight.'

'Goodnight, Alex,' they chorused bleakly. Isobel ran forward and embraced her brother fiercely. 'It's so good to have you home, Alex! So very good.' Then she turned and bobbed to Thomas. 'Goodnight, Thomas. I do hope your chamber is to your liking. We want you to enjoy your stay at Ashbrook.'

Thomas gave a short bow, 'Thank you, Miss Isobel,' and he followed Alexander out of the room.

Mrs Lynch patrolled the corridors of Ashbrook. Her last duties were to ensure that there were sufficient candles burning outside the bedchambers to get through the night. As she passed the quarters of Mrs Milcote and her daughter, she heard raised voices and paused to listen.

'How could you speak to us like that in front of Alexander and Thomas!' protested Melissa. 'I felt so humiliated.'

'Dear girl . . .' Mrs Milcote's voice was so low that Mrs Lynch had to press her ear to the door to hear her. It was clear that Mrs Milcote had ambitions for her daughter. Marriage, perhaps? Mrs Lynch had noticed how Mrs Milcote had been grooming Melissa, paying extra attention to her education and, in particular, her music. Was this to make her eligible – for Alexander? Mrs Lynch smiled to herself as she heard Mrs Milcote chastising her daughter for her lack of decorum. She was as sure as she could be that Sir William would not consider a penniless, minor relative to be a suitable match for Alexander, his elder son and heir, no matter how pretty and talented she was.

Chapter Six

*

The orphanage

L ady Ashbrook frowned. Alexander was, as usual, giving her cause for concern. It was this wretched music. Really! It was so ungentlemanly. He had had four years, four whole years, singing in the choir of Gloucester Cathedral, and it had been clearly understood that, once his voice broke, he would give up his obsession and start learning to run the estate which one day would be his. Tears welled in her eyes as she contemplated her first born, her adored son, on whose behalf she had argued and fought, to protect him from his stern and conscientious father. She thought they had an understanding, that Alexander would repay her devotion with compliance and return willingly to Ashbrook to take up his proper position in obedience to his father's wishes.

She gazed out of the window, feeling truly vexed as she watched Alexander and Thomas canter off down the drive towards the woods, with the dogs at their heels.

He had just that morning asked her to talk to his father about allowing him to stay on in Gloucester as a tutor and assistant music conductor to the choir. He wanted to continue composing and working at the cathedral.

'No, no, no!' she had stamped her foot with annoyance. 'Do you think Sir William would countenance such a thing? Why do you want to incur his wrath like this?'

Whilst Sir William was away, perhaps she could make Alexander see sense. Lady Ashbrook's brother, Geoffrey Maybury, a canon at Gloucester Cathedral was arriving soon to attend her charity meeting. It was he who had encouraged Alexander's great musical gifts, and Geoffrey had promised to watch him and guide him carefully at the cathedral school. Well, now it must be the canon who makes Alexander see sense and give up this fantasy of being a musician. She dreaded the wrath of Sir William if he did not.

A one-horse phaeton came through the gates, trotting up the avenue towards the house. It would be bearing Mrs Forsythe and Mrs Ridley. It passed Alexander and Thomas. The boys both touched their hats and waved a polite greeting. Not far behind the phaeton, the vicar had just ridden in through the gates of Ashbrook House. He reined in his horse to wait for Admiral Bailey, clattering up behind him on his huge horse. The admiral was a large weighty man who, even from a distance, looked pompous and overbearing as he stopped and engaged the boys in conversation before catching up with the patiently polite vicar. Horton, the parish clerk, had already arrived on foot, and was waiting in an ante-room, twisting his hands in his lap as he always did. Finally, they had a new member on the committee, a Mr Theodore Claymore, who had recently taken up residence in the parish and enthusiastically involved himself in local affairs.

They were gathering to discuss the poor of the parish and the orphanage in particular, something which was of great concern to Lady Ashbrook. She sighed. There was more pressure than ever on the almshouses and the orphanage. Somehow, no matter what they did, the poor never seemed to get fewer. Their presence was everywhere, not just on the streets of the city but in the countryside, under hedges and in ditches or caves in the hillside or within the pathetic hovels of their own homes. But it was the plight of little children which exercised her the most: children who had been abandoned, exploited, maimed, orphaned and abused. She knew the committee would argue all over again about making improvements at the orphanage. Mrs Ridley and Admiral Bailey were convinced that the better the conditions, the more it attracted children born out of wedlock – 'an abomination', as she was sure Admiral Bailey would announce yet again. And she knew he was going to oppose increasing the number of children taken in, as she had proposed, and wanted to divert money from the orphanage to renewing the church roof.

He had very little sympathy for the poor or those who 'strayed from the straight and narrow', as he put it. 'These wretched people live Godless lives of idleness and vice. Like leeches, they bleed our communities. No, it is our duty to help them back into the house of God and too much kindness will not do that, it will just pervert them.'

Lady Ashbrook disliked Admiral Bailey, but he was a man of influence as a magistrate and landowner with an estate almost as big as Ashbrook. He had been an MP but now, since his equally pompous son had taken his place, sitting in the House of Commons, he was the chairman of the parish council.

Mrs Ridley always agreed with the admiral. It never ever seemed to occur to her to disagree. Lady Ashbrook sighed. At least there was her dear friend, Mrs Forsythe, always sympathetic and practical, and the vicar, the Reverend Mr Crick. In his shuffling, modest, hand-wringing way, the vicar believed that he was fulfilling God's will by helping the poor and needy, though sometimes, he thought to himself ruefully, God's will clashed with that of the parish councillors. Mr Claymore was yet to make his views known.

When they were all seated in the library round the oval walnut table, having huffed and puffed and divested themselves of their cloaks and adjusted their wigs, Mr Horton, in his nervous, deferential way, opened the books to detail the expenditure for the poor over the last six months. There were fifteen elderly widows and four widowers in the almshouses. The workhouse had five males and eight females made destitute through accident or bereavement. The orphanage at present could accommodate fifteen children. The number turned away last year was twenty-eight.

'Er . . . might I know how many abandoned children under the age of three were found in the parish since we last met?' asked Mrs Forsythe.

The parish clerk fumbled to the right page. 'Eighteen since October last year.'

'And not all of them of *this parish*, I'll be bound!' decreed Admiral Bailey, vehemently thumping the table.

'And of these, how many were dead, Mr Horton?'

'Er . . . six found dead in the countryside and eight died in the orphanage within three weeks.'

The contemplative silence was interrupted by the admiral again thumping the table to reiterate his point: 'Yes – but most infants were not, *not* of our parish, I'm sure. I tell you, our good works have attracted the riff-raff from all the parishes around. I've heard of young women – "women" is too good a word to describe them, for it besmirches all of womankind – *harlots* is what they are – who have come from miles around to exploit our good works and cast their wretched unbaptised babies on our far too tender mercies. But it's got to stop, I tell you. We must enforce the rule that we only admit children from within our parish boundary.'

'Quite right, Admiral, quite right,' agreed Mrs Ridley, vigorously nodding so that her greying ringlets swung furiously from beneath the frill of her lace cap.

'And what happens to the children we turn away?' enquired Lady Ashbrook.

'That, madam, is not our concern, if you don't mind me saying,' snorted the admiral. 'Each parish must see to its own. We can't look after every miserable, sinful creature which is dumped on our doorstep. Caring for our own exercises us most considerably.'

'I agree, sir. It is entirely proper that we attend to the moral state of our own parishioners – that is our duty, madam,' said Mr Claymore bowing his head to Lady Ashbrook.

Lady Ashbrook sighed inwardly. Yet another who would not support her.

'My lady, you must not allow your tender heart to be so seduced by the viler nature of some of our fellow human beings,' urged the vicar.

Mrs Forsythe and Lady Ashbrook caught each other's eye across the table. Years ago, it was they who had instigated a fund to support the parish orphanage which, at that time, had descended to being not much more than a dying house. Barely a week or a month had gone by when some poor infant was not found abandoned in the ditches and hedgerows and brought into the orphanage. No one was under any illusion about their fate, or cared enough to question why over ninety per cent of children brought in were dead within twelve months. Lady Ashbrook and Mrs Forsythe agreed that they wouldn't have known or troubled to find out had not they themselves, when out riding together one day, heard a faint whimpering.

'Perhaps it is a creature caught in a trap,' cried Mrs Forsythe, who could not bear to witness the suffering of animals.

They dismounted and followed the sound deep into the undergrowth, and there found a small girl – barely three – cowering in the middle of a thorny thicket; a pathetic abandoned creature, so thin and starved. How long she had crouched all alone no one could tell but it was obvious that she would not have survived a further March night in the single thin shift which was all that she had on. They gathered her up, took her home, bathed and fed her, then called on the vicar to ask advice as to what they should do with her.

'The orphanage, ma'am,' said the vicar emphatically. 'That is where such creatures go. There is a fund for the poor of the parish – I suppose we must assume she is of our parish – and there she will be cared for.'

Mrs Lynch was asked to take the foundling to the orphanage,

and duly reported back to Lady Ashbrook that the child had been safely deposited there.

Some months later, when Lady Ashbrook and Mrs Forsythe were riding past, they glimpsed the orphanage and decided to see how the little girl had fared, for she had touched both their hearts. It was a shabby, rundown wood and red-brick building standing in the middle of a field, far from the village, as though somehow the sin out of which the children had been born might be contagious. Having knocked on the door, called out, waited, fretted and finally walked round the back, they at last found a bent old man reeking of drink and obviously senile, feeding chickens in a broken-roofed barn. They got no sense out of him, but just as he was about to take them indoors at their request, a large barrel of a woman appeared. She looked furious, until she saw the ladies standing near their horses, then she straightened her hair and bobbed obsequiously.

'We have come to enquire about one of your children,' said Lady Ashbrook. 'Pray, where is the parish nurse?'

The woman wiped her hands vigorously on her smock and bobbed up and down again. 'Why 'tis I, my lady. I am the parish nurse, Mrs Weaver, who cares for these poor orphaned children.'

She invited them into her parlour, apologising that the fire wasn't lit as she wasn't expecting visitors. They entered the damp, dingy hallway, stepping through filth and rubbish and flea-ridden hounds and, within it all, young children, some barely out of babyhood, who scratched continuously and listlessly, barely moving to get out of the way, forcing the ladies to step over them. Mrs Weaver was obviously immune to it all, even though the stench infiltrated even her parlour. Neither of the ladies wanted to sit down, for all the chairs were covered in dog hairs and were probably infested with fleas.

'All we want is to enquire after a little girl who was brought to you in March,' said Lady Ashbrook, clasping a handkerchief to her nose and walking to the window to catch any whiff of fresh air. She gazed out at a filthy yard running with excrement and manure. A single mud-encrusted pig snuffled by and scraggy hens and geese fretfully pecked and shuffled. She could see no children. 'My housekeeper, Mrs Lynch, brought her to you,' Lady Ashbrook's voice was muffled through her handkerchief, 'and registered her in my name – "Ashbrook" – as the child was unable to tell us her name.'

'Ashbrook! Oh, Ashbrook. My lady, if I had realised . . .' Mrs Weaver gave another deep curtsey. When she rose, she clasped her hands to her bosom in great distress and huge tears welled in her eyes. 'Why, the poor wee mite, she didn't last more than a week.'

'What do you mean?' exclaimed Lady Ashbrook, horrified.

'You don't mean she's dead?' cried Mrs Forsythe. 'She seemed quite revived by the time we sent her to you.'

'We had a bout of influenza. It carried away quite a number of our little ones,' explained Mrs Weaver, wiping her eyes.

The two ladies looked at each other in distressed amazement. 'It doesn't seem possible! Did you send for a physician? For how long was she ill?' The questions flowed, and each was returned with an elaborate and effusive answer, which Lady Ashbrook found peculiarly unconvincing – if not odious – and had her making for the door. 'Come, Mrs Forsythe, there is nothing more to be done here.'

As they rode swiftly away, they noticed a couple of thin young boys gathering firewood in the copse. Their bones stuck out through their thin shirts and one coughed all the time. Surely it was a sight they were used to. The poor were always there – the vagrants and beggars and destitutes were as much a part of the landscape as cows and sheep. But, suddenly, it was as if Lady Ashbrook was seeing them for the first time. Perhaps, since giving birth to her own children, she had become more aware of the welfare of the young.

When they had ridden far away from that appalling place, Lady Ashbrook reined in her horse and fell forward over its neck, shaken by what they had seen. 'Mrs Forsythe,' she said weakly, 'I swear I have never in all my days even conceived that such a place could exist. I feel so guilty. Why, it is here on our land, in our parish – and I never knew. How could I have been so blind? That woman! She calls herself a parish nurse? Why, she is nothing better than a killing nurse. How could I not know about such a woman running an orphanage under my very nose?'

'You can't blame yourself, my dear Mary.' Mrs Forsythe drew her horse alongside and stretched out a comforting hand. 'Such affairs are not meant to be part of your responsibility or knowledge. How could we know?'

'You feel the same then?' asked Lady Ashbrook, looking up and seeing her friend's pale and stricken face.

'Feel the same?' She shook her head bitterly. 'You feel the guilt I do. Why, that poor child – and to think how easy it would have been for me to have kept her. Such a strange, pretty, lost child. It is as though she was deposited there by God to test us – and we failed. How can we make amends?'

Lady Ashbrook sat upright in her saddle. 'Amends. Yes, Catherine, you are right. We must make amends and try to save other children from that hell. I will discuss the matter with Sir William, and gain his permission to involve myself in the affairs of the orphanage. It is our duty. Influenza or no influenza, no child could thrive in the conditions that we have just witnessed. I must make Sir William see that this is a matter we must pursue with the vicar, the parish authorities and even the bishop if need be.'

And so they had pursued it. It was not an easy task to

persuade Sir William that his wife should involve herself in such affairs. When she first broached the subject, he was outraged and wouldn't even discuss it, merely declaring that it was not befitting for the lady of the house to concern herself in such matters. She would demean herself; she would risk infection; she would be seen as interfering in matters which were rightly in the domain of the parish council. But Lady Ashbrook was a headstrong woman as well as persuasive. She pointed out that the conditions she had witnessed on their land shamed the Ashbrook name. Surely it could only enhance their reputation if they were seen to care and take action to improve the lot of their own parishioners. After much discussion, Sir William gruffly gave way.

So she and Mrs Forsythe made numerous calls and visits on all parish officers, and invited various local dignitaries to form a committee to look into the welfare of destitute children in their parish. Bracing themselves, they made a further unexpected visit to the orphanage with a parish officer, and insisted they be shown round every corner of it. They found filthy, bare, unheated rooms without beds or blankets, and discovered that the only food fed to the children were leftovers from the dogs. Pitiful children lay immobile on the rough floorboards or sat rocking hour after hour, staring into space. Babies were left unattended, unfed, unwashed, just waiting to die. Indeed, in one out-house in the yard, lying on a piece of cloth was a dead baby, which the old man was about to go into the woods to bury.

Mrs Weaver and the old man were instantly removed and a younger couple installed in their place. Standards were set and more money was promised, which the vicar was to oversee. Lady Ashbrook inaugurated a fund and vigorously began raising money and persuading the wealthier ladies of the parish to give clothes or money for the proper maintenance of the orphanage.

Now here was Admiral Bailey telling them that they were too successful; that infants from miles away were being dumped inside the parish boundaries putting 'much pressure' on the purse. 'An orphanage that does its job too well does no one any favours. Indeed, I would maintain that it only encourages licentiousness,' he declared.

Lady Ashbrook flushed with indignation. 'To lose eight children in our orphanage within three months is hardly a spectacular success, sir,' she retorted, barely able to contain herself. Then, to her relief, her brother Geoffrey arrived.

The admiral became less bombastic now the canon was there. Practical suggestions were discussed, compromises reached. Lady Ashbrook got everyone to agree that parish nurses must be carefully vetted and supervised. Anyone found to be drinking alcohol to excess or who was in any other way ill-suited for the care of infants should be removed instantly. An extra sum of fifty pounds was allocated so another stove could be installed by next winter. Then, after further refreshment of good plum wine and the cook's most tasty savouries, everyone parted on jovial terms, though the admiral couldn't resist a parting shot aimed at Lady Ashbrook, but across the canon's bows: 'Your dear sister is far too soft-hearted. I fear the world exploits her sense of charity. Why, she has created such luxurious conditions in the orphanage that I wouldn't mind my own children going there,' he laughed uproariously.

Lady Ashbrook sighed with relief as she watched the last of them leave – except for Mrs Forsythe, who whispered in her ear at the door, 'Well done, my lady. Once more, you've scored against that man. Shall we ride tomorrow?'

Lady Ashbrook smiled and embraced her gratefully but looked uncertain. 'It may not be possible, my dear. There are one or two matters to be sorted out before Sir William returns. I will send you word as soon as I am free.'

She watched her friend helped into the phaeton and waited for it to trot away down the drive before turning to her brother. 'Geoffrey dear,' she said, linking her arm in his. 'I must talk to you about Alexander.'

Chapter Seven

✫

The cottage in the woods

For the last hour, Alexander and Thomas had been riding in silence. Thomas knew his friend well enough now to know that this was not some surly, sulky silence; it was Alexander disappearing inside his head again.

Thomas had begun to feel a little more at ease at Ashbrook. Most mornings, when the other children were having their lessons, Alexander and Thomas went riding. Today, they reached a high ridge, where the long thin trunks of silver birches swayed like harp strings in the wind coming up from the Severn. They reined back their horses and stopped to look down to a distant farm, its honey-coloured walls glistening in the ripe summer sunlight. It was haymaking time. Farm labourers – men, women and children – were scattered in long rows, wielding their scythes with a relentless rhythm, cutting, gathering and tying into sheaves. Their voices drifted up to them, sometimes breaking into song.

Along the track leading to the farm, a dark brown horse pulled a wagon, and they could just see the bare dangling legs of a boy sitting in the rear.

Alexander frowned. 'Looks like Otis has reached our parish.' Then, almost in the same breath, he said, 'Melissa seems quite amiable, don't you think?'

'She's very pretty, if that's what you mean,' laughed Thomas.

'Hmmm . . .' Alexander nodded and, without speaking further, nudged his horse, Melchior, to move on. They reached a high treeless common where sheep and cows were grazing. Alexander turned round, his face suddenly alive and beaming. 'This is a capital place for a good gallop,' he shouted. Digging his heels into Melchior's flank he yelled to the dogs, 'Come on, Bessie, Zanzibar!' and was off, circling the cattle and heading for the woods beyond. Determined not to be left behind, Thomas's horse, Fedore, followed in hot pursuit with Thomas trying frantically to rein him back. Desperately, he pulled on the bit, certain he would cut through the horse's mouth, he tugged so hard. But Fedore seemed oblivious to anything except the race.

By now Thomas was spread across Fedore's back, arms round his neck, begging him to stop. But the horse was having too much fun and only galloped faster. The hooves thudded across the

Coram Boy ⋆ 91

ground. Thomas saw a blur of field and cattle and the earth tipping wildly as he felt himself slipping round his belly. Suddenly, he was off. Briefly, his foot was caught in the stirrup and he was dragged along, struggling helplessly, the long grass whipping his face – a blur of wild orchids and buttercups and purple scabious. Then he was free. The world stopped. He lay there, staring up at a blue sky. A startled lark rose from the turf, trilling wildly.

He waited for the pain, certain he must have broken every bone in his body, but there was nothing, apart from being a little winded and having to gasp in vast quantities of air.

He heard hooves galloping back and shouts of alarm. 'Are you all right? Good heavens, Thomas, are you hurt?'

The shadow of a horse and rider fell over him, then there was Alexander kneeling anxiously at his side.

Thomas heaved himself up. 'I don't think so,' he muttered, wriggling his arms and legs. Alexander helped him to his feet.

'Sorry, Alex, I'm no rider, you know. Where the devil has he gone?' Thomas looked around for the horse but he was nowhere to be seen.

'Don't worry about Fedore, he'll be hanging around somewhere. Look, we're not far from Waterside, our little play cottage. Let's go there. You can rest while I go and find him. Can you mount behind me? Stand on that log over there.' Thomas heaved himself up behind Alexander and, a few minutes later, he had his first encounter with the cottage in the woods.

Alexander had called it a 'little' cottage, but Waterside was a sturdy two-storey stone house with mullioned windows upstairs and downstairs, and it had twice as many rooms as his own home in Gloucester. It stood beside a gentle, winding brook, trailing with vetch and creeping Jenny, where coots and moorhens paddled in and out of water irises and long reeds. Silky water voles crept out of their homes in the muddy bank to plunge into the water, and a kingfisher of eye-piercing blue sped by in a blink.

The cottage had no garden, just the long grass of the natural clearing in the woods and the wild flowers – hollyhocks, foxgloves, dog-rose and campion – growing in glorious and varied profusion. As the boys slid from the horse and Alexander tethered it to a tree, the sound of a virginals drifted out.

'Someone is playing,' exclaimed Thomas in astonishment.

'If it's Isobel, then she has improved remarkably since I've been away,' declared Alexander, hurrying to the door. He flung it open.

The music stopped abruptly. A chorus of voices called out, 'Alexander! Alex, Alex! You've come!' Little Edward and Alice jumped on him, and suddenly, there were Isobel and Melissa framed in the doorway, smiling with pleasure.

'And look, Thomas's here!' shouted Edward, breaking into a one-legged hop. 'Thomas! You never did finish that story of Dawdley Dan! Finish it, finish it! What happened? Tell us, do!' Little hands grabbed his coat and sleeves and began dragging him, just as the Lilliputians had dragged Gulliver.

'One moment, I beg you!' protested Alexander. 'Thomas took a fall from his horse. He may be hurt. Show him some regard while I go and find Fedore. He's wandered off somewhere.'

The excited voices turned to soft concern. 'Oh, Thomas, are you all right? Are you hurt? Come in and sit down. We can give you a drink of lemonade.'

Thomas allowed himself to be ushered in with the utmost gentleness and told to sit on the sofa. He was more awe-struck by what he saw than troubled by his fall. It all looked like some fairytale. A cottage inhabited by little people. It was perfectly furnished in miniature, with chairs, tables, cupboards, sofas, carpets, curtains, and there in an alcove, the virginals. Even the dogs, two spaniels, were miniature.

He sat awkwardly on the sofa. The least he could do was bend down and remove his boots, but then he was immediately embarrassed by his coarse stockings, which he'd worn because his mother had knitted them specially. Edward and Alice couldn't take their eyes off him. They plonked themselves down on the carpet before him and stared and stared, Alice's thumb creeping into her mouth.

'Thomas, don't finish the story till I get back,' pleaded Alexander before riding off to look for Fedore.

So they waited. Isobel went off to prepare the lemon drink she had promised him, while Melissa asked him what had happened. Thomas described it briefly, saying, 'See, there was nothing to it! I'm not hurt! The grass was soft.'

Isobel returned with a goblet of lemonade. 'You should put your feet up – and be a good patient,' she cried.

Thomas blushed at all this attention. 'Truly, I'm not hurt – but while we wait for Alexander, there is one favour you could do me.'

'Yes?' They looked puzzled.

'Miss Isobel, was that you playing the virginals when we arrived? It was a really pretty piece. Won't you please play it once more?'

'It wasn't Izzy!' cried the little ones. 'It was Melissa!'

Melissa blushed furiously, and Thomas too felt he had gone beyond himself. 'Oh,' was all he could say.

'Melissa doesn't mind playing, do you?' cried Isobel. 'She's so good, Thomas. Much better than I, even though she hasn't been learning half as long.'

'I'd feel much better if we were to play together. We have our duet, don't we?' said Melissa shyly.

Isobel teased her. 'Oh, you are a silly thing. Why be shy in front of Thomas?' But on seeing Melissa's beetroot face she said, 'Oh, all right.'

'This piece is suitable for you – it's a *galop!*' said Isobel. 'One, two, three, four–' she counted them in and they were off with a tumpety-tump!

Edward and Alice leapt to their feet and galloped round the room on their hobby horses in time to the music, and soon Thomas was on his feet too. And when that tune was over, they begged for more and more. Then Isobel played by herself, which gave Melissa the courage to play a solo.

There was the sound of appreciative clapping. Alexander had returned and had been listening unobserved. 'So it was you playing when we first arrived,' he said admiringly. 'Where did you learn?'

Melissa blushed all over again. 'My dear papa taught me before he died,' she said softly. 'He loved music and was an exceedingly good performer at the virginals. Mama plays too – so she encourages me to keep it up.'

'And so do I,' said Isobel emphatically, 'and Melissa helps me with my playing, and we have such fun together.'

'Thomas – story, story!' beseeched the little ones. 'Alex is here now. So finish the story of Dawdley Dan.' They thrust a hobby horse under his arm to use as the peg leg and flopped on to the carpet. The girls curled up on the sofa and Alexander sat on the chair at the virginals.

'Where was I, then?' asked Thomas, winking.

'Dawdley Dan had drunk a lot of rum and wanted to prove he could still swim across the river at Over just as he used to do when he was a boy with two legs,' remembered Alice.

'Oh yes, Dawdley Dan. Well 'e 'opped all the way to the bridge and climbed on to the parapet and swung his legs over – I mean, his *leg* – the other one bein' but a wooden peg leg! Everyone ran after 'im. Some were shoutin', "Dan, Dan, don't do it! You'll drown!" But others were urgin' 'im on. "Let's see you then! Prove it, prove it!" A crowd gathered. People were placin' bets – and soon there were more people interested in winnin' their bet than wha' happened to Dan.

'Dawdley Dan sat on the bridge, laughin' 'is 'ead off, roarin' drunk an' – an' then . . .' Like the first night, Thomas had climbed on to a table and sat there, rocking and swinging and staring down at the carpet as if he stared down into the dark murky depths of the river. 'An' then he just slipped off the parapet an' dropped into the water.'

Thomas paused. The children stared at him wide-eyed, silently asking the question: *and then?*

Thomas dropped from the table and rolled behind a screen. ''E disappeared. Vanished from sight. People ran along the bridge lookin' and callin', "Where is 'e? Dan! Come up. Where are you?" An' the people who'd placed bets were shoutin', "Swim, swim! Get to the other side! I've put five shillings on you. Don't let me down." An' others shouted, "Give up! You can't do it – not now – with a peg leg like yours." Of course, all they really cared about was their money. At last, somethin' came up, somethin' bobbing in the water. 'Is wooden leg it was that bobbed to the surface.' Thomas waved the end of the hobby horse in the air from behind the screen. The children roared with laughter.

'Just the wooden leg?' gasped Isobel.

'Oh, Lord no! 'E was still attached to the end of it – but couldn't right 'imself, see? An' there was this wooden leg floatin' about.' Thomas rolled out from behind the screen with the hobby horse 'leg' in the air, thrashing about as though he was trying to right himself and gurgling and gasping as if his lungs were filled with water.

Amidst all the laughter, Alice asked woefully, 'Was he drowned, then?'

'Lord love us, no, not 'e. 'E was lucky that 'e 'ad a good friend or two who jumped into the river and pulled the silly devil out, an' his friends got him away fast, while those who 'ad lost money fought and argued with those who 'ad won.'

'That's a good story, Thomas!' yelled the little ones. 'Tell us another. Please!'

Outside, bare feet approached through the undergrowth, nail-bitten, rough hands touched the windowsills, moving from window to window round the house. Eyes secretly peered inside the cottage, watching. They moved from child to child, marvelling as though each one was a being from some other star. They settled on Melissa.

Hands gripped the sill. His gasp of astonishment made the dog at his side look up questioningly. 'She's my angel. My angel.' The words were exhaled. If eyes could consume and swallow and fuse into the being, then these eyes would have consumed Melissa. This was his angel. He wondered how she could have stepped out of her window in Gloucester Cathedral and come to this cottage in the woods. What would it be like to touch her? No. Impossible. You can't touch an angel, not if you were alive, anyway. It would be like touching air or light or water; yet *they* touched her as if she were real. And like a living human being, she laughed and sang and chased the little ones, and tenderly played their games of mother and father; and when she cradled a little doll it was as if it were a true baby. But he knew that though she was of real flesh and blood, with living, blushing skin, and those blue-green eyes, she was an angel.

The sound of someone approaching down the path sent the secret spy stumbling back into the undergrowth.

Thomas was just saying that he would go out and find a good

piece of wood to make a new cradle for the doll, when there was a discreet knock on the door. It was the barefooted child of one of the servants telling them that they were to go back to the house now, as tea was ready.

Alexander mounted his horse and took Melissa and Edward behind him, while Thomas, after some persuasion that he should mount Fedore once more, took Isobel and Alice. 'Don't go galloping off this time,' shouted Thomas to Alexander.

The secret eyes watched from within the depths of the undergrowth and followed too. The dogs came tearing out, circling, leaping and bounding. One rushed up to the hiding-place, sniffed the soft-eyed lurcher, which growled and yapped at him.

Alexander called out, 'Bessie, Zanzibar, here! Come on. Heel!'

The dogs rushed back obediently, and the group of children set off back to the house.

The secret watcher fixed his eyes on Melissa. He had no magic powers; he could not become the invisible air which surrounded her, not be a cat and slink along by her side. Yet like a familiar, he shadowed her. From now on, he would be her guardian and protector.

Chapter Eight

⋆

Sir William returns

At supper that evening the children recounted the antics of Dawdley Dan over and over again and everyone laughed – even Mrs Milcote and the serving maid, who nearly tipped the potatoes into Lady Ashbrook's lap, she was giggling so much.

At that moment, Thomas had never felt happier, never more accepted into the heart of this family. He looked round the dining-table: Canon Maybury had stayed for the night and was so jovial and talkative that even Mrs Milcote looked more relaxed, and her lips less pursed. Lady Ashbrook leant across the table and told Thomas in front of everyone how pleased she was that he was their guest. 'You are a good influence on this son of mine, for I tell you I have never seen Alexander more cheerful. Why, he stays in our company – something he would only do if firmly ordered to. He always preferred his own company to that of ours. So we thank you, dear Thomas, for being his friend and turning him into a human being.'

'Huh!' Alexander snorted when he heard this praise being

heaped on Thomas. But he knew his mother was right. Thomas, so natural and unassuming, so funny and kind, made him see the world in a gentler light.

After supper, they adjourned to the drawing-room, where Isobel and the little ones urged Alexander to sing to them. Alexander looked for some approval from his mother. Would she want him to sing? He saw her exchange glances with the canon. But his uncle just patted her hand reassuringly and then went over to sit at the harpsichord. He waved his hand for attention. 'We have had food for our bodies!' he declared. 'Now, let us have food for our spirit or, as the good bard said, the food of love! Come, Alexander! Play on! Sing us a song by Arne.'

And so they performed a number of well-known and well-loved songs, and soon Lady Ashbrook's brow softened, as she couldn't help enjoying her son's clear, flowing voice. After that, Thomas played the violin, with Alexander accompanying, starting with some Bach gigues and ending with sea shanties which got them all up on their feet and dancing. Isobel and Melissa played duets and even Edward and Alice managed to sing 'A frog he would a-wooing go!'

'Now I want to sing a song just for Mama,' announced Alexander with a suddenly sombre voice. 'It's your favourite, Mama. The one you used to sing to me when I was little because I loved it so much.'

Lady Ashbrook looked quietly sad, as if the friction between Alexander and his father were all her fault, because he had inherited her love of music.

'The Silver Swan.'

The canon nodded approvingly and placed the sheet of music on the stand.

It was a sad song.

> *'The silver swan, who living had no note,*
> *When death approached, unlocked her silent throat.'*

Alexander sang and, all the while, his eyes did not leave his mother. The words pleaded with her and, through her, to his absent father. He seemed to be saying, see, this is what I do best!

Sir William had never wanted Alexander to attend the cathedral school. There had been serious arguments and disruptions ever since Canon Maybury had told Alexander about the cathedral school, and how only the best voices were offered scholarships, lightly suggesting that Alexander would benefit from such an education. Once the idea was in Alexander's head, it became an obsession. He begged for a chance to win a scholarship. Sir William had said, 'No, no, categorically no.' He wanted Alexander to go to his old school, Eton, or be educated by tutors at home. As soon as possible, he expected Alexander to be familiar with the affairs of the estate. This passion for music was a distraction and, at best, an indulgence.

But for once, his quiet, moody son would not take no for an answer. He pleaded and pestered and, despite harsh reprimands and the occasional beating, continued to plead and pester. Lady Ashbrook reasoned, and Canon Maybury, too, argued strongly in favour: 'After all, Sir William, he may not win a scholarship. There are only eight for the whole county, you know, and most keenly sought after. Let him at least try. If he fails – and he probably will – that in itself will put an end to his aspirations.'

'Huh,' Sir William had grunted. 'And if he does get a scholarship?'

'Well, it will only be until his voice breaks and then that will be an end of it,' assured the canon.

Sir William reluctantly gave in, though later he often regretted that he had allowed the canon to persuade him. 'There's a conspiracy in my own house,' he grumbled, 'a conspiracy between my wife, her brother and my own son. Well, I agree but once his voice turns from a nightingale into a corncrake, he puts this music thing behind him and takes on the responsibilities of the estate.'

Although Lady Ashbrook had been sympathetic to Alexander going to the cathedral school, he knew that she now sided with his father in being adamantly against him following a life of music. 'Really, Alexander! See sense,' she had implored him. 'You've had four years of music. It's time you remembered your position. You are a gentleman and the heir to Ashbrook.'

Even his uncle Geoffrey shrugged sadly and said, 'I fear now you must obey your father and remember your duties to Ashbrook.'

But the more music Alexander studied, the more passionate he became about it and he couldn't conceive of being happy doing anything else. They could not – must not – stand in his way. This is what Alexander thought as he sang to his mother.

> *'Leaning her breast against the reedy shore,*
> *Thus sang her first and last, then sang no more.*

> *'Farewell all joys! O Death, come close mine eyes;*
> *More geese than swans now live, more fools than wise.'*

Lady Ashbrook held his gaze, transfixed. When the song was over and everyone else clapped with such delight, she continued to sit immobile, silent and pale.

The clapping died away, but one pair of hands went on clapping – not fast with appreciation, but a slow, sarcastic hand clap which made everyone turn round anxiously. Sir William Ashbrook stood in the doorway, his cloak still round his shoulders. His face, wet and flushed from riding through the rain, was unsmiling.

'Sir William, my dear! Why did you not send word that you were on your way?' exclaimed Lady Ashbrook, hurrying to his side. 'You must have ridden the last hour in darkness to get home – and in this dreadful weather. Should you not have stayed the night at the Swan? Have you eaten, dear? Tabitha, run and tell cook the master is home and will require some supper, and tell Mrs Lynch to check that the bedchamber is warm and the sheets dry. I was not expecting you till next week.'

Thomas shrank back with embarrassment, aware that the happiness and conviviality had died away as quickly as a snuffed candle. Alexander moved away from the harpsichord and stood by Thomas and Isobel, while Edward and Alice ran to Polly, their nursemaid, and huddled into her skirts. Mrs Milcote, who had risen and bobbed a curtsey at Sir William's arrival, sat down again on the sofa and continued stitching the sampler she always carried with her. Melissa bent intently over the work basket and fiddled with the coils of silk threads.

'I see our young songbird is in fine voice,' observed Sir William, though his tone was not warm or admiring. Alexander came towards his father, bowed and dutifully embraced him.

'Fine voice? I should say,' intervened the canon, trying to save the situation. 'You should be damned proud of him, sir. In

Gloucester, they are calling him our own little prodigy.'

'Hmmm,' grunted Sir William. 'I've enough songbirds on this estate. What I need is a man with common sense, muscle, guts and strong arms. Perhaps when the voice has flown, we'll make a man of you yet, eh, Alex?'

'Yes, sir,' murmured Alexander unconvincingly. He knew he was not the son his father hoped he would be. Although he rode his horse well, he wasn't interested in hunting and shooting, nor soldiering, nor any of what his father would have termed 'manly pursuits'. The fact that he was a brilliant scholar, outstandingly good at Latin and Greek, cut no ice at all. Such gifts would not run the estate nor be of any value in his father's trading interests. In any case, music was for the serving classes. It could never, never be a profession for a gentleman. It should remain a pleasant pastime and a skill with which to entertain after-dinner company.

'And this young man here is your friend, I take it, eh?' Sir William asked with enforced joviality as he sized up Thomas.

Thomas bowed low and respectfully. 'Glad to make your acquaintance, sir,' he murmured.

'You look a smart young fellow.' He looked him over approvingly, noting that, though still a boy, Thomas already had strong, square shoulders and an open, intelligent face. 'What is your future to be, my lad? Army, navy?' he demanded.

Thomas looked up confidently. 'I hope to be a musician.'

'A musician?' His nose wrinkled as if the word smelt. 'Seems the waste of a fine lad to me,' snorted Sir William, and then turned to allow his manservant to help him off with his cloak and boots. 'I'll have my supper in the library.'

Thomas sensed the relief as Sir William turned away and left them to their own devices, but the jollity of the evening did not return, and soon the younger children drifted up to the nursery to play a little longer before going to bed. Though Isobel and Melissa begged the boys to play cards with them, Alexander frowned and said he would rather read, and Thomas withdrew to his room.

Thomas stared out of his bedchamber window. He thought how strange life was. He, Thomas, who had nothing, was free to follow a life of music, while Alexander, who had everything, was imprisoned by his wealth and class and forbidden the one thing he craved – to be a musician.

The moon was hugely bright, gibbous and almost menacing. Its reflection made the lake mercurial. Dark clouds flared across the sky like horses' tails and he saw how fierce the wind was by the way the trees swayed.

As he watched, a movement caught his eye. Someone stood on the lawn outside, staring at an upstairs window of the house; a raggle-taggle fellow. With the clouds trailing across the moon, Thomas kept losing him in the shadows, then there he was again;

a youth, barely older than himself, he thought, standing stock-still, his legs apart, his arms slightly akimbo, like some half-formed statue. Thomas felt he had seen him before but had barely time to register the figure as the moon disappeared completely and darkness swallowed him up. When the clouds parted again, the fellow had gone.

Thomas shuddered. Filled with unease, he closed the shutters.

Chapter Nine

*

The ball

Here comes a poor woman from baby-land,
With three small children in her hand:
One can brew, the other can bake,
The other can make a pretty round cake,
One can sit in the garden and spin,
Another can make a fine bed for a king;
Pray ma'am will you take one in?

Otis and Meshak had been on the estate for a few days, touring the villages, bargaining and dealing as pedlars do. They had found a clearing in the woods where they had unharnessed the wagon. It was not far from the stream, and they could camp there for several days and make it a base from which Otis could tour the hamlets and villages around.

The wagon was full of pots and pans and china and tools, and three more young children. The two little ones they had picked up earlier had been sold to a pinmaker in Gloucester. Up here in the wild hills there was a demand for labouring children, and as Otis scooped up runaways or abandoned children from the highways and byways, he disposed of them to eager employers looking for cheap – if not slave – labour in the isolated farms and the many mills which were scattered all around.

They took the three new children to a cloth mill where they were to be put to work in the weaving and dyeing sheds. Meshak had glimpsed about twenty such young children working in the cold gloom; thin clothes, bare feet, bowed heads as they pulled the threads and wound the shuttlecocks.

On the same day, Meshak noted that there were more little squealy bodies stuffed into the panniers and saddlebags, which Otis had collected from around the district, calling in at parish orphanages and the remote dwellings and hamlets where such unwanted creatures also came into the world. Now that Otis was known as a Coram man, desperate women pleaded with him to take their babies to London where, it was heard, they would be well cared for at the Coram Hospital. They paid him what he asked for; some gave him everything they had, such was their desire to know that their babies would be cared for by the finest institution in the land.

Otis had no compunction in taking money in exchange for the babies; always giving earnest assurances that he would take them to Coram. But, in reality, hardly any ever survived a week, let alone the month or two he always took to get to London. Otis would follow a meandering route so he could take in as many farms and hamlets as possible. 'What the eyes don't see, the heart doesn't grieve for.' That was his motto and, though his panniers were always full of babies, by the time he got to London, they were rarely the same ones he set out with.

Surely there would be no unwanted babies here at Ashbrook? thought Meshak. Not in this paradise in which my own angel lives.

Meshak had taken to wandering – so much that his father had commented that he was like a dog on heat, and tried to beat some sense into him. But it was no use; ever since Meshak had spied Melissa in the cottage, he had hung around, trying to be wherever she was. He watched her in the cottage and up at the house; he followed her when she and Isobel went roaming the woods or out riding. Meshak didn't understand his feelings. When he was so near and could almost have reached out and touched her, he wanted to rush about, jumping over logs, singing at the top of his voice, 'She is my angel!' But if a day went by and he didn't see her, he would hurl himself face down on the ground, weeping and murmuring, 'Dead, dead, dead,' and wish he could be lying beneath the earth if it meant his beloved would walk over him with her dear feet.

He stood on top of the common, looking down on Ashbrook House about half a mile away, with Jester panting at his side. The house was teeming with activity. There was to be a ball to celebrate Lady Ashbrook's birthday and to mark the end of Alexander's holidays, for in two days he and Thomas would be returning to the cathedral school in Gloucester. It seemed that every man, woman and child on the estate was engaged in the preparations. Sir William Ashbrook led a deer shoot to provide venison, and a posse of young lads including Meshak had been out rabbiting days before with their dogs and traps, not just for the fun of it but because they would be paid twopence for every rabbit they brought back.

A continual flow of horses and wagons moved round the estate: to the fields for vegetables, wheat, barley; the mills for flour; the orchards for fruit; the slaughterhouse to which they took the heifers; and the dairy for butter, cheese and curd. A Gloucester black spot pig had been slaughtered and preserved in the ice house, and already the pantry was hung with hams and sausages and filled with bacon, brains, liver, kidneys and trotters – in fact, every bit of the pig except the tail. Gradually, sufficient food was assembled to feed a multitude of guests.

In the kitchens, there was a frenzy of peeling, chopping, stirring, boiling, frying, roasting, baking, kneading, blending and rolling out, while, bit by bit, pastries and pies and sausage rolls and all sorts of savouries began to appear. The smell of cooking pervaded the kitchen area and out into the yard, attracting all the dogs, who hung around with slavering tongues and pleading eyes.

On hearing that a party was being prepared, troupes of actors, entertainers, jugglers and travelling minstrels began trickling into the neighbourhood, setting up camp in nearby fields, attracting villagers from miles around, adding to the air of festivities. Heinrich the dancing bear came all the way from Rodborough. A travelling freak show on its way to London pitched camp and displayed their charges – penny-a-peep – to see the two-headed baby, the bearded woman, the conjoined twins and a man whose heart you could see beating because he had been born with it on the outside. That was tuppence a peep, which most people thought worth it, to see the organ and all its mysterious tubes and muscles expanding and contracting, giving life yet looking as if it had a life of its own.

Meshak gazed at the traffic grinding up the avenue. One after the other, a stream of pack horses, wagons and horses laden with instruments, costumes and props for the musicians and entertainers headed for the house. He tracked them across country, scrambling over walls, crossing fields of cattle and sheep, keeping the avenue in sight until he reached a high wooded ridge from where he had an even better view of Ashbrook House. There, he watched goods being unloaded and carried into the house, and the strange-costumed people milling around like swarms of butterflies.

As the sun began to set, the wagons gave way to shining carriages with proud plumed horses and liveried coachmen and menservants in attendance on horseback. They processed up to the front of the house, where they were greeted by the Ashbrook footmen, who came hurrying down the steps to open the carriage doors. Other servants held flaming torches to light their way in the fading light.

Meshak made his way down to the house and crept round the side, peeping in through the windows. A flurry of housemaids and footmen rushed up and down the corridors, completing last-minute tasks, but there was no sign of his angel. As he completed a tour of the house, he found himself back at the front, in time to observe a small, dark-green, one-horse carriage drawing up. He noticed the coat of arms – a leaping stag – painted on its side and remembered seeing it before. Where was it, now? he thought. Oh yes, it was the same carriage which had come in the night to the Black Dog. As before, someone else was watching discreetly. He saw Mrs Lynch drawing back behind a pillar to observe who would emerge.

A footman opened the carriage door to reveal a broad, middle-aged gentleman who descended first. He held out his arm. A young woman's hand extended to rest on his brocade and lace sleeve. She was barely sixteen and looked pale and nervous. She was dressed rather soberly for a party, wearing a full, dull-green gown, as if she had recently been in mourning. The couple walked stiffly up the steps without looking at each other, and could have been strangers but for the fact they had arrived together in the same coach, and now walked into the house arm-in-arm.

As one of the grooms passed nearby, Meshak heard Mrs Lynch ask casually, 'Amos, to whom might that phaeton belong?'

'Mr Theodore Claymore, the district magistrate, and his ward, Miss Price from Barnsley,' he replied, not succeeding in hiding a smirk on his face, before he hurried away.

An hour later, music streamed out with the sounds of laughter and merriment as the ball got under way. Outside, Meshak sensed that the night sky was full of angels. But the only angel he wanted to see was Melissa. He crouched in the shadows of the stables, waiting until the nightwatchman's swinging light had turned the corner before moving cautiously round to the west side of the house. He knew the children's nursery overlooked the back gardens. Perhaps there he would glimpse her.

He sidled up to the walls of the house, sheltering beneath their gables and cornices, and found himself passing the housekeeper's quarters. The shutters were not quite closed and, as it was a warm night, the window was slightly open; he could hear voices talking and laughing. Standing on tiptoe, he peered in. He could see his father quite clearly, lounging on a sofa, beer tankard in hand, pipe in the other. Mrs Lynch had drawn up a chair nearby and, also with tankard in hand, was leaning forward earnestly talking. 'I can put business your way and be of use to Mrs Peebles too,' she was saying.

Otis was trying to brush her aside with teasing. 'Come now, Mrs Lynch. Mrs Peebles and I have no *business*, as you put it. I pick up stray brats and take them off the hands of the parish. It's as simple as that. Mrs Peebles is in a position to know which parish has a problem. Occasionally, she gets gentlewomen coming to her for help. When she knows she has a bastard to get rid of, she passes them on to me. That's all!'

'Yes, but *she's* in Gloucester and *I'm* here,' wheedled Mrs Lynch softly. 'Don't you think I don't know what's going on round these parts? Or do you think farming folk are too poor to warrant your attention and stir your compassionate heart?' There was a long pause. Mrs Lynch poured more wine into Otis's tankard. 'There's money out here, Otis. Big money. I'm not stupid. This isn't just about doing favours for the parish – or favours for silly young women who get themselves into a pickle. This is about influence and money. It involves big and powerful people . . . If you count me in,' she continued softly, 'I can put big business your way. Better than foundlings. I know things about a lot of people – a lot of high-up people. Why, right here in this very house, Lady Ashbrook runs a committee in support of the parish orphanage.

Do you know who else is on that committee? Admiral Bailey, Canon Maybury and Mr Theodore Claymore.' She paused to see if Otis recognised the last name but he showed no sign, so she continued. 'Just benefactors? I don't think so. They wouldn't like it if what I know got around. You see, Otis, my job is to know the needs of the people of this house.'

Otis smiled. Yes, he could see that Mrs Lynch was good at listening and probably overhearing too. He was sure she displayed understanding and that, above all, she understood the frailties of others. She would have made herself indispensable. She probably had Lady Ashbrook in the palm of her hand and made herself invaluable to her mistress by being the fount of all information about the parish. If anyone required a position or a loan or had a problem of any description, it was almost certain that Mrs Lynch would know about it. If Lady Ashbrook was looking for 'good quality' and 'reliable' parish nurses to attend to the poorhouses and the orphanage, it would surely be Mrs Lynch to whom she turned for advice. Otis smiled, but his eyes were cold. He could see how well it would be to keep in with Mrs Lynch.

'I may not be as experienced as Mrs Peebles in these matters,' Mrs Lynch said to Otis with soft modesty, 'but I can offer you useful information in exchange for a small cut of your – how shall we call them – profits?' Then, with the perfect timing of an actress, Mrs Lynch suddenly stopped being business-like and turned coquettish: 'Eh, Otis? Aren't I making you a sensible business offer, eh?'

'Now, that all depends,' murmured Otis seductively. He opened his arms and drew the giggling Mrs Lynch towards him, but before she succumbed to his embraces, she slipped coyly away and went to the window.

Meshak ducked out of sight, as she closed the shutters so that there was not one chink between them, though he heard Mrs Lynch ask sweetly, 'Otis, what was the carriage which came to the Black Dog the night I was there?'

'What carriage?' Otis casually murmured.

'The one which came to the Black Dog the night you were there. Mrs Peebles knows about it. Must have been important to get Mrs Peebles from her bed in the dead of night. It was to do with your *business*, wasn't it, Otis? Well, I think I may have more information about that mysterious visitor about whom you appear to know nothing . . .' Her voice became muffled and Meshak knew they were kissing and cuddling.

The nightwatchman's tossing light came back into view once more. Meshak patted his thigh, which brought the patient Jester to his side, and slipped away round the house to the west side where the ballroom was.

He gazed through the long elegant windows downstairs. It was like peering into fairyland. The people were so beautiful in their satins and silks and lace and velvet, their slippered feet and gloved hands, their lacquered wigs and bejewelled curls. He clearly saw the dancers facing their partners as they lined up for a whirling gavotte. He broke into a dance too, jigging up and down like a half-formed puppet. Still dancing, he moved on and, through another window, saw the dining-room with its long table laden with food. White-gloved footmen moved slowly round, checking the cutlery, plates and glasses, making sure there were no smudges or imperfections, and that each was perfectly positioned.

But where was *she*? He couldn't see Melissa.

Meshak continued his search. There were so many windows at Ashbrook House, especially higher up where the bedchambers were, but, apart from briefly catching sight of a boy in the west wing, he did not glimpse that flash of auburn hair or that sweet angelic face.

A large dog came flying out of the darkness from nowhere, snarling and baring its teeth. Jester lunged at it and, for a moment, it looked as if the two animals would hurl themselves into a fight. Meshak flung his arms round Jester's neck and pulled him away. But the alarm was given: he saw the nightwatchman hurrying towards him, ready to confront an intruder.

With his hand gripping Jester's neck, Meshak fled towards the stables, where the stable lads were gathered in a clump, sitting on hay bales, drinking ale and telling boisterous stories. He would like to have sat with them and been one of the lads. He would like to feel he was normal, that they saw him as normal, but instead they jeered at the sight of him. 'What 'ave you been up to, turnip head?' they scoffed. 'Ditching babies? Why didn't your da ditch you? That's what we want to know?' Their faces were cruel in the glow of the brazier round which they sat. 'Shall us put some business your way?' they laughed with their broken, cracked, young lads' laughter. 'Come round these parts in nine months' time and us'll have some more babbies for you!' One of them chucked a stone at his feet and sniggered as Meshak jumped out of the way, and another struck Jester and made him yelp. Then they all joined in, splitting their sides as Meshak hopped this way and that and finally was forced to flee with two or three guard dogs barking and leaping after him.

'Call them blasted dogs off,' groaned the lads to the nightwatchman, who had come heaving and panting round the house, his cudgels at the ready. ' 'Tis only that loon, Meshak.'

He ran low, like a fugitive, with Jester at his heels, away from the house and across the gardens to a point where the stream runs along the edge of the gardens of Ashbrook House and under an Italianate bridge which curved over the water, linking the smooth lawns and terraces with the wild woods. Meshak crossed the bridge and picked up a track on the other side.

He didn't want to go too deeply into the trees, for there were always gamekeepers who roamed the woods, heath and riverbanks on the lookout for poachers. They laid snares and mantraps, and to be caught could mean dire consequences; not just because you might break an ankle or rip open the flesh of your legs but, if you were suspected of poaching it meant the law and the assizes, and that in turn could mean deportation or even the gallows. He kept close to the water's edge so that he and Jester could lose their scent in the water and foil the vigilant nostrils of the gamekeepers' dogs. He blundered on. The stream entered the deeper darkness of the trees and he lost sight of the star-strewn sky.

He saw a pale light. It came from the little play cottage. Surely the children weren't there at this hour? Would they not all be up at the ball? Tentatively, he crept forward. He could hear music; a voice sang with piercing sweetness accompanied by the soft tones of a virginals. He knew instantly who it was. He knew, he knew – yet he had to see. His heart tightened in his chest. He could hardly breathe with the emotion which surged through him. The shutters were closed, but still he prowled round from window to window, seeking one small chink through which he could gaze. When he reached the back, he pushed at a door. It opened. He did not reason, but just followed his desire to see. He motioned Jester to stay and stepped inside. He was in the little kitchen. A fire smouldered in the grate and a kettle hung from a hook, steaming softly. Ahead was the little room where the children played their games and pretended to be grown up. The door was ajar.

He saw them. He saw his angel. She played and Alexander sang. The song ended and Alexander was standing behind her now. He put his hands on her shoulders and kissed the top of her head. Meshak's angel turned, her face tipped upwards. She was streaming with light and joy just as she did when she stood in the window in Gloucester Cathedral; her eyes gleamed, overflowing with happiness, and then their arms were round each other and they were kissing. Kissing. Mouth on mouth. Arms, cheeks, hair, neck.

A howl filled the cottage. A sound so raw and harsh that no one could say it came from a human being. Meshak fled away, his wretched, wrenching howl scuttering and trailing through the night, leaving behind the two people in the cottage blood-chilled, transfixed with horror and guilt, as if somehow they had done wrong and all the demons of hell had found them out.

He fled through the woods and climbed up the steep banks, out of the deep valley, up and up into open pasture above the woods where the cows slumbered like great statues in the darkness. Still howling, he flung himself down to be dead among them, yet his heart thudded so hard it could have burst from his breast. The huge beasts with their great swelling bodies, smelling of milk and flesh and grass, stirred out of their moonlit reverie. They bowed their slow heads to see who lay there, while Jester gently nuzzled him with soft, moist, questioning nostrils.

For a long while, he lay dead, lying on his back, staring sightlessly at the vast fishing-net sky in which stars seemed caught like silver fishes. And he too was caught, his limbs entangled; his hair and eyes and all four limbs were being stretched and pulled and pinned down between sky and earth. Hours may have passed, years, eternities with Jester patiently at his side. Finally, dew-drenched, he stumbled to his feet. He didn't want to come alive. He would have stayed dead if he could. But he couldn't control the deep pain in his heart which brought him alive, weeping and howling.

'She's *my* angel!' he bellowed.

Dawn was streaking the eastern sky when he returned to the wagon. Otis was still not back. Meshak climbed up inside and pulled the flap to. He crouched tight as if he were back in the womb, his arms hugged round his knees, and rocked and rocked and rocked, while outside Jester whined pitifully.

Chapter Ten

★

Jealousies

After the boys had returned to Gloucester, Isobel knew something had changed. It wasn't just that Ashbrook seemed unbearably empty, or that Edward and Alice were fretful and quarrelsome and missed Thomas, who had spent so much time with them, making them laugh with his silly voices and funny stories. Everyone missed Thomas. Nor was it that Lady Ashbrook was preoccupied and could sometimes be heard humming 'The Silver Swan', as though she missed her son more than anything. Something had happened to all of them through that August holiday and in particular to Melissa.

The day the boys left, Melissa hadn't even come out to say goodbye, sending word that she had a headache and was confined to bed. Isobel had wondered how that could be, when she had danced so merrily most of the evening at the ball. True, Isobel had lost sight of her towards the end. If she had felt ill, why hadn't she told her? Isobel was used to Melissa being her closest friend and couldn't conceive of her even having a headache without her knowing about it. And wouldn't Melissa have had to have been at death's door not to come out and say goodbye to Alexander, whose company she seemed to have enjoyed so much? Indeed, as Isobel sat at her dressing table and studied her own reflection staring back, she knew, that for the first time in her life, she had felt stirrings of jealousy.

Before he went away, Alexander had always been Isobel's closest friend. They had done everything together and, even though she had nothing like his musical talent, she had been able to share his passion for music, play duets and sing with him. Isobel knew that she understood her brother in a way that no one else did. Brother and sister had always confided in each other; protected and sympathised with each other, especially she with him when their father could be so stern and demanding and critical of his son. It was with her alone that Alexander shared his secret hopes that one day he could be a great musician.

But by the end of the holidays, something had changed and she wasn't sure what. Had Melissa taken her place as her brother's confidante? Was she jealous because Alexander spent so much time with Melissa, or upset because Melissa's behaviour on that last day seemed to indicate that she no longer liked Alexander? Either way, it left Isobel feeling upset and confused.

Finally, she resolved not to just sit there fretting. She would ask her. Isobel leapt to her feet and ran to Melissa's room. Melissa was seated in a chair in the window, reading. She looked up, startled, as the knock on the door was almost immediately followed by Isobel bursting in.

Melissa's face broke into such a broad welcoming smile at the sight of her, tossing her book aside and leaping forward to embrace her, that all those questions, those accusations with which Isobel was going to accost her, just drained away. Instead she said, 'Melissa, dearest! Look – the sun is out again at last. Let's go for a walk. I feel half stifled. We seem to have been indoors for days and days.'

'Oh yes, I'd love to. I'd really love to,' exclaimed Melissa.

Minutes later, wearing leather boots because of the mud, but otherwise lightly dressed in cotton frocks and bonnets and summer cloaks tossed over their shoulders, they set off arm in arm across the grass towards the trees on the other side of the stream.

They followed the path through the woods and for a while postponed talking too deeply, although each felt there was something which needed saying. They stopped to examine and identify the tracks of animals; they wobbled and laughed as they tried to balance on fallen logs; they leapt from stone to stone across the winding stream; and only after they seemed to have relaxed with each other, joking and chatting, did they begin to talk about the month of August and the holiday.

Isobel started it by expressing her concern about her father.

'He hates Alexander's music so much, I fear there will be bad feeling at first when Alexander comes home.'

'Perhaps when Sir William attends the Christmas concert and hears the Christmas anthem Alexander has composed, he will understand,' said Melissa. 'Surely he can't fail to be impressed at hearing his son's music performed in that great cathedral?'

'He's never been impressed before,' sighed Isobel. 'It's not the first time the choir has sung Alexander's music. He has written something for them every year. My father has attended many times, and all he can say is, "Yes, yes, very nice but it won't bring in the harvest." '

They had broken out of the woods now and were following a drover's track towards the open moor. Sheep grazed on the steep slopes around them, their white fleeces like gleaming snow against the summer grass. Isobel could contain herself no longer. 'Melissa! Why did you not come out to say goodbye to Alexander and Thomas the day they left? Why? I am most troubled and fear you may have quarrelled. Don't you like him any more? Is that why you didn't come out to say goodbye? Is it why you are so distant with me?'

'Quarrelled?' Melissa stopped dead in her tracks. 'Quarrelled? What, me and Alexander? Oh, Isobel!' Melissa threw an arm round the younger girl. 'Why, nothing could be further from the truth. I think he and I have a . . .' she hesitated and flushed a little, trying to find the right words. 'We are good, good friends, believe me. How could I ever fall out with him when I admire him so? But there is something which has happened and perhaps I should tell you that . . .'

Suddenly, they heard the thud of hooves behind them. The girls instinctively flattened themselves into the hedgerow as two riders cantered into view with empty saddlebags flapping at their sides. The first one, a sharp-faced handsome man wearing a broad-brimmed leather hat, his dark unwigged hair flowing round his shoulders, reined in his horse. The youth behind – who rode a mule and was much less gainly, with his overly large head of bright red hair, florid face and drooling mouth – did the same and the two riders passed the girls at a walking pace. The first rider made a great show of doffing his hat and emulating a low extravagant bow from his saddle, looking directly into Isobel's eyes, as though he knew it was she who was of superior station, while the red-headed boy could only gabble and drool. He fixed his large, blue watery eyes on Melissa and could not take his eyes off her even after they had passed by, till it looked as if his head would be twisted off.

At the bend, they heard the first man shout, 'Get thy mind on the road, you loon, and stop gawking at the ladies!' Then, with an almost insolent wave of his hand, the rider kicked his horse's flanks and the two of them cantered on and disappeared out of sight.

Still leaning back into the hedgerow, the girls didn't move until the sound of hooves had died away.

'Who were those awful fellows?' exclaimed Isobel. 'Did you see the way they looked at us? And the red-headed one! Why, Melissa, I thought he would scoop you up and gallop off with you, he stared so. I've never seen such insolence. But the older man – why, I think I loathed him more. There was such a lack of respect in his bearing . . .' she trailed off, unable to express the abhorrence she felt.

'I think that is Otis Gardiner and his son, Meshak,' said Melissa. 'Tabitha told me about them when I saw them hanging round the house on the day of the ball. She said Otis is an acquaintance of Mrs Lynch. They are known round these parts. I believe they are nothing but pedlars so don't be alarmed.'

The girls once more took the track, brushing down their skirts and straightening their bonnets, and continued their walk. Despite the interruption in the conversation, Isobel hadn't forgotten where they had left off. 'What was it you felt you should tell me?' she asked Melissa warily.

'It's that . . . well . . . it's "the flowers", that's what they call it. You know, when a girl stops being a child. Once a month she bleeds.' Isobel looked stunned and horrified. 'Just as you will too,' Melissa reassured her. 'It's best you know so that you do not panic as I did. It's natural, I promise you. Just nature's way, you'll see soon enough. The night of the ball, I felt something . . . I thought I was . . . I thought I was dying. Mama got all fussed. She didn't seem afraid, yet she didn't know how to tell me and went rushing off to find Mrs Lynch.'

'Mrs Lynch? What could she know? Why didn't she call a physician? She should have dispatched one of the servants to get Dr Wallbridge. What did Mrs Lynch do?' cried Isobel, still alarmed.

'No, no! It's not an illness, I tell you. She sent Dorcas to the kitchen for a pail of warm water for me to bathe. She bundled up all my soiled clothes to take to the washerwoman, and she got strips of cotton and wool which I was to use to stem the flow.'

'I wish you'd told me.' Isobel shook her head with guilt. 'I thought so many bad things when you just took to your bed like that and never sent for me. I thought you must have quarrelled with Alexander and didn't like me any more.'

The track on which the girls had been walking now dipped down out of the wooded valley and opened up to flat pastures, and ahead of them they saw the orphanage. It was quarantined beyond the pastures; bleak and isolated on a piece of rough scrub ground and, although Isobel knew her mother had worked hard to make it a more caring and agreeable institution, the building was ugly. Its red brick was not glowing and warm like so many other brick buildings in the area, but grubby, damp-looking and unwelcoming. They saw the horse and mule which had passed them by, tethered at a water trough. A straggle of children wandered about, doing tasks in the yard, but with little energy.

'What business would this pedlar have at the orphanage?' asked Isobel curiously.

'Who knows,' said Melissa. 'I suppose they have need of goods as much as any other place. Come, let's get away from here in case we have to pass them once more on their return.'

The girls left the track and cut across the fields to their left, heading for the line of distant trees which made up Ashbrook Wood. 'I think we might get to Waterside in time for tea,' murmured Isobel, looking up at the sun and guessing that it was about three o'clock in the afternoon.

Edward and Alice were in the play cottage being supervised by their old nanny and Ruth, one of the nursemaids.

'Isobel! Melissa! Oh good, you've come! Eddie and I are playing mothers and fathers,' cried Alice. 'Look – this is our baby. We've put her in the cradle Thomas made. Ruthie's been sewing sheets for her and Nanny gave us a blanket. Isn't she lovely? Eddie and I want to have a christening. Ruthie says we must have a christening robe. Can you make one?'

'Well . . .' answered Isobel doubtfully.

'Yes – we can!' asserted Melissa. 'You're wonderful at embroidery, Isobel, and I can cut and sew. Between us, we'll make a perfect christening gown. Ruth can help us, can't you, Ruth?' Melissa addressed the young nursemaid.

'Yes, miss. I'll do me best, miss. I sewed one for our Michael, miss, when 'im was baptised, and me mam said it was good as like I'd been a seamstress meself, miss,' she answered confidently.

'Here, Melissa,' cried little Alice, tenderly picking up the doll from out of the cradle, 'hold my baby. I've called her Arabella. Rock her, otherwise she'll cry.'

'Like this?' laughed Melissa, rocking the doll in her arms.

'If we make the gown well enough, Alice will be able to keep it for her own real baby,' cackled old Nanny.

'Oh!' laughed Melissa, handing Alice back her baby. 'And who is Alice going to marry when she grows up?'

'I'm going to marry Alex,' answered Alice stoutly.

Everyone burst out laughing. Bewildered, Alice ran to Nanny. 'Why are they laughing, Nanny?'

' 'Cos you can't marry Alex, silly!' shouted Edward. 'You can't marry your own brother.'

'Well then.' Alice paused and thought a while. 'Then I'll marry Thomas.'

Everyone laughed again.

'Now why are you laughing?' cried Alice, looking red-faced and distraught.

'Now, now, children. Don't get our little Alice all upset,' said

Nanny soothingly. 'Leave the little mite alone. She'll learn soon enough who she can marry and who she can't.'

Alice ran to Edward and whispered in his ear. 'Why, Eddie? Why can't I marry Thomas?'

' 'Cos he's not a gentleman,' Edward whispered back – which everyone heard and burst out laughing again.

'Will Izzy marry a gentleman?' asked Alice.

'I hope so,' laughed Isobel.

'Can Melissa marry Alex, then?'

Everyone turned and looked at Melissa, who turned a beetroot red then fled into the kitchen. 'Nanny! Have you been making some of your delicious cakes again?' she called with a muffled voice.

'Oh my goodness! I forgot my cakes!' exclaimed Nanny, heaving her great body up out of the easy chair and hobbling after Melissa into the kitchen.

'Izzy? Can Melissa marry Alex?' asked Edward thoughtfully.

'I don't know,' replied Isobel slowly, as if suddenly she realised perhaps this was something she should think about. 'I think Mama and Papa hope that Alex will marry Lady Sarah.'

'Oh no! She's horrible!' exclaimed Edward emphatically. 'She smells.'

'Hush, Edward, that's no way to speak of a lady!' chastised Nanny, shuffling back into the room. 'Now, come on, there are two cakes each!' The children fell upon the cake dish and, for the moment, forgot the dilemmas about who to marry.

After tea, they played. Alice kissed and cuddled her doll, tenderly swaddling it and unswaddling it, and gave it to Melissa to tuck into Thomas's cradle. But her maternal games could switch rapidly from her dolls to wanting to play with Edward, and she would suddenly abandon her baby and push Edward off the rocking-horse so that she could ride. 'I know. Let's play highwaymen,' and Alice would laugh with stifled terror, and she and Isobel would hide behind the sofa as Edward rode the rocking-horse, and then they would jump out with pistols drawn, crying, 'Stand and deliver, your money or your life!'

It was in the midst of such a game that Alice, who was hiding behind a chair near the window, suddenly jumped out with a scream.

'Too soon, Alice! Too soon!' yelled Edward.

Then they saw her face. 'There's someone out there. Right below the window. He was peeping at us,' she whimpered.

Large, fearsome Nanny got to her feet, clasped the poker from the grate and thrust open the cottage door. All the children ran out, except Melissa, who hung back, looking suddenly terrified. They couldn't see anyone, but the sound of someone scuttling off like a wounded animal trailed away into the undergrowth, and there was that same howl, much lower this time, more stifled, but

Melissa recognised it. 'Sounds like a hound,' she whispered as the others came back.

'Thomas told me a story about a headless ghost dog which runs through the village when there's a full moon,' stated Edward. 'He said it's a sign that someone is going to die. Do you think a headless dog can howl – even if it's a ghost?'

'Now now, me lad. Let's have no talk of headless dogs, if you please. Little Alice is already upset enough,' muttered Nanny. 'Thomas is a naughty boy to fill your head with such stories. They're probably out with the dogs looking for a runaway from one of the mills. I hear there was an escape from Mr Merryweather's quarry. Nothing to worry about. These youngsters take off in the summer but go back in the winter. I'll tell Josiah the gamekeeper about it. We'll go back to the house now, but mind you children don't leave the path in the woods. Don't want you falling into any of Josiah's mantraps now, do we?'

They gathered together their cloaks and set off along the trail.

Meshak stood utterly motionless, his eyes rolled up into his head. He had come back to the wagon in the woods like an animal, bounding on all fours, howling frantically. Then he had stood up, taken one huge gasp and become rigid as if turned to stone.

'Wake up, damn you!' Otis roared and flicked a horse whip across his son's shoulders with a stinging swish. 'Move yourself, you great lump, and give me a hand with the mules! I want to get on the road.' He lashed the whip again.

But Meshak hardly even winced. He could neither hear nor see, feel hot or cold, or respond to any kind of stimulus. Many a time Otis had beaten, kicked, whipped, slapped – inflicted all sorts of pain on his son to wake him up – but nothing worked. Many people wondered why Otis hadn't abandoned the idiot boy long ago, to which Otis had replied with deep sincerity, 'Why, how could I do a thing like that to my own flesh and blood?'

Now Otis whipped him again and again but in frustration, as he roared around the wagon, getting it hitched and stacked and ready to leave, lashing out at the animals, causing them to bray in distress, and the children inside to quake in terror.

Deep inside his brain, Meshak stood in a wasteland beneath a black sky. It was a place of nothingness; of non-existence.

When finally he was ready to go and Meshak still hadn't moved, Otis grabbed the lad, humped him over his shoulder and threw him like a sack of potatoes into the back of the wagon.

Chapter Eleven

✫

The Coram Hospital

'Coram, Coram. That's the name. I've heard of him. You are the Coram man, aren't you? You will take my baby, won't you? You will deliver her safely to that kind gentleman? It is true, isn't it, that he never turns any baby away? And they look after them until they are ready to work? It's true, isn't it? Tell me it is. They feed them, clothe them, train them for work? That's what I've heard. Girls as well as boys. That dear good man, Captain Coram, like Jesus – suffer the little children – I would kiss and wash his feet if I could, and thank him for taking in my little one. Will you guard her with your life? I'll pay you – I'll pay you whatever I have, only take care of my little daughter, my darling angel. And here, will you take this lock of my hair and this little bead necklace? Make sure they stay with her. Make sure you tell them there at that place, tell the captain, God bless him, that this is her mother's hair and that she should know one day that her mother loved her and only parted from her to save her from starvation and cruel public abuse. You will, won't you? And bring me word, will you? Next time you're round these parts. I'll look out for you – only bring me word from time to time that my darling is safe and well . . . I'll pay you . . . I'll pay . . . I'll pay you all that I have if you will just take her to Coram . . .'

The weeping, pathetic voices of distraught mothers became an increasing chorus in his head, night and day, night and day, so that often Meshak didn't know whether he woke or slept, dreamt or really heard the anguished voices like rain streaming through leaves, mingling with the kitten-like mewlings of newborn babes – in those woods – those dark, deep, leafy, muddy, root-entangled woods; or in mire-filled ditches, or on high, deserted moors, or by lonely wayside hedgerows.

They dumped so many little bodies along the highways and byways on their way to London, and all the time the name, Coram, Coram, Coram was repeated and repeated like a prayer, as though the very name invoked Paradise.

They reached London and crossed its teeming carriage-filled thoroughfares, squeezing through narrow, rat-infested alleys and lanes, and skirting the piles of rubbish. They ignored the drunks and down-and-outs, the men, women and children, slumped in doorways or under arches of bridges, dying of gin and starvation. Otis eyed the fine ladies and gentlemen in exquisite wigs and hats, jackets, gowns and silver-buckled shoes, who picked their way through the city or skimmed lightly over the mayhem in their carriages like glittering fairies, as if all the filth and sorrows of the world were completely invisible to them.

They were invisible to Meshak too, for all he saw in his mind's eye was the little play cottage in the woods and Melissa, his beloved angel; Melissa kissing Alexander. Even now, after two months, his stomach turned over. She was *his* angel. Pain and anger merged like waves crashing in a storm. Only now, gradually, the anger was fading. Somehow, she began to rise up out of it and, once again, in dreams and fantasies, it was her face alone which hovered over him, and he imagined her walking at his side or smiling with her heaven-blue eyes into his face.

On a certain morning, Otis and Meshak left the stench and smoke and raucous sounds of the city behind them, and made their way northwards towards Lamb's Conduit Fields. They drove alongside cow-cluttered fields and meandered between orchards and pastures to the outskirts of the city, where the air was cleaner and where wealthier people lived in their large mansions, keeping their distance from the murk and din of the teeming populace.

'I've come to see Sarah Wood, the chief nurse,' Otis told the gatekeeper when they arrived at the large wrought-iron gates at the head of a long avenue which led to the Coram Hospital. As usual, there was a throng of desperate women pressing at the gates of the hospital; begging not to be forced to drop their babies in the street to die, begging for a chance in the lottery. They had to dip their hands in a basket and draw out a ball: a white ball denoted entry, a black ball meant denial and a red ball meant they could wait in the hope that one of the chosen babies would fail the medical test they all underwent.

Otis had left the train of mules grazing on a piece of common land nearby, and come with the wagon, clanking and clinking, filled to the brim with pots and pans and metal tools, for kitchen and garden. Hidden from view were three or four bundles of babies, the only ones still alive from their travels, but too weak even to mew. The watchman recognised him and cheerily waved him through. 'She's somewhere round the back – or else in her parlour all the worse for gin,' he grinned.

Otis and Sarah Wood had an understanding. He kept alive the babies from well-to-do families which he had picked up on his journeys, and on whom he would lean from time to time for money and more money – 'For the welfare of the children, you understand.' There was always the unspoken threat that if they didn't pay up, the babies would suffer, and their sinful daughters be left exposed to a pitiless society, disgraced and unmarriageable.

It had been Otis's idea that Sarah Wood should take in the infants he brought to the back door instead of the front. This way, they wouldn't be counted in and registered by the officers of the charity, who would not have admitted more than thirty foundlings at a time. But so many foundlings died within the first few days of admittance that it was easy for her to slip in two or three extra ones to take their places. Otis put himself in charge of the extortion. Although he couldn't read or write, he had a notebook in which he had his own signs and markings to list the people who fell into his power, and he always collected the money, out of which he paid Sarah a goodly sum. So she was generally satisfied with her part of the bargain.

In the back yard, Otis yelled to a Coram child, recognisable by his brown serge jacket and breeches, trimmed with red, and the white cap bound to his head. 'Oi! Go tell Mistress Wood, Otis is here.'

The boy vanished obediently, and Otis got down from the wagon and hitched it to a post. 'Stay within earshot,' he commanded Meshak.

Hearing the sounds of children, Meshak waited till Otis had been summoned inside, then wandered off in the direction of the voices. Across the kitchen yard, full of pecking hens and waddling geese and farm dogs slumbering in the sun, he came to a well, around which a group of Coram girls laughed and squealed as they wound a winch which drew a pail clanking and slopping up to the top. Then, like sparrows, they dived into it, their sleeves thrust up to their elbows, washing and drinking and splashing each other with sprays of water which sparkled like diamonds in the sunlight.

Meshak rocked backwards and forwards on his heels, clapping his hands with pleasure; and he laughed too – loudly, like a donkey – longing to share their fun. But when they saw him, they pulled faces and their laughter became mocking and cruel. 'Go, go, go,' they jeered, and dashed the remainder of the water in the pail at him as if he were some flea-ridden hound come in off the street. And so he scuttled off out of their sight, round the back of the cowsheds. He saw the chapel and the graveyard. Here, at least, children who died were given a Christian burial and had their names chiselled on headstones to prove that they once lived. Away from the graves of Coram foundlings were those of the farmworkers and surrounding families. Some of the graves were quite grand, with high plinths and ornate headstones or sculptures of angels. It was quiet. No one here to laugh and jeer at him. So he stretched himself out on a tomb, like a crusader knight, and decided to be dead for a bit and try to talk to the angels.

His eyes rolled upwards, tracing the length of an elm, up, up its knobbly trunk, into the branches and leaves where the sky glistened in a patchwork of blue; and he penetrated its blueness till he was absorbed into it. When he began to hear the sound of voices singing anthems and psalms that reverberated in all the corners of his brain, he felt he hovered among the angels. Oh, how good it was to be dead up there among them. His awakening

– how long after, he could not know – was rude and rough. A gravedigger came by, hollering at him, and shoved him off the tomb with the sharp edge of a spade so that he crashed to the ground face down, his heart thudding fit to burst. Meshak was amazed that he could still hear the angels' singing.

'Get out of here, you heathen idiot,' ranted the gravedigger. 'Don't you know this is hallowed ground?'

Half crawling, half stumbling, he fled again, zigzagging among the graves, and found himself at the chapel door. Music poured out. He pushed open the great oak door and crept inside. Crouching among the pews, he only saw the heads like cherubs, with ruffs round their necks. He could glimpse the brown and red colours of the Coram uniform. But still he was hardly aware of whether he was alive or dead, until their conductor, a large stocky man, rapped a stick against the lectern and rasped in a heavy German accent, '*Nein, nein, Knaben! Nicht so. So!* Dum de da de da de dum. Like ziss. *Noch einmal!* Again, again!'

'From which bar, Mr Handel?' called out the voice of the organist.

'*Fünfzig!* Feefty!' he roared back. A huge sound filled the air: 'For unto us a child is born!'

When the choir practice was over and the boys went racing outside with cassocks flapping, like doves freed from their dovecote, Meshak followed them, warily keeping his distance. He was hungry and so were they. He heard them shouting that it was time for food. He did not dare follow them through a side door that led into their dining-room, though he glimpsed the long wooden tables and benches at which they all sat. Instead, he went round to the kitchens, where dozens of loaves were being drawn out of the ovens to be served with thick vegetable broth. A cook girl saw him and roughly tried to send him away like some troublesome beggar, but another cried out, 'Let 'im be, Sal, 'e's Otis's lad. 'Ere you. 'Ave some o' this!' And she gave him a wooden bowl of broth along with a chunk of bread. Gratefully, Meshak accepted the offering and consumed it with the speed of a ravenous hound.

Otis seemed pleased with himself when he emerged from Sarah Wood's parlour. First of all he had made a hefty profit from his last transaction. Secondly, they had spent the last few hours poring over his notebook with the list of foundlings he had brought in from well-to-do families who would be willing to pay a price to protect their honour and cover up the sins of their fallen daughters. But he had another list: a list of children who should have been apprenticed out but for whom there were no places in the trades of the city. It would have been a headache for the hospital had it not been for the likes of Otis Gardiner, who recruited for the army and navy, and the many merchant ships – 'For a small fee, you understand.' Today, Otis said he would take four boys and, while he consumed a tankard of ale and smoked a pipe with Sarah Wood, the boys were made ready.

Some time later, Otis emerged with the four young boys in tow. One or two of them were weeping quietly and looking round as if in the hope that someone would come out and say it was all a big mistake, and that they should not leave the safety and shelter of the hospital.

Meshak ran to the wagon and opened up the flaps, and the boys tumbled in, followed by Meshak, whose main job would be to ensure they didn't abscond. Otis climbed up on to the seat and took the reins. He looked pleased with himself and patted a large pouch of money strapped to his waist. The whip flicked with a crack across the mule's back and the wagon lurched forward. They headed back into the city, taking the road that would lead to the docks.

If Meshak was afraid of the dark wild forests and moors of Gloucestershire, afraid of the body hanging from the gibbet at the crossroads, afraid of marauding vagabonds, highwaymen and witches, and of the blue-stained woad men who were said to be able to cross between the living and the dead, nothing looked more terrifying to him than the London docks of the River Thames.

Sloops and barges, coasters and fishing-boats scuttered up and down the river. He had to tip his head upwards to see the merchant ships with their ropes and masts and rigging and drooping sails, looking like some kind of spider's web within which people struggled and scuttled like insects as they climbed and swung among the masts and yardarms. Others endlessly shinned up and down ropes between land and water, hauling baskets and bundles, cattle and sheep and crates of chickens – everything that would be required to sustain a full ship at sea for weeks on end. And when night fell, the outlines of these ships loomed even more menacingly, flickering with flames from the myriad lanterns and oil lamps and fiery brands; some swinging from poles and prows and yardarms, others carried by boys, flashing to and fro like fireflies.

Meshak had no idea that there were so many people in the world – let alone in London. By those manic, swaying, fleeting lamps he saw faces he could never have conceived of before. Faces of every hue and shape and size: broad-browed and squat, spoon-shaped and moon-shaped; long-nosed, broad-nosed, narrow-eyed and round-eyed; skins that were yellow, brown and olive, skins that were as black as night. (That there were distant lands over the ocean, he had no notion.)

Otis stopped the wagon and climbed down. 'Keep an eye on them, Meshak,' he ordered, and was gone.

The Coram boys were terrified. They peered out of the wagon between the flaps. 'What's he going to do? Can we go back to

Coram? We're not going on them things, are we?' They stared in horror at the huge hulks and, seeing other young boys scampering about, began to fear the worst.

Then Otis was back, accompanied by a wigged gentleman in a smart long brocade coat, with a sword at his side. His cold eye swept over the boys. 'Get out! Let's have a look at you!' he rapped. 'Free of disease, are they? Can't have disease aboard my ships. Bare your chests.' The boys clambered out and pulled up their shirts. He looked over their skin for signs of a rash, peered in their mouths at their teeth, felt their bones and joints for signs of rickets, and then nodded. 'I can take two.' He prodded the two older ones with his baton.

'Take me too, 'e's my best friend!' wailed a younger one.

'Shut up,' snapped Otis, and whisked the two remaining boys back into the wagon.

As Otis and the agent made a deal over the boys, a group of black men and women, all chained together, shuffled by, shivering and all but naked. They were a cargo of slaves who had just come in from Africa and who were to be put on board a slave ship bound for the West Indies. One of the women clasped a newborn baby in her arms. The sailor in charge stopped nearby. 'This one gave birth.' He addressed the overseer. 'What shall we do? We had four of them on this voyage.' He snatched the baby from the mother's arms, who gave such a heart-rending shriek that even the hardened sailors stopped what they were doing and glanced over with pity.

'I'll take it, if it's a boy,' declared Otis. 'Straight exchange, these boys for the brat.'

'It's a boy all right,' said the overseer and handed the baby to the agent.

'It's a deal,' said the agent, who handed it to Otis, who passed it to Meshak.

'Put it in your jacket, lad, we don't want it freezing to death.'

Meshak held the little creature, staring at its black quivering body. It was human, wasn't it? He licked his finger and smoothed it over the baby's skin to see if the black would come off. He looked into its bawling face. As he tucked it into the warmth of his jerkin, it stopped crying and looked up at him with huge black glimmering eyes and, feeling a strange tenderness, he held it close.

There was money in black infant boys. Otis knew that. There was nothing a wealthy family in society liked more than to have a little black boy as a plaything. He was such a pet, just like their lapdogs, only more enchanting. The ladies loved to bounce him on their knees; to marvel at his black skin; to run their white fingers through his extraordinary jet-black, tight-curled hair. And later, as he grew older, if he was lucky and was still charming and lovable, he would become a page boy, all dressed up like a fairy prince, with a silken turban, embroidered garments and jewels in his ears and nose, taking the coats and cloaks from visitors, handing round sweetmeats during drawing-room gatherings. So long as he behaved himself and wasn't returned to slavery, as an adult he could become a footman or a gentleman's manservant, or an army mascot and be taken into battle. He might even be freed.

Satisfied with his bargain, and ignoring the slave mother's anguish, Otis and the agent shook on it and Otis came away puffed with self-satisfaction. He would deliver the baby to Coram for rearing and education. It would be his first 'long-term investment'. He ordered Meshak back into the wagon to stay and mind the baby and the two remaining boys, while he headed for the tailor to order a suit. It's time, he thought, that I looked like a gentleman trader rather than a pedlar.

Chapter Twelve

✫

When the voice breaks

Because this would be Alexander's last, the whole family had made the journey from Ashbrook to Gloucester for the Christmas concert, even though the weather was bad and it looked like snow. Mrs Milcote had stayed behind but Melissa, excited by the outing, had gone too. They had travelled with plenty of horses, servants and provisions, prepared for the worst eventuality.

They had taken up their quarters at Canon Maybury's house in the close and then trooped across the green into the cathedral, where they sat right up at the front.

As the choir filed into the stalls, they craned their heads to identify Alexander.

'Where is he?' whispered Isobel, her eyes scanning the faces of the choristers.

'I can see Thomas,' said Melissa, 'but not Alexander.'

'I can't see Alex,' hissed Edward loudly.

Sir William and Lady Ashcroft quietly exchanged concerned

words and, finally, Canon Maybury slipped from his stall and disappeared into the vestry.

Minutes went by. The audience shuffled and pulled their cloaks tighter round them. The cathedral was a vast and cold place. Coils of breath spiralled into the air. The few charcoal braziers glowing at intervals in the bays along the aisles hardly took the edge off the chill, and a murmur of restlessness rippled along the pews.

Canon Maybury returned. The family looked at him expectantly.

'What's happened? Where is he? Is he all right?'

'Alexander can't sing,' said the canon. 'He woke up this morning to find he had no voice. He thought at first it was a sore throat and was treating it with a remedy, but it is now apparent that his voice has broken. He didn't tell anyone at first, hoping he could manage to get through the concert, but it's impossible. He's out there in the vestry quite distressed, I'm afraid. The concert will now begin without him. At least the anthem he composed will be performed,' he said consolingly, seeing their distraught faces. 'It had to happen. We all knew that.'

Sir William leant forward. 'My dear Geoffrey, be good enough to return to Alexander with a message from me. Request him to prepare himself to return to Ashbrook with us in two days' time.

There is no point in him continuing on here now that he can no longer sing in the choir.'

'But, William . . .' Geoffrey Maybury protested. 'He has many other duties here at the cathedral. Isn't this a bit precipitous? Why not let the boy stay until next August as he expected.'

'William, my dear, Geoffrey is right,' pleaded Lady Ashbrook, with a sudden sense of foreboding. 'This is too sudden. Let him stay till August.'

But Sir William was coldly adamant and waved his hand to quell any further argument. 'I see no point in prolonging his absence from Ashbrook. I agreed that he could stay at the cathedral till his voice broke. Well, now it has broken. Kindly do as I say without further ado.'

As Canon Maybury returned to the vestry, people might have observed how a quiet smile of satisfaction spread over Sir William's face, even though the others looked alarmed and disappointed. 'I think we have our son back at last,' he murmured to Lady Ashbrook.

In an explosion of disbelief and fury, Alexander rushed from room to room, from one end of Ashbrook House to the other. Every single musical instrument had been removed. The harpsichord had gone from the drawing-room, the virginals from the nursery, the spinet from the west wing; the collection of instruments – the violins, the viol da gamba, the haut boy and horns – all had gone; even the scores, albums and the blank sheets of manuscript paper had been removed from the music room. Nothing in the house was left which could show that music ever existed in any shape or form.

Alexander burst into the library and confronted his father: 'Why, why, why have you done this to me? Isn't it enough for you that you have bagged me like some pheasant and bundled me away without even time to say goodbye to my friends and teachers?'

His father took up his cane and laid it across his back.

'This is the only way I know to get that music madness out of your system,' gasped Sir William between strokes. 'You had your way while you were a boy – you and your mother and the canon – and I kept my side of the bargain. But now, sir, the voice is gone; the bird has flown. You are a man – at least, I hope to make one of you.' He flung the cane across the room and stared into the tearless, unfathomable eyes of his son. 'You are the heir to Ashbrook,' Sir William sounded pleading now, 'and we have four years of catching up to do. See sense, man. From tomorrow, you will involve yourself solely with duties on the estate. You will ride with Elias Wick, our head forester, to be instructed in the management of woodland and forestry; Jonas Bingle will show you the workings of the mills; Stephen Dean, my chief shepherd, will explain the mysteries of the sheep industry to you, and I have instructed Martin Staines to keep you by his side so that you can learn all the details of this estate and the names of every man, woman and child who works for you. You would be wise, sir, not to think even for one moment of music, and you can thank me that I have aided you in this by removing every single instrument and every reminder of music from the house. When you are master of Ashbrook, you can do what you like, but while I am master you will do as I say.'

Standing transfixed outside the library, Isobel overheard everything. Choked with distress, she hurried almost fainting into her mother's arms. 'Can't you stop it, Mama? Don't you realise this will kill Alex?'

'Nonsense, my child. Don't overdramatise things, it helps no one,' said her mother, trying to maintain her composure. 'Alex has got to take responsibility now. He must accept his status and birth. Ashbrook must continue as it has for the last three centuries. Ashbrook has meaning. It is our life, and we are responsible for everyone who lives and works here. Who will manage it after your father dies if not Alexander? You must not encourage or sympathise with your brother's selfishness. Later, when he has rid himself of this madness, he can allow music back into his life. He was truly fortunate that his father allowed him the opportunity to give his childhood to music, but now he is a man and must behave like the future master of Ashbrook.'

When Alexander finally emerged from his father's library he stared blankly at his mother as if she were a stranger, then through her, as if she no longer existed.

'Alexander! Alex!' She reached out to touch him. 'Please . . .' But he turned away, and left the house as if he no longer lived there. 'Go after him, Isobel,' she whispered. 'Watch over him!' Filled with remorse, she felt that she, who had given birth to him, could do nothing for him.

Everyone was affected by the gloom that hung over the house; it billowed around like a great fog in which people and objects lost their identity and became just disembodied shapes. Tension and suppressed anger were as palpable as a storm brewing in the hills, when sheep huddle together and cattle make for the shelter of trees, when dogs bark meaninglessly and flocks of birds fly in confused circles in the sky.

Meal-times were almost silent. Edward and Alice stayed confined to the nursery with Mrs Milcote and Melissa. Only a silently distraught Isobel was allowed to be present at meals, on condition that she said nothing that referred to Alexander's past life as a musician.

Canon Maybury didn't call, and no contact was allowed with the cathedral, even with Thomas.

Alexander appeared like one dazed. He looked without seeing. He offered no conversation but only answered when he was spoken to. During snatched moments, Isobel tried to cheer him up and to bring back their old relationship, but he was listless and unreachable. It frightened her. He began to look more and more tired, and Lady Ashbrook feared for his health.

'Perhaps, sir, we could relent and allow him at least the use of a virginals?' she mooted anxiously to her husband.

But Sir William was implacable. 'He'll get over it. Why not organise another ball? What he needs is a young lady to take up his mind rather than music. Invite Lady Sarah. You know, I believe she would make a good match for him.'

Each morning, Alexander was roused from his bed by a manservant and told with whom he was to ride that day and what part of the estate he was to observe.

One night he awoke, startled out of a dream. A shape stood at the foot of his bed. He wondered why Bessie and Zanzibar, who slept nearby, hadn't barked or given warning. Unafraid, he sat up, ready to confront the phantom or intruder. 'Who the devil . . . ?'

'Hush, Alex, it's me. Melissa. I had to come. I had to talk to you. I feel so wretched about what has happened.' The shape glided round towards him.

'Melissa!' Alexander jumped from his bed.

She held out her hand to him, shaking uncontrollably with cold. 'I'm so so sorry. How could this happen to you? It's wicked to keep you away from music . . .'

'My God, you are like ice,' he whispered. 'Here. Come, get under the blankets.' He drew her on to the bed, tucked a blanket round her and then held her until her body stopped shaking. 'You have taken a fearful risk coming here like this.'

'I had to talk to you, Alex.'

'Oh heavens. It's so good to be with you,' Alexander kissed her and kissed her, his pent-up misery giving way to the sweetness of having Melissa in his arms.

'I can't stay, Alex, you know that. I just wanted to remind you of Waterside. You haven't been there since your return, have you?'

'Waterside? Our play cottage?' he whispered. 'Is it better to be children for ever, Melissa? Just play at being grown up?'

'Hush, Alex. Don't give up hope. One day you'll be in charge of your own destiny.'

'One day! In ten years? Twenty years? When it's too late?' he muttered bitterly.

'In the meantime, Alex, there is one instrument your father overlooked.'

'Where?' His voice hung in the darkness.

'In Waterside. Go and see.' Then Melissa threw aside the blanket. 'I must go before Mama . . .'

'Come and see me again. Please.' He kissed her outstretched hand, then released her, and she disappeared.

'Waterside!' Alexander did not go back to bed but quickly dressed, pulling on warm clothes and tossing his winter cloak round him. Bessie and Zanzibar stood up and stretched. He patted them reassuringly. 'Come, Bessie, come, Zanzibar!' Then, taking a taper and flint, he quietly left his bedroom, with his two dogs padding faithfully behind.

It was no good trying to leave by any of the usual exits – all would be guarded, though the servants on night duty often slumbered, propped up against the doors like stringless puppets. Alexander went instead into the winter room, whose long windows looked out towards the woods at the back. He didn't need the taper. The moon was high. He waited ten minutes or more for the swinging light of the nightwatchman to appear so that he could calculate his round. Alexander then knew how much time he had to climb out and cross the grass without being seen. With suspended breath, he unlatched one of the windows but held it to. He heard a soft tread. An arc of light swung round the corner. Alexander shrank back into the heavy folds of a brocade draped over a screen. The man whistled one long wailing whistle, ending abruptly on a short one to identify himself to anyone who might be awake at that hour. Then the light was extinguished from sight as the man turned the corner.

Soon, Alexander, Bessie and Zanzibar were running across the grass. Finally, they entered the dark skirts of the wood.

A poacher, creeping through the woods that night, with traps over his arm and a bag on his back, heard the sound of a virginals strumming. It gave him more of a fright than any gamekeeper, and sent him hurrying away empty-handed as fast as he could.

It was mid-January. The winter was raw and cold. Sharp crystals of ice swept in with the north winds, cutting round the escarpments, piercing through the Cotswold walls and stiffening the brown, coarse grass up on the moor. Each morning, Alexander was dressed and ready with his horse to accompany his father or Martin Staines across Ashbrook. Once he and the bailiff rode to the farthest edge, where a drover's track entered the estate. Alexander looked down through the trees to the plain below, where Gloucester Cathedral seemed to float in the low, wintry haze. It was like a confirmation of the plans that had been forming in his mind.

'Yes!' he said out loud.

'Pardon me, sir?' asked Martin Staines.

'Nothing, Staines. It's blasted cold. Shall we ride on?'

'Indeed, sir. I said we would meet up with old Elias at the blacksmith's in the village. His orders are to take you through Ashbrook Woods to mark the trees he will be coppicing.'

Alexander was glad that the snow had not as yet fallen, so there would be no telltale tracks across the hard ground and through the woods when he stole out at night to go to the play cottage. But now he had made a decision, there was no time to lose. The sky had already gone leaden and the wind had begun to drop. 'Sure sign of snow,' remarked the bailiff. 'Day after tomorrow, I reckons.'

It was time. There was no problem about staying awake. He had made his plans. He did not undress, but sat at the writing desk in the window before a sheet of writing paper and, by the light of a single candle, he dipped his quill into the inkpot and began to write. For an hour, there was just the sound of his scratching pen and the owls hooting outside in the elms.

He wrote two letters. He took a long time over the first, making several false starts and having to begin all over again. He paused at every sentence, needing to ensure that every word he used was the right one and conveyed the right meaning. It must have taken over an hour before he reached the end and was satisfied.

> *My dear Papa,*
> *I cannot live without music. You must blame the Almighty for having given me not just the talents and gifts to be a musician but the overwhelming need for music – as great a need as a starving man has for food. Without music I cannot be a man, least of all the kind of man you want your elder son to be. I*

love Ashbrook, of that there is no doubt. But I love it in my way – as a composer. When you ride through the woods, you see the investment you have made in timber, what trees need felling, coppicing or clearing; when I ride through the woods, I hear the music the trees make when the wind blows and the trunks sway and creak and sing. When I see the land changing with the seasons from red earth to soft green and then to the yellow of summer, it is my inspiration, and my spirit is moved to compose; you will be calculating the yield and what profit can be made and what you should invest in the following year. That is the irreconcilable difference between us. But God made us both, for both of us are necessary to this world, I believe.

You must have an heir who can do the same as you, for otherwise I know Ashbrook would fall into neglect and ruin. The land must be cared for as you care for it. But I am not the man to do the job. It will destroy me, and in turn, I would destroy Ashbrook. My brother is far better suited. I have watched him and seen how, already, he is a farmer at heart. He understands the land as a farmer, and it is only because I know this that I am able to take the decision to leave Ashbrook and leave my inheritance.

I dare not ask your forgiveness. I know that I will not only incur your wrath, but also your grief that I, your son and heir, should abandon his duties, his parents and his brother and sisters. *The only way I may one day earn your forgiveness is to prove to you that I have chosen the right path and become a musician, and a man who commands as much respect in my chosen profession as you do as a preserver and conserver of the land.*

I leave Ashbrook not as an act of rebellion, but an act of love. I pray that one day you will understand. I pray that Mama, Isobel, Edward and Alice will understand – especially Edward, to whom I pass on the responsibility for Ashbrook.

Perhaps you will no longer call me your son, but you will for ever be my father.

I will not tell you where I am going – for, indeed, I hardly know. I throw myself into God's hands. It was He who gave me these gifts and so surely He will show me how I can use them and where I must go. One day, when I feel I have justified my existence, I hope you will allow me to return, not as a prodigal son, but as Lazarus, brought back alive and blessed. Till then, I beg you not to search for me.

I pray that you do not wish me ill; that you believe me when I say I love you and my mother, Isobel and Edward and Alice as the most treasured beings on this earth. I leave so that their love for me does not turn to bitter disappointment when my incompetence demonstrates my complete unsuitability to be master of Ashbrook. One day I hope that they, and you,

will be proud of me and not scorn my profession, which I
believe to be Divine, and so demands a higher and greater duty
even than that I owe to you.
  I am for ever, your most loving and grateful son,
                                Alexander

The second came more easily. He wrote fast; his strokes dashed
across the page with emotion: *My dearest, sweetest and most*
treasured Melissa . . .

When the ink on both of them had dried, he folded each carefully
and sealed it with wax. The letter to his father he propped up on
the writing desk. The second he pushed into the breast pocket of
his jacket.

By the time his letter writing was done, the whole house was
enveloped in a deep slumber and now there was one last thing to
do. He took from the top of a cabinet a large, polished walnut
box. At first it looked as if it had only one lid, which opened up
into a velvet-lined interior, but Alexander did not open this lid.
Instead, he felt round the body of the box and squeezed a highly
carved corner of it. Immediately, a hidden base swung out in
which glittered a number of gold and silver coins. He scooped
them all up and put them in his inner breast pocket, then closed
the box and returned it to its place on the cabinet. As if going

through an inventory in his head, he looked carefully round the room – and finally it was on dear Bessie and Zanzibar that his eyes came to rest. He fell on his knees and cuddled them both. 'Dear Bessie, I would take you if I could – and you, Zanzibar – but I fear I would be doing you no favours where I'm going.' Zanzibar grunted affectionately at his voice and Bessie licked his hand as he held her face and kissed her. Then, slinging his cloak round him, he took up his bag and quietly let himself out of the chamber.

As before, he went through the window of the winter room, crossed the grass into the woods and made his way to Waterside. There, he was filled with grief and uncertainty. Coals still glimmered in the grate, casting a low soft light. He sat at the virginals and lifted the lid. He placed the letter inside. Would Melissa understand? *It is not enough for me to have an instrument to play*, he had written. *Music is my life, not just an amusement.*

Sadly, his fingers touched the ivory keys and played the tragic chords of Dido's farewell from Purcell's opera, *Dido and Aeneas* – music he loved and had sung in Gloucester. He was so absorbed in it that he did not hear the door open behind him or realise that someone had entered, until he reached the words, 'Remember me, remember me,' and, like a dream, Melissa's voice came in, singing with the utmost tenderness.

They lay in each other's arms all through the rest of the night, not knowing where affection ended and passion began, or which was the child and which the adult. They hardly knew what happened or how; just that feelings and sensations and emotions beyond their understanding overwhelmed them, and carried them outside the boundaries of anything they had ever experienced. And even when Alexander finally stumbled to his feet, groping in the darkness for his breeches and boots, they still didn't realise what they had done. She lay motionless. Tenderly, he raised her to her feet. She was silent; dazed. He smoothed down her dress, covered her with her cloak and quickly led her back along the moonlit path, back to the house all silver beneath a wintry sky. She said nothing when he kissed her mouth and whispered, 'Farewell.' Then she was swallowed up into the house and both were obscured from each other.

Chapter Thirteen

★

A quickening

Alexander had gone. Gone, gone, gone. He had left his father, begging forgiveness, and asking him not to look for him. But the whole estate was galvanised into a massive search and a party set off for Gloucester, the obvious place to look. Sir William Ashbrook himself went to the cathedral. He questioned Thomas, the choristers, his teachers and, of course, his brother-in-law, the canon, desperately seeking any clue as to where Alexander had gone. No one had any information.

As Martin Staines had predicted, the snow came down. Gently at first; soft, curly, fluttery flakes, slowly drifting to the ground and tumbling about in the thin wind. Then the sky turned an opaque grey against which the snow fell like a thick, blinding white shroud and soon, whatever tracks might have been discovered were covered up and any harshness of a winter landscape was smoothed over. The dips and dells, walls, fields, ditches and drovers' roads, all lost their identity beneath the innocent snow, the beautiful snow, the snow which seemed to eradicate and cleanse all the imperfections of the world.

Lady Ashbrook, gazing in despair from her window, knew it was all an illusion; nothing had really changed. When the snow melted, everything would be as it was before – the good, the bad, the ugly and the beautiful. Happiness too, but especially the sadness.

Indeed, when the snow melted and revealed the first snowdrops shyly clustered, bowing their drooping heads among long, pale-green leaves, when yellow primroses arranged themselves along the paths through the woods, Alexander was still absent, still gone; still vanished without a trace.

Melissa read his letter over and over again. After he was declared missing, the first place she went to was Waterside. The first object she touched was the virginals. When she lifted the lid and found the letter, she didn't know whether to laugh with joy at his freedom or weep with anguish because he had gone, and she didn't know when she would ever see him again.

> *My dearest, sweetest and most treasured Melissa,*
> *I am not telling you where I have gone so that you need not be burdened with a decision about where your loyalty and duty lie. Suffice it to say that I have gone. I have to seek a life of music. It is not enough for me to have an instrument to play. Music is my life, not just an amusement. Without music, I*

can have no life worth living. But I love you, Melissa, and as soon as I am established in my chosen profession, I will send for you and, if you still love me, will ask you to be my wife.

Believe in me.

Your ever adoring,

Alexander

Melissa showed the letter to Isobel. Isobel read it, and then stared at the words for a long time. Her fingers gripped the page so tightly that Melissa wondered if she might rip it up into little pieces. Then Isobel had rounded on her furiously. 'How could you let this happen? You could have stopped him. You've ruined our lives. Papa is so angry he has disinherited Alexander. Mama is ill with distress. And all this talk of love and marriage – why, how selfish of you! Can't you see it would never be allowed? If Mama and Papa were to hear of this, you and Mrs Milcote would be instantly banished from here.' She burst into angry tears and threw the letter to the ground.

'I'm sorry, Isobel. I'm so sorry!' wept Melissa, horrified.

A month later, Melissa began to be sick. It was Mrs Lynch who came across her vomiting into the chamber pot, and knew instantly. She had seen too many young girls in that situation not to know. She didn't inform Melissa or Mrs Milcote of her suspicions. There was time enough. Instead, she began to scheme. She would play this carefully. A lot was at stake, and she needed time to think of a strategy. 'It looks like a chill on the stomach,' she told Mrs Milcote. 'I have a remedy of comfrey and ginger which will do her the world of good, you'll see.'

But Melissa wept even more during that night and the nights that followed, quenching her terror so that neither Mrs Milcote nor her maid, Tabitha, would hear. 'What is happening to me?' she asked voicelessly into the darkness. Mrs Lynch had told her she had a stomach upset, no more, no less. But it didn't feel like a stomach upset. Something frightening and mysterious was happening to her body. Though she eventually stopped vomiting, there was something else taking place outside her control.

She became obsessed with getting fat. Some of her waisted dresses did not fit her any more, yet she was hardly eating. In bed, Melissa would lie with her hands on her belly, compulsively fingertip-touching the roundness which she was sure had increased since a month ago, even though everyone commented on how thin she had become. Nanny noticed her reluctance to eat. 'Miss Melissa, little petal, eat up your tatties now, or else you'll fade away. What's wrong with you, child?'

One day as Melissa changed for bed, she felt a small bulge move in her stomach beneath the surface of her skin. She shrieked with horror. Tabitha was in the room, sorting out her clothes. She leapt up, startled. 'What is it, miss? Have you seen a spider or a mouse?'

Melissa stood in the middle of the room, her hands over her belly, staring down at herself in horror. 'There's something inside me! God help me, am I possessed? There's something alive moving inside. Feel.' Melissa dragged Tabitha's hand and placed it on her stomach. 'Can you feel it?' she whispered hoarsely. 'There's something there. Feel it? It moved. Do you think I'm possessed by the devil? Am I a witch? Oh God in heaven. What is it?'

Tabitha pressed her hand over Melissa's stomach. She felt the small bulge. Then stood back with a smile. 'Why 'tis only your baby quickening,' she said.

'My baby? My *baby*, did you say? Quickening? What baby? How can there be a baby?' Melissa's voice rose hysterically. 'What are you talking about?' She grabbed the girl by both shoulders and shook her. 'How dare you talk so insolently.' She slapped the girl hard round her face.

'I'm sorry, miss! I'm sorry!' Tabitha gasped, tears flowing down her cheeks. 'I thought you knew.'

Melissa stood with her face turning from red to ashen. Her eyes were wild and her hands clutched her belly. 'Have I a baby inside me? Am I with child?' She could hardly speak the words. 'How, Tabitha? How?'

'I'll try and explain, miss.'

She went over and over Tabitha's words, over and over again in her head, and replayed that night with Alexander. That closeness, that special closeness, that love, that passion. Some blood, yes – but that was the bleeding of flowers, wasn't it? 'Oh God!' she wept. 'It's not true. Tell me it's not true! How could I have not known?' And if Tabitha knew, then did the whole of Ashbrook know?

'No, no!' Tabitha swore on her life. 'I only knew it was a babby because I've seen my mammy with child so often.' And she burst into bitter sobbing because her mammy was dead in childbirth, her father was at sea and no one knew if or when he would return, and she and all her brothers and sisters had been separated, some to go into orphanages and others sent into the army or to work in the cloth mills. Tabitha was one of Lady Ashbrook's orphan girls. 'I would never betray you, Miss Melissa. Don't send me away, I beseech you. I would never tell. Cut out my tongue if ever I did.' Tabitha knelt on the floor before her and bowed her head.

'And Mama? What about Mama? The disgrace. We'll both be thrown out. Destitute. Oh God, Mama.'

'You should tell her, miss,' whispered Tabitha.

'No, no! I can't! She mustn't know. Never. Oh heavens! What am I going to do?' Melissa sobbed quietly as she began to realise their terrible situation.

'You should tell someone, miss. Tell Mrs Lynch?'

'No, no, no!'

'Then Miss Isobel?'

'Isobel? She was my friend. But I've hurt her already. Oh God, how she will hate me. Oh help me.'

Tabitha looked up at her young mistress. 'I'll do everything I can, I promise. I helped my mammy give birth to four babbies. I can help you.'

'Yes.' Melissa turned away. 'Now, go. But tell no one, do you hear? No one.'

After Tabitha had gone, Melissa stood staring out of her window. The more she thought, the more she condemned herself and the more she felt there was only one way out. She fled from the house into the woods, plunging off the track into the thicket. There seemed only one place; one place which seemed a suitable punishment. Hidden in the wildest part of the woods, overhung by ancient trees whose eyes had seen hundreds of years, whose creepers hung like giant spiders' legs, was a single small but deep, deep pond. It was a place full of terrors; full of stories of ghosts and goblins and tales of suicide. She reached its edge, stood trembling on the rim, staring into its dark, still, mirror eye. Mesmerised, her body swayed. Just one step. That's all it would need. Just one step . . .

The water quivered. An image rippled towards her. For a

while she waited for the tumbling, glancing shadows to still themselves. And when the surface was flat and even once more, the image was still there: a figure, shimmering as if reduced to molecules, penetrated by shafts of light, and water and reflections. It must be the devil himself, waiting. She slowly lifted her eyes and, with one wretched scream, turned and ran.

Life went on even though, to begin with, everything had been turned upside down in the frantic search for Alexander. There had been sightings – in Gloucester, Bath, Bristol and various villages here and there. Sir William had scrupulously followed up every lead, only to find that it was mistaken identity or that the person had gone. Every day he seemed to veer between fury and despair; accusation and remorse. Most frightening was when his anger cooled to a detachment.

'He is no longer my son,' declared Sir William. 'If he can run away like a common coward, leaving a note as if he were some eloping lover, and after all this time send us no word of his whereabouts or welfare, then by his own actions he has disinherited himself from my fortune and my name. He is no longer a son of mine.'

Sir William ordered that Alexander's name be mentioned never again. He summoned everyone into the library and unlocked the family bible in which were inscribed all the names of family members for two hundred years. He took a quill and rattled it in the inkwell, then dashed through Alexander's name so fiercely that the ink splattered across the page. 'From now on, I have only one son, Edward, and Edward is my heir.'

Melissa shunned everyone, even Isobel. She stayed for hours in her room or went down to Waterside to play the virginals and weep.

Mrs Milcote was sure she knew the reason why. 'The child misses Alexander,' she confided in Mrs Lynch. 'Alas, that he should have left in such a manner,' she exclaimed as her ambitions crumbled. Mrs Lynch nodded sympathetically, but said nothing.

Then one day, as Melissa was once more alone, playing some of the music which she used to play with Alexander, the door opened and Isobel quietly entered.

'I have to know.'

'Know what?' Melissa's face blushed guiltily as she stood up.

Isobel burst into tears. 'What's wrong with you?' she wept. 'For pity's sake, don't be ill. You're missing Alex, I know you are – but so am I and Mama – we all are – even Sir William. I see him pacing up and down in the library and, at church, I sometimes see him weep when the choir sings.'

'I'm sorry, Isobel. I'm so sorry,' Melissa trembled.

'What is it, dear friend?' Isobel clasped her arm. 'Are you ill?

I am so worried. You are looking so pale. Why don't you tell me? Do you think I haven't forgiven you over Alexander? It is you who should forgive me for being so jealous, but that is all past. You are my dearest friend, Melissa. Please say you forgive me.'

'No, Isobel,' said Melissa quietly, taking her hand. 'It is I who must ask you for forgiveness.'

'I cannot imagine anything in the world you could do for which I could not forgive you,' declared Isobel.

'For what I have to tell you, there is no forgiveness. I tried to kill myself. But . . . but . . . I swear I saw the devil. I know it was the devil. He was watching me . . . wanting me . . . Oh God, Isobel. I am damned . . . and whether it is now or later . . . I will surely go to hell.'

'Shall we walk?' suggested Isobel to calm her.

Watching from the top of a ridge, watery blue eyes saw them walking first together then apart; then, after a long time of stopping and turning, of walking, and stopping again, the two girls embraced each other. It was a long, long embrace of such great comfort, friendship and love, that fountains of tears spurted from the eyes of the watcher.

All through that late spring and summer, Isobel and Melissa were inseparable once more. They walked together, rode together and spent much time in the play cottage. They watched Edward and

Alice playing their games of mothers and fathers, and entered their games, forgetting about the real world.

Melissa and Isobel together, always together; whispering, laughing, withdrawing into a private, secret world which no one else could penetrate. And if Melissa slipped into despair, there was Isobel to comfort her, give her courage and shore up her belief in a merciful God. And when Edward and Alice had gone back to the nursery, they would take over playing with the dolls, dressing and undressing their doll babies in the clothes that they and Nanny had stitched. How they nursed them, kissed them, loved them, and put them to sleep in the wooden cradle that Thomas had made. And what long hours they spent talking feverishly, planning how they would bring up the baby.

'What name shall we give it?' asked Isobel one day as she stitched another little frock. 'I want to embroider its initials on every garment,' she said. 'And I shall incorporate the letter into our family crest – the swan.'

'If it is a boy, then it should be named after Alexander. If it is a girl, then she shall be Alexia,' said Melissa.

So they talked and planned as if they thought they could simply conceal a crying, burping, messing, hungry, demanding infant; as if they could wash it, dress it, feed it like one of their dolls and then put it away in a chest when the day was over. They lived in a dream, a game, a make-believe world. They didn't count the months or comprehend that soon the fantasy would become real.

And so the autumn came. The long warm days of an Indian summer were followed by fierce gales that swept in and stripped the trees.

It was easier now for Melissa to disguise her shape, bundling herself up in many layers of pantaloons, petticoats, bodices and voluminous skirts, all of which could be enveloped in her shawl or cloak.

Time slipped by inexorably.

And all the while, Mrs Lynch watched to see if her suspicions were correct. On her next visit to Gloucester, she went to see Mrs Peebles.

'Kindly tell Otis Gardiner to call at Ashbrook next time he's passing.'

Chapter Fourteen

✫

Autumn apples

Before he reached the hem of the woods, a single tree appeared. It gleamed in the moonlight. It was a crab apple tree. An autumn tree stripped of leaves; golden apples hanging from bare silver branches; bark shining moon-bright . . . And it sang. The tree sang; and its singing became a wailing and the wailing became a choir of sobbing voices which seemed to come from within itself. And twisted in among the apples, within the boughs of the tree, he saw little bodies; white naked bodies of babies. Their tiny fingers fluttered like leaves, their limbs merged with the twigs and branches, their heads nodded like blossoms. He didn't want to pass by it but, somehow, as if he were in the grip of a dream, he had no choice and found himself going nearer and nearer, and their crying became more pitiful, and he saw their large eyes staring at him. He looked away; thrust his head into his jerkin. To look into those eyes would be to be swallowed up into their damnation, so he ran and ran, unsure if he were awake or asleep.

When he reached Waterside he was surprised to see a light glowing from inside. A thin coil of smoke rose from the chimney into the star-silver sky. He was about to go closer and look for any chink between the closed shutters, when two women came hurrying through the darkness, their lantern swinging with agitation.

'Oh my God, oh my God!' one woman repeated over and over again in a distressed voice.

The other woman, who was slightly ahead, said nothing. When they arrived at the cottage door, the first woman pushed it open, and a thin, high-pitched scream escaped into the night.

'Melissa!' the second woman cried out, before the door was slammed behind her as she crossed the threshold.

'Melissa!' Frantically, he scurried round the house, seeking a crack, the tiniest opening which would enable him to see in. But this night, the back door was bolted and every shutter pulled to. He ran round and round, like a demented animal. He wanted to batter on the door, smash the windows, anything to get inside and help his beloved angel. But he knew, he knew; an inner voice warned him, restrained him, 'No, no, no.' So he must listen. He moved from window to window, pressing his ear to the slatted shutters.

Another scream; shuddering, high as a rabbit caught in a trap.

He had dozed and dreamt and shivered helplessly in the cold

autumn night. Once, a door opened at the back. Tabitha hurried down to the stream with a pail and scooped up some water. He would have accosted her but, suddenly, there was Miss Isobel in the candlelit doorway, urging her to hurry.

'Will she die? Will she die?' Tabitha wept.

He didn't hear the answer as the door slammed shut again.

Die? His angel die? No. She couldn't. She was one angel who was alive and made him want to be alive, not dead with the other angels. She had come down to the dark pool in the middle of the woods, looking as if she wanted to die. He had waded into the water, ready to save her if she threw herself in, and the whole surface of the pool had rippled and sent his reflection to her. She saw him. For one second like a bolt of lightning, her glance had fallen upon him. But she had mistaken him for a ghost or a demon or some unquiet spirit – for nothing else could have caused her to scream with such terror.

'Come back, Melissa. Be not afraid of me, my angel, my treasure.'

'Oh God in heaven, what will happen to us?' Mrs Milcote rocked and wept, massaging her daughter's ice-cold feet. What kind of fortune was this? Yes, in her deepest dreams she had hoped that there could be a union between Melissa and Alexander – wouldn't that have solved all their problems? Given them security for ever? Yes, she had dreamt of being a grandmother to the heir of Ashbrook, God willing. But not like this. This could ruin them completely. For Melissa to bear a bastard child, even though it was Alexander's, would most likely have them thrown out. They would have been destitute had it not been for dear good Mrs Lynch.

When Mrs Lynch warned her, just a few days ago, she had fainted, overwhelmed with fear and anxiety. Since then, she had hardly been able to breathe, waking up with panic attacks, clutching her throat, terrified she was going to suffocate to death. Dear Mrs Lynch, good Mrs Lynch. Mrs Lynch had called at her bedchamber constantly, bringing her soothing concoctions and murmuring reassurances. 'There is a way out of this, Mrs Milcote my dear,' she had said. 'No one knows about the child except the four of us. Remarkably, the secret has been well kept. As soon as the baby is born, I can arrange to have it taken away to an orphanage. No one need know.'

'Oh no! No, no!' wept Mrs Milcote. 'Not there.' She was thinking of the parish orphanage, which for all Lady Ashbrook's good intentions and charitable works was still a dire place for children. 'If I abandon it, it will surely die and if I hand it in, then my name will be known and I and my daughter will be ruined.'

'I was thinking of something else.' Mrs Lynch's voice coiled as slithery smooth as a serpent, but to poor Mrs Milcote it sounded like honey. 'The Coram man is in the district.'

'The Coram man? Coram?'

'Yes. You surely know the name? Captain Coram. In London. He has the whole of London society supporting his charity. Even parliament. Yes, the Coram Hospital,' explained Mrs Lynch. 'What better place? The child would be succoured at the breast of a wet nurse, fostered, educated, apprenticed out and prepared for self-sufficiency. Given a future.'

'You mean a Coram man is here? Could take this child?' she asked in a dazed voice.

'Indeed, Mrs Milcote. For a small fee, of course.'

'A small fee? Yes, of course. Anything, anything. I'll pay.' She did not try to comprehend what a *small* fee was. 'Yes, let the Coram man take it to London.' She almost laughed with relief.

'But it is best we say nothing to anyone – especially not Melissa. She is in too delicate a frame of mind. She expects to keep the child – when she is still a child herself, poor mite – and has no idea of the consequences of her folly. So say nothing.'

Then late in the night, Isobel had come running, sheltering her candle flame with one hand, scooping up her nightgown with the other as she ran to Mrs Lynch's chamber. 'It's Melissa. I think she's going to die.'

They had tried to manage on their own. Tabitha recognised the signs that the baby was imminent and she, Melissa and Isobel had gone down to the cottage in the night. But Melissa had got into distress and, as the fierce pains of labour swept over her, she drifted in and out of consciousness, and the baby was not yet born. In a panic, Isobel rushed to fetch Mrs Lynch.

There was no time to lose. Mrs Lynch sent Isobel back and said she would collect her bag of remedies and follow immediately. Then she went to fetch Mrs Milcote.

Before they reached the cottage, Mrs Lynch stopped and looked at Mrs Milcote. She did not hold up her lantern, but held it downwards, so that no light fell upon their faces. In the dark gloom she said, 'To make our plan work properly, you must let Melissa believe that her baby has died. It is the only way. If she thinks it lives, she will be for ever blighted by the knowledge. It is far better that she believes it to be dead – if, if it has not already died, of course.'

'Yes, yes. You are right,' agreed Mrs Milcote, wondering if this nightmare had an ending.

Even as they burst through the doorway, Melissa gave a piercing shriek and a small, blood-smeared body slithered into Tabitha's hands.

There was the cradle Thomas had made, and there was the willow basket lined with down and cotton sheets and, nearby, the pile of baby clothes: the shawl Nanny had crocheted for the dolls, the woollen jackets which Melissa had knitted and the christening dress Ruthie had made for Alice's baby, which Isobel had embroidered with the initials AA entwined with the Ashbrook swan.

Tabitha thrust the baby into Isobel's arms. Isobel stared and stared. 'I can't believe it, I can't believe it.' It was so damp and sticky, its uncut cord trailing from its belly. Alexander's baby. A boy. 'Melissa, it's a boy!'

How pale; how still; his frowning face set like sculpted marble and his fingers clenched as if with determination. The room receded; the anxious voices dimmed. Standing in her own universe, Isobel held the baby wonderingly, hardly aware of Tabitha knotting the cord or Mrs Milcote kneeling desperately at her daughter's side, stroking her head and massaging her arms.

Then Mrs Lynch came to Isobel and snatched the baby away from her. She was taking away the silent baby. With rapid movements, the housekeeper scooped up the snow-white shawl from the basket and wrapped its unwashed body tightly in it, then hooked up the basket of clothes into her elbow.

Isobel held out her arms to take back the baby but Mrs Lynch said, 'I'll see to it,' and she went out into the night.

'Wait!' Mrs Milcote left her daughter and followed Mrs Lynch outside. 'Let me . . .' A wind had whipped up as she took the baby from Mrs Lynch. 'My grandson.' She cradled him in her arm and stared at his white, frowning, blood-smudged face with eyes clenched shut. She passed a hand over his damp, matted hair – as dark as Alexander's – yet was not that a glint of auburn beneath the candlelight, just like Melissa's? 'Oh God bless you,' she wept and held him passionately to her breast. 'Forgive us.' She took a ribbon on which hung a silver locket, and slipped it round his neck.

'There's no time to lose, Mrs Milcote. Don't forget. The baby is dead.' Then Mrs Lynch hurried off along the path that led towards the clearing in Ashbrook Wood, leaving Mrs Milcote standing immobile, as if she stood on the edge of an abyss.

He gawped in bewilderment. A baby? Melissa's baby? Mrs Milcote had held it, kissed it, and given it back to Mrs Lynch. Dead, he had heard her say? The baby's dead? Meshak leapt out of the shadows and stood before Melissa's mother, face to face, glimmering eye to glimmering eye; like two frightened animals, they stared in frozen confrontation. Then he looked over his shoulder down the path into the black void of the wood, spun round on his heel and sped after Mrs Lynch.

Once more he passed the crab apple tree all silver and gold. He heard the crying. 'Dead babies don't cry,' he yelled as he stumbled on. And when he came to the clearing, there was their wagon, with the horse standing stock-still in sleep. And there was Mrs Lynch handing over the baby to Otis, Melissa's baby.

'She thinks you're taking it to London to the Coram Hospital. It's your business now. Here's the money, and she'll pay you the same every time you call, so long as she believes the baby is alive.'

When Mrs Lynch had gone, leaving the basket of clothes on the ground before the wagon, Meshak edged slowly forward, braced for a beating because of his absence. At the sight of him, Jester, tied up to a tree and neglected, began to howl and jerk at the string which held him, trying desperately to reach his master.

'Here, take this baby and bury it. It's dead anyway.' Otis tossed it over to Meshak, its white shawl unravelling a little as he did. 'Get rid of the basket too,' he ordered.

Meshak put the baby into the basket.

'And shut up that blithering dog of yours before I do.'

But Meshak didn't seem to hear his beloved friend Jester, he didn't even glance at him. As if in astonishment, Jester stopped barking. Just a soft whine lodged in his throat. Meshak stared at his father and backed away. He clutched the basket close to his chest, as if Otis might change his mind and snatch it back again, and went lolloping off into the woods as he had done so often. But all the time, he was whispering into the baby's face. 'Dead? No, not you. My angel's baby. My baby. Not dead.' He went down to the pitch-black pool. With such tenderness, he lifted the baby from the basket and flung aside the bloodied shawl. Like a christening, he dipped the motionless infant into the water. One, two, three. The shock of the cold water made it gasp and a juddering, feeble cry escaped into the air. A startled wood-pigeon flapped noisily among the trees. And it seemed as if the whole wood was crying; beneath his feet, where he knew the bones of so many other little children lay, their voices came up through the earth.

'Hush, babby! Hush. Don't let my da hear you. Hush.' He washed the blood away. From out of his jerkin pocket he took a knife that his father had made and cut the umbilical cord, which was still attached to the baby's stomach. It sank down down; spiralling slowly through space, down through the dark waters. He rolled the baby up in the christening robe which he took from the basket. 'I'll be your mammy now, and your da. I'll be your guardian angel.' He tucked the swaddled child into his jerkin.

Meshak looked east. The night sky had splintered from end to end into a thin silver crack. 'Coram,' he said softly. 'Coram.' And, as the crow flies, he plunged straight into the rough, up the hillside, heading into the dawn and London.

Part Two – 1750

Chapter Fifteen

✫

Mother Catbrain

'Can you see her?'

Two boys lay side by side, belly down in the grass. They peered over the edge of a ditch to a small gutter of a stream, alongside which they could just make out the humped shape of a dwelling. They knew it well by daylight. They also knew the name of the old woman who lived inside it. Mother Catbrain. They weren't sure if that was really her name, but it's what everyone called her. They said she had the brain of a cat; that she could think like a cat and knew all the mysteries that cats knew; and when she moved, she sidled, and when she sat, she seemed to be stalking as if braced to pounce. They said she was a witch.

She was a common sight. Every day, she would take up a large piece of folded cloth, tuck one end under her bonnet and wrap the rest round her shoulders. Then she set off walking, heading for the city. All day long, from dawn to dusk, she scavenged through the streets of London, sometimes being seen as far afield as Blackfriars, Spitalfields or the vegetable stalls of Covent Garden, picking up any bits and bobs and storing them in her piece of cloth. Along with the pigs, stray dogs and other down-and-outs, she scoured the rubbish tips, especially those outside the butchers, bakers and fishmongers. All would get tossed into her cloth together. At the end of the day, before sunset, she would sling the bundle over her shoulder and return to her hovel.

It was suspected that she stole turnips, carrots and kale from the Coram gardens and apples from the orchards, but, either through pity or fear, no one did more than chase her off if they saw her sneaking among the furrows.

The boys had often spied on her in the evenings, sitting before a small fire just outside her door, on which she stirred her potato broth in an iron pot balanced on stones and, in whispers, they exchanged stories about her.

On certain nights, when the moon was full, it was said she would turn herself into a black cat and consort with demons and witches. That's why, for a dare, the two boys were lying on their stomachs in the darkness, spying on Mother Catbrain's cottage.

'Let's go closer.'

They wriggled forward and tumbled over the edge of the ditch, roly-polying down into the soft earth below. Mother Catbrain's cottage was more of a hovel than a cottage. Its four stone, windowless walls were not wattled together but full of piercing gaps, which she stuffed with rags so that the wind could not penetrate. Its roof was just plaited reeds and earth on which, over time, moss and grass had grown. It was held down by a number of large stones, heaved out of the stream.

Moonlight riffled the softly running water. They edged nearer. The entrance to the hovel faced the stream and was, for the moment, out of their sight.

Except for the bubbling water, there was not one sound.

'Aaron,' one of the boys whispered. 'Should we? I mean, what if she really is a witch? If she sees us, she could turn us into mice and eat us.'

'Are you scared?' chided Aaron. Although the younger of the two, he was the bolder.

'I just don't want to be turned into a mouse and eaten,' hissed Toby.

'Well you go back, if that's what you want. I'm staying.'

'I ain't not leaving you. We go together or stay together.'

Aaron scrabbled round in the darkness and found what he wanted. A sizeable stone. He held it up, and the moonlight glinted on its silvery sheen.

'What yer gonna do?' asked Toby.

'Chuck it on to the roof.'

'And then . . . ?'

'Let's see. I don't know. Maybe nothing. Perhaps she's already turned herself into a cat and gone out. We've been here a great while and we ain't seen nothin'.'

Aaron got to his knees, swung back his arm and, with a good bowling action, threw the stone in the direction of the house.

It landed with a thud. The boys pressed themselves flat into the grass.

Nothing happened.

They waited a little longer, then Aaron said, 'You stay here with this stone.' He held out another, a sharp-edged flint. 'I'm gonna creep round and chuck another stone inside the doorway.'

'Be careful,' hissed Toby fearfully. He ran his thumb along the sharp edge of the flint stone, then turned to watch Aaron creeping like a low fox, closer and closer to the hovel. Now he was at the corner. Now he was out of sight. Toby raised himself to his knees, ready to throw his missile. He heard a loud crack coming from inside the house. Then he heard a devilish shriek, followed by a blood-curdling yell. Aaron came hurtling round the corner and up the ditch. 'Run, run!' he screamed. But Toby saw the cat. A big, dark, emerald-eyed creature, which sprang up the bank behind Aaron. Toby flung the stone with all his might and struck the cat on its front leg. The cat's forward motion was halted violently and, with a yowl, it flipped upwards, four legs in the air, twisting and writhing.

'I hit it, I hit it!'

The two boys scrambled, whimpering and stumbling, all the way back across the fields and through the orchards and past the pig sties and cow sheds and chicken runs. Dogs started barking. A few sleepy voices cried out, 'Shut up!' and 'Who's there?'

As they passed the barn, a figure suddenly loomed before them and the two boys were scooped off their feet, gibbering with terror.

'Whatchya doing, whatchya doing? Oh, it's you, little angel, izn't? And you Tobykins, Tobykins, Tobykins, whatchya doing out of bed? Bad boys, bad boys!' The voice cackled softly and hugged them close.

'Mish!' The boys laughed with relief and wrapped their arms round their captor's neck.

'Mish, we did it, we saw her! She *is* a cat – we saw with our own eyes,' Aaron babbled on.

'I hit her with a stone. Got her on the leg, I did!' boasted Toby. 'D'you think she knew it was me? D'you think she'll come after me?'

'Will she turn us into mice and eat us?'

'Gobble, gobble, gobble,' chortled Mish, gobbling into their arms and necks and making them wriggle with laughter. 'Mish will save you. I'm good at killing witches. I'll steal their broomsticks and drown their cats – ugh, ugh, ugh! No one will get my little angel or my Tobykins. No, no, no. Come now, before

Mrs Hendry catches you – and then there'll be trouble.'

With a boy in each arm, tall-as-a-stripling, the young man loped across the yard towards the large building whose shape dominated the sky. He took them to a side door and pushed them through. 'Bed. Bed!' he ordered, and shut the door on them.

'I saw her. The cat. I saw her,' Toby repeated, wide-eyed. 'She was coming after you. I hit her with my stone.'

The boys stared at each other in the darkness, full of pride and terror.

To the right of them, a narrow flight of wooden stairs led upwards to the dormitory on the first floor. Aaron led the way, his breath still coming out in gasps, and they crept back into the long thin room in which rows of pallet beds lined the walls.

Heads bobbed up, visible by the thin streak of light which fell through a skylight. 'Did you see her? Is she a witch? Did she turn herself into a cat?' Whispered voices came from all round the room.

'Yes . . . we did . . . she did . . . a cat . . . a big black cat with green eyes. She came after us. Toby hit her with a stone.'

They huddled under their blanket and shuddered, glowing beneath the other boys' admiration, but fearful too. Perhaps they should have considered her powers more deeply before attacking her? They dreaded what possible revenge Mother Catbrain might take, even though Mish had promised to defend them.

Aaron was unaware of sleep secretly invading his mind, his thoughts becoming dreams. When the cat flipped into the air, twisting in agony, it turned into a witch. A broomstick propped against the wall flew up to her, and soon she was astride it, streaking after him, waving an axe. Mish was trying to save him, running along, flapping his arms like a scarecrow. But his gangly legs kept flopping and folding as if they were made of rags. The witch flew nearer and nearer. Now the axe was whirling close enough to chop off his head.

Bong, bong, bong, bong, bong!

It was not the bell ringing for his funeral, it was the chapel bell striking five, and soon it was followed by a faster, more erratic clanging, as the porter went round the courtyard ringing his handbell to wake them up.

Their lives were ruled by the bell. The bell to wake them up; the bell to send them to bed; the bell to call them to prayers; the bell to begin and end their lessons; the bell to despatch them to their many tasks; the bell to start play and the bell to end play. Sometimes Aaron heard the bell in his sleep and would sit bolt upright, ready to rush off at its command, but this one was real.

'Not already,' groaned Aaron, pulling the blanket over his head.

With much yawning and protesting, the boys staggered from their warm beds.

Toby noticed the state of Aaron's feet sticking out from under the blanket; mud and grass clinging from the night's escapade. He looked at his own and saw they were the same.

'Quick, Aaron, quick. Don't let Mrs Hendry see our feet, they're filthy. She'll know we've been out.'

'Oh, no!' exclaimed Aaron, leaping from their shared bed with dismay.

'And look at our bed!'

They tried desperately to beat away the dirt which had rubbed off their feet on to their blanket. Mrs Hendry appeared. The boys dashed past her as she began her daily morning hustling to get them washed and dressed. Like a mother hen, she flitted from one to the other. 'Ow! Ooo! Eee!' they exclaimed as she checked behind their ears and in their eyes, examined their fingernails and the nape of their necks, and parted their hair to look for nits. From checking their bodies, she scrutinised their clothes to see if they were clean, as they put on their shirts, neckcloths and brown and red-trimmed uniforms of serge jacket and breeches. Satisfied at last, she herded them into the chapel for morning prayers just as the bell began ringing.

Twenty or more boys stood on one side of the aisle, while an equal number of girls in brown and red-trimmed skirts and bonnets stood on the other. The rest of the congregation were the steward, the matron, governors, clerks and the apothecary, nurses, the schoolmaster and schoolmistress, cooks and cleaners, and all the numerous people who were part of the Coram Hospital for the Maintenance and Education of Foundling Children. Sometimes, there were grand visitors, lords and ladies in fine clothes, who came to observe how their money was being spent. How solemnly the children had to stand there before the vicar, upright and looking straight ahead. How slowly and with due seriousness, they intoned their prayers, and sang their hymns. Their music master, Mr Ledbury, conducted them.

> *'Left on the world's bleak waste forlorn,*
> *In sin conceiv'd, to sorrow born,*
> *By guilt and shame foredoom'd to share*
> *No mother's love, no father's care,*
> *No guide the devious maze to tread,*
> *Above no friendly shelter spread.'*

Every day, they sang hymns. Some which had been specially written for them; hymns which were supposed to remind them that they were all foundling children – abandoned, born out of shame, nameless, picked up off the street or left at the stone fountain by the gates of the hospital by people unknown. They were never to forget that they bore the sins of their iniquitous mothers and fathers. And there were other hymns too, whose words were full of reproof and condemnation. But Aaron never related the words to himself. He believed that the words were there for no other reason than to put music to them. He loved singing the syllables 'foul offence' or 'Sin and Shame', although the words, 'no mother's love, no father's care' made him feel inexpressibly sad. What Aaron loved most in this strict, solemn hospital school was the music.

After chapel it was into the yard to be allocated chores before breakfast. From the west block, the girls and boys streamed out. Briefly, their worlds met. 'Thread the needle, thread the needle!' they cried and, linking hands, went into the game, the girls forming an arch through which the boys had to pass:

> *'Brother Jack if you were mine*
> *I would give you claret wine*
> *Claret wine is good and fine*
> *Through the needle-ee go!'*

'Go, go, go, go,' the girls chanted, jerking their arms up and down until, 'Gotcha!' They dropped their arms right down over a boy.

> *'Jack, Jack, look in my eye*
> *What do you like best*
> *Plum pudding or plum pie?*

Plum pie! Do you want to go through?
Here's my black and here's my blue,
Open the gates and let me through.'

The boy kissed the girl on the plum pie side of the arch and joined it.

And so the game continued until a clanging bell made them scatter, boys on one side, the girls on the other. As usual, there was an exchange of catcalls and good-humoured insults, with a lot of face-pulling and sticking out of tongues.

Then roly-poly Mr Rawlings appeared, with his round face red beneath a flowing white wig, his round Humpty Dumpty body tightly contained within his shirt, waistcoat and jacket, and his stick-out arms. His legs looked as if they had been stuck on later within his breeches, stockings and shiny silver-buckled shoes. But, as always, he was in command and only needed to rap his ivory-tipped cane for an instant hush to fall over the children.

Mr Rawlings' eye roamed over the boys, then he hammered out instructions. 'You, you and you,' he pointed, breaking the boys up into groups, 'to the barns to fill sacks with grain. You, you and you muck out the pigs, clean the yard, you and you collect fuel for the kitchen.' The older boys he got chopping wood and grooming the horses and he picked a contingent to go out to the fields and take their orders from Mr Barrington. Alongside him stood Mrs Burgess, the matron who supervised the girls. She allocated them chores, sending the older ones to the dairy to help with the milking or to Mrs Hendry, the housekeeper, who would put them to work in the kitchen or laundry room, or polishing floors or ironing, stitching and mending clothes. The very young children fed the chickens, collected the eggs and checked on the ducks and led the goats to pasture.

Aaron and Toby were in a group going to the fields. They looked at each other and grinned. They didn't mind when the weather was dry. They chucked out stones from among the furrows and collected vegetables for the kitchen. They raced each other across the yard, clambering over a five-barred gate and out into the fields.

In the distance, they saw Mish standing in the middle of a cabbage field shooing off the crows. The morning mist rose all around him, sun-bright white. The boys waved at him. He waved back, gleefully leaping up and down, rotating his arms like a crazy windmill, and Aaron remembered his dream.

Mish, though a man nearly six foot tall, with red hair and watery blue eyes like chunks of rainy sky, was nothing but a child in a man's body. A simpleton. He had been taken on by the Coram Hospital out of charity eight years ago, when he arrived, starving and practically at death's door, with a baby boy tucked into his jacket. On examination, the baby proved to be so well-cared for, so clean and healthy, that they could hardly believe such a fellow had taken care of it and wondered if he had simply abducted it from somewhere. But when he held the baby and kissed it and hardly wanted to part with him, some were convinced that he was the father. 'Mine, mine!' he had repeated over and over as they tried to remove the infant from his arms.

Others were suspicious. Round the baby's neck hung a silver locket containing a strand of auburn hair, and it was dressed in a christening gown of finest French cotton. Embroidered on the lacy collar were the initials 'AA' entwined with a swan. When they asked him what was the baby's name, he looked puzzled and unsure. He kept prodding his own chest and repeating the name, 'Mish,' adding, 'turnip face' and 'pig stew'. Then he had wept and rocked to and fro in great distress repeating, 'Mine, mine, mine. My angel.'

Sarah Wood the chief nurse, who would have known Mish, had been sacked for corrupt practices the previous summer. So only one or two workers on the staff would have remembered a red-headed lad who had turned up with a certain Otis Gardiner from time to time. But Otis was only one of many pedlars who would call at the hospital with babies stuffed in their saddlebags, and when word had reached them via other pedlars and traders that Otis Gardiner was dead, executed for murder and blackmail somewhere in the West Country, the news was so common it caused no more than a shrug. No reason for him to be retained in their memory, and especially not his boy. 'A halfwit, wasn't he?'

Until the mystery was solved, the hospital board decided to take in the baby and allow Mish to work on the land. They registered the infant and gave him the name Aaron, partly because of the AA embroidered on the swaddling clothes and because the only thing Mish called him was 'my angel', and also because Mr Aaron Dangerfield, cabinet maker, had agreed to be his sponsor.

The baby was then fostered out to Mrs Camberwell, a wet nurse in the country, much to the young man's agitation. He disappeared, though the authorities reckoned he had gone to be near the boy. Four years later, in accordance with the regulations, the boy was returned to the Coram Hospital to begin his education, and Mish reappeared. He was allowed to earn his keep by working with the hospital's animals and on their land.

At the sight of the boys, Mish came trotting forward with his odd gambolling gait. He scooped up Aaron and hugged him tight. 'Hello, angel!' he exclaimed, swinging him round. 'Look what I've got for you.' He fished into his pocket and brought out an apple. 'And one for friend Toby,' he said, producing another. 'Night and Day, Night and Day,' he chortled. Everyone at the hospital called Toby and Aaron 'Night and Day', for not only were they inseparable friends, but where Aaron had a pale white skin with silky auburn hair and deep-set, ink-blue eyes, Toby was African black, with round black eyes and black tightly curled hair which covered his head like moss covers a stone.

Mish watched with a great grin as the boys sank their teeth into the apples' crisp flesh, and juice spurted round their lips and ran down their chins.

'I dreamt Mother Catbrain came to chop off my head,' Aaron told him. Aaron always told Mish his dreams.

'Chop, chop, chop!' gurgled Mish. 'I'll chop her up into little pieces if she hurts one hair of your head,' he cried, swiping the air with his invisible axe.

'She's a witch, Mish,' whispered Toby, still fearful from the night before. 'We saw her. We saw her! We saw the cat, and I hit her with a stone.'

Mr Barrington's voice bellowed out across the fields. 'Get on over here! Come on, lads!'

'See you later, Mish!' cried Aaron, slapping a kiss on his cheek.

'We'll sneak you a turnip!' added Toby, knowing Mish loved eating raw turnips.

For the next two hours, the boys worked with stooped backs, moving among the great clods of earth, chucking out stones and collecting up sackfuls of potatoes and turnips.

The chapel clock struck eight times. The boys straightened their backs. At last: breakfast. They were starving now. Today it was porridge day. Aaron much preferred porridge to gruel. But before they could eat, they must wash off the mud. So, stripped naked, the boys plunged into the brook, losing their breath with its early morning chill.

The sunlight struck the stream with dazzling force as the boys dashed their hands into the water, sending showers of spray at each other. Their shouts and laughter echoed through the willows as they swam and dived, leapt and twisted and played as merry as young frogs.

Then Aaron stopped, his hand in mid-air. Just beyond a great weeping willow, he glimpsed old Mother Catbrain. She was hobbling with great difficulty, a pail in one hand and a willow stick in the other. She limped to the edge of the stream and eased herself painfully down on the bank, allowing the pail to lie at her side in the grass.

'Toby, look!' Aaron grasped his friend and pulled him to a stop.

The boys watched as Mother Catbrain wriggled herself closer to the water, then she lifted her skirt up one side to expose a leg. It was bound with a filthy piece of rag. She unwound the rag and rinsed it in the water. A stain of blood floated among the sunbeams, and the boys clearly saw a wide, open wound on her leg as if she had been struck by a sharp object.

'She *is* a witch!' breathed Toby, backing away with horror.

'Quick. Let's go from 'ere. I ain't not never coming down this end ever again.'

Aaron couldn't move. He felt rooted to the bottom of the stream, where he could feel the weeds trailing round his legs and the mud squishing up between his frozen toes.

After she had bathed her wound, she dabbed it dry with the edge of her skirt, then awkwardly got to her feet and, paddling at the water's edge, tried to reach for her pail.

At that moment, the old woman lost her balance. As she fell backwards on to the bank, her pail slid into the water and was carried away, filling with water as it went.

'Come on, Aaron, before she turns us into mice and eats us,' begged Toby.

The old woman flapped helplessly on the bank. The bucket, which drifted downstream towards Aaron, was now nearly full of water and slowly sinking. All he had to do was reach out and get it. Toby was tugging at his arm. The other Coram boys had already got out and were chasing each other about to dry off. He took a step backwards and was about to flee, when she looked up and caught his eye. Aaron's heart stood still. Her eye seemed to suck him in. The bucket was descending to the bottom of the stream. Aaron made a swift movement forward – if only to release himself from her eye – and caught it. Now that he had it, Aaron knew he had no choice but to wade over and give it to her.

'No, Aaron, no!' he heard Toby's panic-stricken voice.

How many steps did it take? Wading upstream against the current, he felt in the grip of a dream. Once more, her eye held his. He tried to give the bucket back quickly and get away, but suddenly her hand whipped out, claw-like, and grabbed him.

Without a word, she drew him nearer. She twisted his arm round so that his palm was upturned. She bent her head over it and looked hard and said nothing. Seconds, minutes, hours? Time passed, he had no idea how long. He felt doomed. All he could think was that she knew he was partly responsible for her injury and would exact some dreadful retribution.

She just dropped his hand and muttered, 'A gentleman you were born, a gentleman you are and a gentleman you will be.'

As he backed away, she made a further attempt to fill her bucket and she neither looked at him nor spoke to him again.

They ran, dressing as they went, towards the sound of the breakfast bell.

Chapter Sixteen

✫

Meeting in the chapel

They had been at lessons all morning, learning their alphabet and numbers, but Aaron was bored. He already knew it all. His foster mother, Mrs Camberwell, could read a little and during those early years when he lived with her, she had taught him everything she knew. She also taught him to recite from the Bible and sing songs. That was best – singing songs. How she used to bounce him up and down. 'A farmer went riding upon his grey mare, bumpety bumpety bump!'

From his desk, through the slightly open window he heard strains of music coming from the chapel. He had been hearing the same music over the past few days, when musicians had come to practise, and now he knew almost every single note well enough to hum. It was different from the hymns and religious music they were used to. Today, there were horns, trumpets, flutes, oboes and sackbuts as well as the organ. These were also adult singers. Aaron would have given anything just to climb out of the schoolroom window and join them.

There was often music in the chapel, and it stirred such feelings inside him; sometimes of happiness, of gaiety and energy, but sometimes of an indescribable sadness. It made him wonder who he was. Who had his mother been? Had he got a father somewhere out there in the big wide world? Some orphans like him had brothers and sisters, aunts and uncles, grandparents and cousins.

He didn't belong to anyone except the Coram Hospital – and that wouldn't be for ever. Nothing was for ever. Not even Mrs Camberwell. She had suckled him and reared him till he was nearly five years old, and he could still remember the warmth of her arms and her loving bosom; the strange farmyard smell of her and her rough, hard-working hands which not only cared for him, but milked cows and herded goats and slaughtered chickens and mucked out horses and fed pigs. On wash day down by the stream, he would play along the banks while she swirled and slapped the clothes against the stones, and on ironing day she pushed her heavy charcoal-filled iron up and down, and at night he would sleep between bedclothes smelling of woodsmoke and charcoal and listen to her singing.

When the day came that she had to send him back to the Coram Hospital, he remembered how he had clung to her skirts screaming. They had to prise him away from her and bundle him on to the wagon, and he would never forget how, for a while, she ran down the track after him, shouting, 'Remember, I love you, little Aaron. I'll always love you, my dearest sweet boy, my baby!' As the horse broke into a trot to put distance between them, she had thrown her apron over her head and howled. He had sworn then that as soon as he was grown up he would go back and see her.

Once he asked Mish, 'Do you know where my mummy is?' And when Mish repeated over and over again, 'She's an angel, she's an angel,' Aaron thought it meant his mother was dead. So he never had dreams of going out to find her.

Sometimes, he and Toby would lie side by side in their shared bed in the dormitory and try to imagine their families. Toby said he came from Africa.

'Where is Africa?' Aaron had asked.

'It's far, far away over the dark green ocean,' whispered Toby mysteriously. 'Old Benjamin told me.'

Toby had been wet-nursed and fostered by old Benjamin's daughter, Mary, and they all lived with Cobbler Jack. Old Benjamin was a freed slave who worked for Cobbler Jack, making shoes for the Coram children, and was so old that his black hair was like silver ash.

'But my mammy is in America,' Toby told Aaron with awe.

'Where is America?' Aaron had asked.

'It's far, far away over another dark green ocean. I told old

Benjamin when I grow up I'll go and find her. But he said, "No, Toby, no. They will ship you off to the plantations. They will make you a slave just like your mammy, and put you in irons and brand you like a bull. It's best you stay here and forget her. You can be a free man here." But I said, "I'm not afraid. When I grow up I'll find her. I'll go and get a magic spell to make my skin white so no one will know, and I'll go like a white man and find my mammy." '

Aaron had stayed silent for a long while, thinking about these things and then he asked, 'How will you go to America and Africa?'

'On a ship, a big, big ship with lots of sails. I've seen them on the river. Do you remember that time I was a server? I served for Mr Philip Gaddarn when he held that big party which went on for three days. We were on barges – twelve barges – full of fine ladies and gentlemen, and there was musicians playing wonderful instruments, and they set off fireworks, and I saw the ships, the huge merchant ships, and I heard the gentlemen talking about them ships. They owned some of them, and said they went to America and Africa with their masts taller than trees and flapping sails like giant birds. I'll go on one of those ships, I will.'

'Me too, Toby,' whispered Aaron, excited at the prospect. 'I'll go with you.'

'But what about Mish?' asked Toby. 'How can you leave Mish?'

Ah yes, Mish. Once Toby had asked, 'Is Mish your daddy?'

'I don't think so,' Aaron had replied – a little uncertainly. 'Nobody said he was. Mish says he's my guardian angel. But he's just Mish.' He fell silent again, for Mish had always been there, even when he was sent to Mrs Camberwell's farm. Mr Camberwell had died and she could always do with a helping hand with the animals, so when Mish turned up one day after Aaron was fostered out to her, she took him on, even though he was a simpleton.

Aaron used to think of Mish as a grown-up, but now that Aaron was eight, and could read and write, Mish no longer seemed grown up, even though he was giant tall and had whiskers if he didn't shave, and had a deep voice like a man. He had the ways of a child, the thoughts of a child and he could laugh and cry as easily as children do. Somehow, Aaron knew that, one day, he would have to be Mish's guardian angel. Yes, Toby was right, he couldn't leave Mish.

'Well then, Mish will have to come with us.'

Aaron stared out of the window, thinking about how strange life was. Toby had been sent out again to serve in the city. All the children envied him because he was often collected from the hospital and taken to some grand house where a party or banquet was being held. Toby would be dressed like a miniature prince, in silk trousers and embroidered jacket with curling slippers and a bejewelled turban on his head. He would be given a silver platter laden with sweetmeats which he had to hand round to all the guests. The ladies adored him, and loved to bounce him on their knees, feed him sweets, and push their fingers under his turban to feel his extraordinary crinkly hair. There was never a shortage of demand for little Toby, who had a ready smile and black flashing eyes. A general, who was also one of the patrons of the Coram Hospital, wanted to take Toby as his regiment's mascot and carry him off to war, but the Coram board of governors drew a line at that. Better that he be trained as a good manservant, they said.

So the children thought that Toby was the luckiest of all of them, destined to live a life of luxury, while the rest of them would be fated to toil away as apprentices in back-breaking trades. But one night, lying there in their narrow pallet bed, Toby had finally confessed to Aaron that, for all the silken clothes and sweetmeats and petting that he got, he'd give it all up just to be a cobbler's boy even. 'In their eyes, I'm nothing but an animal – no different from one of Mr Gaddarn's poodles. I hate being picked up and stroked and cuddled by his fat-fingered women; undressed to see if I'm black all over or having my skin scraped to see if I am white underneath my black. I am just as easily pinched and kicked if they feel like it. One night the party went on till five o'clock the next morning and I fell asleep. I couldn't help it. I tried and tried to keep awake. Mr Gaddarn had me whipped. I hate it, Aaron, I hate it!' he wept. 'And I know that I am soon to be taken on in Mr Gaddarn's household for ever.'

Aaron hoped that Toby was not being whipped this time. No one ever beat them here in Coram, except if a child had been very, very bad, and then only the governor could administer the punishment. Sometimes, children who had been apprenticed out had reported being beaten by their employers and the Coram authorities had stepped in and either sorted out the problem or moved them to another employer. Aaron urged Toby to tell the governor how he was being treated. But Toby didn't dare. 'Mr Gaddarn is one of their benefactors,' he cried. 'They'll never believe me. They won't want to believe me.'

The sun moved out from behind a cloud. A swath of golden light fell across the courtyard. A movement caught his eye. It was Mercy Bligh, one of the older girls, skilfully fingering her sightless way along the wall till she reached the chapel door and slipped inside. Being blind, she was not with the other girls stitching and weaving. Instead she came with a dusting cloth to polish the pews. He sighed with envy. He knew Mercy loved music. She often pumped the bellows for Mr Ledbury, and he often allowed her to play the little organ in chapel. Her recorder playing, too, thrilled everyone, not just with the dum de dum tunes most of them could play, but with melodies which made her fingers flutter up and down with great speed. She learnt to play scales and arpeggios and trills all by ear. So Mercy found any excuse to be in the chapel when music was being played, and she and Aaron often crouched among the pews together to listen.

A bell clanged. At last the lesson had ended. They were ordered out into the yard to play in the fresh air, and the children needed no second bidding. But Aaron didn't follow them. As Toby wasn't there, rather than pitch in with the other boys in a game of cricket or tag, Aaron slipped along to the chapel.

The music had stopped. Perhaps they were just resting. He pushed the door – it opened silently – and slid inside, keeping his back to the wall, as if somehow he could merge into the stone if anyone came. He couldn't see Mercy but he knew she must be hiding somewhere.

The singers were filing out and the performers were packing up their instruments. Aaron frowned with disappointment. It was over. How he wished he could have seen them play. Then, suddenly, as the men trailed away calling their goodbyes, someone began playing the organ. It was the new organ with its array of shining pipes, all glistening gold, looking like a temple between garland-strewn pillars.

He looked up into the organ gallery, expecting to see Mr Ledbury, but instead he saw a hulk of a man. The figure was hunched over the keyboard, an untidy wig perched on his head.

Scattered around were sheaves of manuscript paper and, from time to time, he interrupted his playing to grab a quill – dipping it into an inkwell – and scribble notes on to the page while humming hoarsely.

Aaron crept closer and closer, hardly aware of anything except his fascination with the music and the man who was making it.

Crouching among the pews, he listened as the musician played through the work. Wondrous chords and melodies reverberated all around, and when the organist pulled out all the stops and played right down in the bass, everything throbbed and vibrated. The sound came through the soles of Aaron's boots and the tips of his fingers; it made his heart and guts and every fibre in his body twang and resonate, as though he himself had become a musical instrument. Then, suddenly, the sound dwindled till it was like a single reed, piercing sweet, blowing in the wind by a riverbed. Aaron shivered with the magic.

A side door flew open and a manservant came in, clanking a bucket. The organist swore loudly. '*Du liebe Gott, Dummkopf! Sei ruhig! Raus mit dir, bitte, raus! Ich muss Ruhe haben.* Qviet wiz you!!' He swung round on the organ stool and leant over the gallery rail. A manuscript slipped from his hands and fluttered down to the chapel floor, and the fierce grunts were even louder. '*Raus, raus!*' He pointed fiercely at the door, and the man made a hasty exit, bowing and apologising.

'Sorry, sir, sorry, sorry. I thought the rehearsal was over.'

By this time, Aaron was very close. He quickly scooped up the fallen sheets, tidied them together and held them up to the smouldering musician with a respectful bow.

'Shall I bring them up, sir?' he asked.

'*Ja, ja!*' The organist didn't sound in the least grateful.

Aaron nervously climbed the stone stairs to the gallery, afraid of the anger which still reverberated round the chapel. When he reached the organ gallery, he approached cautiously, and as the man swivelled round to face him, Aaron thrust the sheets of music into his hands, then turned nervously to run away. But a hand gripped his shoulder.

'Ah, ah, ah!' The big musician growled as he towered over him. 'Zank you, my boy! Vhy do you rrun avay von mir? I vill not eat you. Vat are you doing hir, creeping rrround like a leetle mouse? Heh?'

'Sorry, sir, sorry, sir!' stammered Aaron. 'I heard the music and came to see.'

He tried to pull away again and run, but the man still held him. 'You like music, huh?'

'Yes, sir.'

'Can you play?'

'No, sir.'

'Can you sing?'

'Yes, sir.'

'Sing you in ze choir?'

'Yes, sir.'

'Sing me somzing zen.' He lifted Aaron up as if he were no more than a toy and placed him on the organ stool. Then he stood back with arms folded. 'Go on! Sing!'

'How beautiful are the feet of men . . .' sang Aaron. It was the song he had heard being rehearsed in the chapel, over and over again, and he had memorised it himself. 'That bring the gospel of peace . . .' His voice was strong and pure, his intonation was perfect, and he sang with a deep feeling and conviction which seemed beyond his years. He sang, not just a few bars, but all the way through. He sang from his heart, from his whole being.

When he stopped, there was silence. Aaron stood uncertainly on the organ stool, wondering if he should get down, but the big, red-faced man was gazing at him intently, as if he remembered how, when he was a boy, he had wanted to play music more than anything else in the world.

Finally he spoke. 'How do you know zis music?'

'I've heard it here, sir. I can hear it from the schoolroom.'

'You love music?'

'Yes, sir.' Aaron sighed with longing as he replied.

'I see you haff not only a gut voice, but you sing like a

musician too. Ve must see about you. Vat is your name?'

'Aaron, sir. Aaron Dangerfield.'

'Ach, *ja*! I know zis man. He is your benefactor, *ja*?'

'Yes, sir.'

Below them, a door opened on the south side. A young man entered. He was dressed as a gentleman, though not extravagantly. He wore a long coat of broadcloth trimmed with lace; a white shirt gleamed beneath a waistcoat; his brown wig was modest and his walking boots, though of leather, were well worn. At his waist, a sword hung in its scabbard.

This man was not shooed away, but warmly welcomed. 'Ah, Herr Ashbrook. Gut, you haff komm. Ve haff much vork to do.'

'Your servant, sir!' The young man bowed respectfully.

Aaron continued to stand on the organ stool, feeling forgotten. 'Please, sir, may I get down now?'

'*Ja, ja* – now so – run along. I vill speak to your Mr Dangerfield.'

Aaron leapt from the stool and ran down the steps, passing the young man but not looking at him.

He burst out of the gloom of the chapel into the brilliant sunshine. Inexplicably, he felt a sudden sense of joy so great, it almost lifted him off the ground. 'And bring glad tidings!' he sang.

Chapter Seventeen

✴

Old friends

All across the city, link boys with flaming torches in their hands lit the way through the dark, menacing alleys and narrow streets. Bobbing like glow-worms, they moved through the darkness, the light flaring across the faces of huddled figures whose eyes shone briefly then were extinguished as the link boys moved on.

Coming late out of a tavern, Thomas Ledbury found a link boy to light him to the home of Mr Burney, with whom he had an appointment to discuss the placement of a Coram boy as Mr Burney's apprentice.

It had been raining earlier. The rutted road was sloshing with potholes of water, excrement and mud. He had to keep leaping to one side as a carriage would lurch by, churning up a spray of brown liquid, or a carrier overloaded with timber creaked and groaned behind a pathetic half-dead mule. A train of mules clanking with pots and pans, thrust its way past him, led by a young boy urging the weary beasts onwards with a high raucous voice and a stick of willow with which he flicked their haunches. Thomas's pace slowed down even more when they arrived in St Martin's Lane, which was teeming with sedans, horses, hollering street traders and scurrying messengers.

They crossed the lane and entered a narrow side street and soon stopped before the door of a house. A watchman stood at the top of the steps and cheerfully enquired what their business was.

'Please inform Mr Burney that Mr Ledbury has arrived for his appointment.'

While he waited for the watchman to return, Thomas gave a ha'penny to the link boy and dismissed him.

The sound of a harpsichord drifted out of the window of an upper floor. It was a pleasing sound and he wondered who had composed the music.

The fellow reappeared. 'You're to go up,' he said. 'Second floor.'

A flickering lamp fixed to the wall gave a wavering light as he climbed the flight of stairs. The sound of the music grew louder. He reached a broad oak door and knocked.

It was a youngish man who welcomed him with a broad smile. 'Ah, Mr Ledbury. Do come in,' he cried.

The music stopped abruptly mid-bar. Thomas took off his cloak and set his walking-stick in the corner. Charles Burney called to the unknown player, 'It's all right, Alex. Carry on practising. You won't disturb us.'

But the music didn't continue.

Mr Burney led Thomas into a well-furnished room with carpets on the floors, walls full of pictures, and two high bookcases bulging with books and documents and manuscripts. A fire burnt in the grate. He waved him to sit down on a couch, which was reluctantly vacated by a large, shaggy dog, who proceeded to flop with a great sigh on the floor at his feet. Thomas gave it a friendly pat, while Mr Burney called for some wine, then settled himself in an armchair.

'So, Mr Ledbury. I am to take on a young scamp and teach him my trade, eh?'

'It's Mr Handel's idea, sir. Came across this lad in the chapel – and you know what the old man's like with children. Always has a soft spot for them.'

'Should have had some of his own. It might have changed his opinion,' laughed Mr Burney. 'So, he's musical, this boy?'

'Most definitely! He sings in my choir and I was hoping that he would be apprenticed to a musician. He has a splendid singing voice but, more than that, a good ear and a great passion for music, which is why Mr Handel recognised these qualities in the briefest of encounters . . .' Thomas paused.

The housekeeper came in, bearing a tray of wine and cakes.

She placed it on a side table and was about to serve them when Mr Burney said, 'Thank you, Annie. I'll see to it.'

She bobbed and left, passing someone in the doorway to whom she murmured, 'Good evening, sir.'

'Ah, Alex!' Mr Burney beamed up at the young man who had entered the room. 'It seems we've disturbed *you* rather than the other way round. Our business will not be prolonged, I assure you. Will you join us for a glass of wine? After all, this boy concerns you, too, as I hope he will learn much from you.'

Thomas got to his feet. He turned to greet the other inhabitant of the house as Mr Burney said, 'Mr Ledbury, allow me to introduce you to my fellow musician, Mr – '

'Ashbrook!' Thomas completed the name in a whisper of astonishment. 'Alexander Ashbrook?'

'Thomas? Thomas Ledbury.'

The two men looked at each other like ghosts who had materialised unexpectedly in the same place. They circled each other as if to be sure. Then, with a shout of joy, they clasped each other's hands and embraced.

'It seems my introductions are unnecessary,' laughed Mr Burney, pouring out three drinks. 'Do we drink to a reunion?'

Chapter Eighteen

★

Partings

'Aaron, Aaron!' Toby went careering through the long grass of the orchard, yelling frantically for his friend. He knew Aaron was often in the orchard, scrumping apples when he wasn't collecting them for Mrs Penny, the cook. But he wasn't there. So Toby went along to the cow sheds and pig huts. Perhaps he was with Mish. Toby had been away for three days and now he just wanted to find his friend. Usually, in the afternoons, the boys would be out working somewhere on the hospital estate, but he had looked everywhere.

Mish was pouring swill into the pig troughs, surrounded by snorting, squealing, snout-shoving beasts, who rubbed their thick bristly bodies impatiently against his legs. Toby didn't go into the sty but stood on the fence and tried to make himself heard above the noise. 'Have you seen Aaron?' His breath shuddered unsteadily.

'Angel's in the chapel!' answered Mish when he finally heard and looked up.

Toby looked bewildered. Why would Aaron be in the chapel at this time of day? But if Mish said he was, then he was. Mish always knew where his angel was.

'Toby sad?' asked Mish, noticing that Toby's face was not smiling as it usually was and that his eyes were red as if he had been crying.

'Yes, Mish, Toby sad,' and the tears began to fall again. 'They're sending me away for good. I'm to join Mr Gaddarn's household permanently; for ever – or for as long as 'e wants me. I'm goin' away, Mish. I won't hardly ever see you no more.'

Mish came sloshing over to him through the mud and lifted the boy into his pig-smelling arms. 'Oh, Tobykins, Tobykins!' He hugged him tight. 'Leaving your Mish? Leaving angel? No, no, no. Don't leave angel.'

'I don't want to. I don't not *never* want to leave Aaron or you. Oh, why must I? I hate it at Mr Gaddarn's house,' sobbed Toby.

'Ah, yes. Mr Gaddarn,' Mish nodded, stroking Toby's head quietly. 'Mr Gaddarn. *Mister Phillll-ip.*' He played around with the words as if they mesmerised him. 'You going to Mr *Phil*-lip's house? Not good man, *Mr Philiddle* diddle diddle?'

Toby shook his head then pressed his mouth to Mish's ear. 'He ain't a moral man – not a Christian man. He ain't a gentleman. I've seen bad things at his parties, Mish. Drinkin', fightin', swearin' and,' Toby spoke even more quietly, 'and many bad women. Mr Rawlings would be shocked to see it . . . I'm sure 'e wouldn't send me there if 'e knew. But 'e doesn't know, and I can't tell 'im. 'E would never believe me. Everyone 'ere thinks Mr Gaddarn is so good and generous.' Toby wiped his nose along his sleeve. 'But I've seen 'im. 'E pretends to be kind and generous in front of the right people. Some people think 'e's a saint because 'e's a benefactor of the hospital but I know 'e 'ates children. I've seen the way 'e treats 'em. I think 'e's a devil. 'E's cruel. 'E's even killed people; I've 'eard the servants talking – and they 'ate 'im too. 'E 'orse-whipped Joseph, the old butler, just because 'e tripped and spilt some wine. 'E's struck me too, and often kicks me as if I was a stray dog. 'E's bad, Mish. Bad.'

'Yes, bad. Bad man,' Mish repeated softly. He put Toby back on to the fence, then taking Toby's face in his large rough hands he whispered, 'Mish is always your friend. Always.' Then he turned back to the pigs, shouting, 'Go find angel in the chapel.'

Toby headed back to the hospital and crossed the quadrangle to the chapel. He could hear the sound of children singing. He pushed open the large oak door and crept inside. Fifteen children clustered round Mr Ledbury, who was conducting them, listening to each child in turn.

Toby liked Mr Ledbury. Everyone did. He was young and funny and often made them laugh when he taught them hymns. He didn't know any other adults who would share a joke with the children. But Mr Ledbury did, and even sometimes mimicked Mrs Hendry.

The voices sounded so cheerful. Toby crept down the side aisle to get closer.

Aaron was in the centre of the circle, right in front of Mr Ledbury, and singing his head off. Toby could hear his voice rising above the others.

Fingers plucked at his sleeve. It was Mercy. She had been standing by a pillar. Her fingers flew rapidly over his face and hair. 'Ah, Toby! It's you,' she whispered. 'Are you going to sing?'

'No,' murmured Toby sadly. 'I don't sing no good.'

'Yes you do, I've heard you,' she hissed firmly.

'Aaron sings. Aaron has the voice of an angel.'

'Yes, that he does,' agreed Mercy. 'Mr Handel thinks Aaron is musical and should be trained. I heard him say. I wish I could sing in Mr Ledbury's choir,' she sighed. 'They're to give a concert soon. They are performing Mr Handel's *Messiah*.'

The anthem ended. Thomas Ledbury smiled. 'Good. Good. We'll soon have you sounding like songbirds instead of crows. We shall meet three times a week for the next six weeks and at Christmas we shall give a concert for all our generous benefactors, governors and supporters. If the concert goes well, we propose to take you on a tour into the country, where we also have many benefactors, and we will give more concerts to raise money.'

The children murmured excitedly.

'We are so honoured to be performing *Messiah* by Mr Handel, who will also conduct us. I hope you will all appreciate this, as he is our greatest living composer, and a man whose interest in your welfare is beyond calculation. In fact, this is his idea. He believes music is good for your soul and as essential to your well-being as eating and drinking.'

A bell rang. Choir practice was over. The children dispersed. But Mr Ledbury held Aaron back. Toby wondered what he was saying. Aaron was nodding and then looking pleased. At last he was dismissed but, rather than running out after the others, Aaron seemed dazed and almost walked passed Toby without seeing him.

'Aaron!'

Aaron jerked back to reality. 'You're back!' he exclaimed warmly, and clasped his friend. 'You stayed away three days and do you know what happened? Mr Ledbury just told me. I'm to be apprenticed to a musician – a composer. Isn't it wonderful? I'm going to live with him soon and learn to write music and play the harpsichord and . . .' Aaron was bursting with excitement until he saw Toby's face. 'You were away so long, I was beginning to think I'd never see you again.' His voice became subdued as he saw Toby's anguished expression. 'Toby? What's wrong?'

'Perhaps it's no matter to you,' Toby muttered, holding back tears. 'Do you care if we never see each other again?'

'Toby!' Aaron was aghast. 'You're my friend. My greatest, greatest friend . . . I . . .' He faltered. He hadn't thought about it. He didn't know what to say. Everybody knew the day would come when they would be apprenticed out, but Aaron had thought it would be far in the future. Everything had happened so fast since he sang for Mr Handel. He had wondered from time to time what kind of trade he would be put into and whether he would have a kindly employer; he just hadn't considered that it also meant leaving Toby, who was like his brother. And what about Mish? Would he have to leave Mish, too? Suddenly he too was overwhelmed with horror.

'It's not just *you* going away. I am too,' said Toby, distraught. 'In three days they're sending me to Mr Gaddarn. He put in a request to the governors and they have agreed to it.'

'You can't! You hate it there.'

'We'll run away, won't we, Aaron? Run away so that no one can find us. Mish will help. He can come with us and we'll all go far away and be together always, shan't we?' cried Toby desperately.

'We could . . .' Aaron agreed uncertainly.

The two boys rushed back to find Mish and tell him their plans, but they were told that Mish had gone to the farrier to sort out some horses. They wandered disconsolately back towards the courtyard and saw Mercy playing her recorder under the oak tree.

'Hello, Mercy!' said Aaron, sitting down next to her. Toby stayed standing to pull down the branch of a tree and strip a twig of its leaves.

'What's wrong?' asked Mercy.

'What do you mean, what's wrong?' demanded Aaron.

'I can tell by your voice. What's wrong, Toby? Why don't you say hello to me?'

Sometimes it was as if Mercy had eyes everywhere that could see except the two in her head. 'Stop stripping that poor tree,' she chided him.

'Me and Aaron are going. We're leaving Coram. We won't never see you no more.'

'Ah yes! Well that happens to everyone,' sighed Mercy.

'Everyone 'cept you,' retorted Toby. 'You're still here.'

'That's just because I'm blind. When are you going?' asked Mercy after a pause.

'Friday. Unless we run away.'

'Hush, Toby. You shouldn't have said that,' cried Aaron worriedly. 'No one was supposed to know.'

'Mercy won't tell on us, will you, Mercy?' pleaded Toby. But he was longing to talk it over. He stopped stripping the leaves and knelt down next to her. 'We want to run away, me an' Aaron, 'cos we're best friends. We're brothers. We could go on the ships to America or Africa, couldn't we, Aaron? And I could find my mother.'

'Yes!' agreed Aaron slowly. But already he had begun to wonder. 'I suppose so.'

Toby heard the change in his voice. 'Aaron? We are running away, aren't we? Didn't you always say you would come with me on the big ships? And just now you said we should run away, you did. Don't you want to no more?' Toby cried like one betrayed.

How suddenly everything can change. Just one encounter with Mr Handel and, like a blinding flash, Aaron had realised that he wanted to be a musician more than anything else in the world. He wanted to be apprenticed to Mr Burney. Yes, he also wanted to run away so as not to be separated from Toby – but the thought of fleeing across the ocean to Africa or America no longer seemed as appealing as before and he faltered with confusion.

'I don't know what I want,' stammered Aaron. 'I want to be with Toby. And Mish – what about Mish? How can I go away from him?'

' 'E was goin' to come with us, remember?' pleaded Toby.

'But . . . I do want to be a musician when I grow up.'

'A musician?' Toby was astonished. 'You never said that before?'

'I never thought it before,' said Aaron. 'Not till I met Mr Handel and then Mr Ledbury told me what they planned for me: that when I go to Mr Burney, I'll help him and learn to copy music, and I'll be taught to play the harpsichord by a friend of Mr

Ledbury. I don't know that I could learn to play the harpsichord in Africa?'

'Then I'll run away on my own,' shouted Toby, the tears falling down his face. He leapt to his feet as if to take flight straight away, but Mercy reached out a hand and pulled him back.

'No, Toby, no.' She stroked his head. 'Don't run away, Toby. All you have to do to be free is grow up. Then you won't need to run away, you can walk away. You too, Aaron. Do you think I don't know how painful it is to part? Every friend I've ever had has had to go.'

Aaron looked into Mercy's face. Why was he so blind? He had never bothered to look at her properly before. She was just poor sightless Mercy, who loved music and played the recorder. But though she was twelve years old, she was as old as the hills; she could see more than any of them. She seemed to know all about sadness and hopes and feelings as if she had been a grown-up all her life. He didn't know how long she had been at Coram. She had always been there. So she must have had to say goodbye to lots of friends because, in the end, everyone had to leave, unless the governors thought you could not cope outside because of some disability.

'Do they ever come back to see you, Mercy – your friends?' asked Aaron.

'Some do. Sarah does. Margaret, and Anne. Anne works for a

seamstress, really kind she is, and when clothes need delivering to Coram, she lets Anne bring them so that she can see me.'

'There you are, Toby!' cried Aaron, clasping his friend. 'We will see each other. We will. Perhaps we don't need to run away.'

'I don't think you're my friend no more,' whispered Toby.

'Yes, Toby, yes I am. You and Mish are my friends for ever and ever. We swore it. We can swear again. Cut our palms and mix blood. I am always your friend,' insisted Aaron.

To soothe their feelings, Mercy began to play her recorder again. The music was sweet.

And then the bell clanged.

Chapter Nineteen

★

Mementoes

Aaron and Toby had been summoned to Mrs Hendry's parlour. They were nervous. What had they done? Usually, children were only summoned to the housekeeper if they had done something wrong. Perhaps Mother Catbrain had been to complain; perhaps Luke the gardener had counted the apples in the orchard and realised many were missing because they had gone scrumping. Perhaps it was to do with the fight: Sammy Painton had challenged Aaron at the back of the sheep barn. It had been a long fight, ending with both of them bleeding from the nose and no clear victory, but they had got so muddied and bloodied that Mrs Hendry had noticed and given them a right royal ticking-off.

Aaron glanced nervously up the main staircase where hung a great portrait by one of their patrons, William Hogarth. It was of their founder, Captain Thomas Coram. Each morning and night, whenever he whispered the Lord's Prayer, Aaron thought it was to this man they were praying. They knew it was thanks to him they got shelter and education and their daily bread. Would his kindly eyes suddenly look into theirs and become full of disappointment and reproach because they had been naughty and ungrateful? Yet he looked such a kindly old man with his white hair and his gloves in his hand, as if he had only sat down for a moment before setting off again to help some abandoned child. Our Father, which art in Heaven . . . Aaron desperately repeated the prayer silently in his head.

The maid who had fetched them knocked on the housekeeper's door. The boys stood elbow to elbow and bowed their heads.

'Come in!' they heard Mrs Hendry call.

The maid opened the door. 'I've brought the boys, ma'am,' she announced, then skipped out, shutting the door after they had taken one cautious step inside.

'We didn't mean to, ma'am. They made us . . . It was them big boys.'

'Tetch, tetch!' Mrs Hendry shook her head. Heavens, she was smiling. She got up and went to a large oak cupboard. She opened the double doors and revealed a set of long wooden drawers. She lifted one right out and placed it like a tray on the table. The boys stared at it uncomprehendingly. It was full of oddments: rings and lockets and handkerchiefs, a comb, a ribbon, brooches, pins, buttons and bits of metal. Some were valuable, like a baby's shirt of cambric and lace, or a tiny pair of white brocade shoes; there was a locket of gold, a hat pin of silver, a comb of mother-of-pearl. Others you wouldn't look at twice if you saw them in the street: a brass button, a cheap string of glass beads, a grubby piece of material lopped from a dress. Yet each item was meticulously labelled.

The boys shuffled closer, twisting their heads to read the tags. As well as the name and date the child was brought in, some had scraps of paper attached with hastily scrawled words: *Cruel Separation; Taken from a broken-hearted mother; Good sirs, Protect my poor innocent child.* There were even poems:

> *If Fortune should her favours give*
> *That I in Better plight may live*
> *I'd try to have my Boy again*
> *And Train him up the best of Men.*

'You are in no doubt as to how you came to be here.' Mrs Hendry sat down behind her desk and folded her hands in front of her. 'All of our children are foundling children; children who were found by the wayside or in porches and doorways, or secretly dropped at our gate by mothers unwilling or unable to care for them. But that is not to say that all the mothers were heartless and had no love for their babies. For many it was heartbreak and anguish. Many wanted to leave some token for their child, so that it would know that though it seemed to have no identity other than being a Coram child, in fact, a grieving mother loved it and would have cared for it if she could.

'Both you boys were delivered to us in person and each of you knows who brought you here. Toby was brought here by Mr Gaddarn, who rescued you from your poor mother when she was being taken as a slave to the Americas.' Mrs Hendry reached into the tray and took up one of the strings of beads. 'This is what your mother left for you, and which we now give you as you leave our institution to join the household of your benefactor. We give you this because it is yours which we kept in trust, and because we want you to be as responsible to us as we have been to you. Do not disgrace the Coram name. Do not let down the fine hopes your unknown mother had for you, nor the man who has succoured and ensured your well-being all this time.'

It was just a simple row of beads on a thin string and tied with a knot to form a bracelet. They were small brightly coloured beads in red, green, yellow and black. Mrs Hendry put it into his hands.

Toby let it lie in his open palm. He was touching Africa. He was touching his mother. He scrutinised the dusty brown tag on which his name was clearly written in ink and hardly dared close his fingers in case, once out of sight, they would disappear. He just stared and stared. He tried to imagine Africa and, in feeling their delicate weight on his skin, to experience through them his own mother's touch.

'Is my mother alive?' he asked. 'Can I go and see her now?'

'We do not know if she is alive or even where she is, except that she was taken as a slave to the Americas . . . I'm sorry, Toby, this is all we have.'

'And my mother, she's dead, isn't she?' said Aaron, hardly daring to look at Mrs Hendry. 'You have nothing for me.'

'We do have something. We are not sure about you, though. You were brought here by Mish, but we were never able to discover from where or from whom he had brought you. He has never claimed to be your father, only your . . .' she smiled, 'guardian angel. But we have two things which he brought with you.' Mrs Hendry opened a side drawer and took out a bundle roughly wrapped in brown paper. 'This is the christening robe in which you were wrapped. It is finest French cotton and stitched into a corner are the initials AA and a crest of a swan. There was also something round your neck – a locket on a ribbon. Not a cheap locket, but solid silver, and inside we found this lock of hair. We think it could be that of your mother. She must have been a lady of substance.'

'A lady of substance.' Aaron wasn't sure what that meant.

She handed him the locket. Like Toby, he took it tentatively as if it were unreal and might dissolve at his touch. He opened the locket. A single coil of dark auburn hair gleamed within a white silken lining. 'My mother!' he murmured. 'My mother's hair.' He stroked it with his little finger. If only, if only he could see the face which this hair had framed.

Mrs Hendry was talking. But they didn't hear her. Each was soaring through time and space with his thoughts – back to the past before he was born, forward to the future, wondering, wondering, wondering. Each raking through his memories, wishing that there was one tiny shred he could remember of his mother.

'You two, who have been such close friends, have the good fortune to be apprenticed to two good people. Toby, you will take up duties as a permanent liveried servant in Mr Gaddarn's household. You will be housed and fed; you will be allowed to attend church on Sundays and have one day off a year.

'Aaron, although you are barely eight, and normally too young to be apprenticed out, Mr Handel believes you to have superior talents in music. This is supported by Mr Ledbury. They see no reason why this talent should not be nurtured immediately. Although your patron had wanted you to be apprenticed to a cabinet maker in one of his workshops, in view of Mr Handel's intervention, he agrees that you should be apprenticed to the household of the musician, Mr Burney. You will be instructed by him in the art of music copying, harpsichord tuning and assist him in any way that he requires. But you will also be given musical instruction.

'Now that you have taken possession of your mementoes, it is up to you to keep them safe. Go now, both of you. Pack your bags with your uniform, Sunday clothes, shoes, stockings and comb. Tomorrow you will appear before the board, where you will thank them for their care of you, and then you will take your leave of this place.'

Toby burst out crying and flung himself into the housekeeper's arms. 'I don't want to go. Please let me stay. I don't want to serve Mr Gaddarn.'

The housekeeper sternly took the boy by both arms and lifted him away from her. 'Come, come, Toby. This is no way to show gratitude. You are privileged indeed to be taken into the house of one of the most esteemed gentlemen in London and one of our most generous benefactors. Face the world like a man and learn the manners of a gentleman, and you will go far. Make no mistake, it is a cruel world out there, and if you fail to take up the opportunities which are offered you, only God could preserve you from the crime, poverty and degradation which awaits any weak sinner.'

'What about Mish?' asked Aaron at last. He had been standing silent as a statue. 'What will happen to him when I've gone?'

'Nothing, dear boy. Nothing. He will stay here. He earns his keep by working the farm, and we do not believe he can survive alone outside the hospital,' said Mrs Hendry.

'I wish he could come with me. He will be so sad without me.'

'You may visit him on your day off. The governors will not object and I'm sure Mr Burney will allow it.'

'What about 'im and me?' burst out Toby. 'Will we ever see us again?' He grabbed Aaron's hand. ' 'E's my friend.'

The housekeeper sighed. 'Take my advice. Work well. Grow up honestly. Follow the ways of the Lord. When you are grown into men, you will find more freedom to fulfil your wishes.'

'That's what Mercy said,' muttered Aaron, holding Toby's hand tightly.

'God bless you, Toby. God bless you, Aaron,' said Mrs Hendry, kissing each boy on the top of the head, and then she gently ushered them out to go to their pallet bed and spend their last night in the Coram Hospital.

Chapter Twenty

✫

Apprenticed out

Toby left first. A manservant came from Mr Gaddarn's house with a horse and carriage. He was a sullen sort of fellow, and more or less chucked Toby and his bag into the carriage. Then, without a word, he climbed up next to the driver. All the children clustered at the portico, shouting and waving and yelling goodbye. It wasn't often a Coram boy was taken off grandly in a coach. Aaron ran after the coach, all the way down to the front gate, until it turned into the thoroughfare which led to the city, his eyes fixed on Toby's distraught face. 'I'll see you again soon, Toby. I'll see you soon. You'll always be my friend,' he shouted as the carriage quickly sped away. Then he rushed off to a dark corner in the sheep barn to cry and cry and cry.

Early that afternoon, a young woman arrived on foot to escort him to the home of Mr Burney.

A servant was sent first to Mish. He was disturbed and bewildered. 'Are they taking my angel today?' he asked, his huge brow dropping over his eyes till they darkened almost to black.

'They shouldn't take him away from me. He's my angel.'

It was Mercy who found Aaron, suddenly remembering that he and Toby liked to hide in the sheep barn and eat their stolen apples. She found the great wooden door ajar. She stepped inside, smelling the hay and the animals, and hearing the pipping house martins diving in and out among the rafters. She listened, and soon heard an intermittent sniff.

'Aaron?' she called softly. 'Aaron, it's me, Mercy. I've come to find you.'

'I ain't going nowhere,' sniffed his tearful voice from deep inside. 'I can't leave Mish.'

'I know. Mish is upset too.'

Mercy took her recorder from out of her apron pocket and, standing in the warmth of a shaft of sunlight pouring through the doorway, she played and waited.

She knew he would come, approaching slowly like a shy animal. When finally he, too, stood blinking in the same shaft of sunlight, she sensed his presence and said, 'Poor Mish. You will have to console him, Aaron. You will have to explain to him how you must go away, so that when you are grown up and a man with a living, you can care for him in his old age. He'll understand if you make him see. Will you come with me now? He's waiting for you.'

She held out a hand. Aaron came up quietly, still sniffing, and took it. Then they went outside to find Mish.

Just as Mercy wanted, Aaron explained to Mish, held tightly in the great bear hug of his arms, why he must go and Mish must stay. 'I've got to go, Mish. But I'm not far away, and Mrs Hendry says I will be able to see you often. And when I'm a man, Mish, I'll be rich and famous, and we'll get a house and live together for ever. But Mrs Hendry says it's better you don't come with me. It's best for me if you stay here. You're safe here and they look after you. So don't ever go away, will you, Mish? Otherwise I won't know where to find you.'

Mish had promised. Promised, promised. They both made promises. Then said their goodbyes.

The young woman from Mr Burney was waiting patiently when finally Aaron, dressed in his Coram Sunday clothes with cap on head and bag in hand, came out.

'Good day to you, Master Aaron,' she said. 'I'm Martha Baines, and I've come to take you to Mr Burney's house. We should get going as the sun is dropping and I would like to get back before nightfall.'

He heard their voices as they walked down the long avenue. 'Bye, Aaron! Goodbye, goodbye!' And, above all, Mish's voice calling louder and louder than the rest.

'Farewell, my angel. God go with thee till we meet again. Goodbye, my angel, goodbye, my angel . . .'

* * *

Martha kept up a fast pace, with Aaron at times having to break into a trot to keep up with her. His bag got heavier and heavier, and every now and then he was forced to stop and change hands. But soon, his hands were sore and his legs ached, and he got slower and slower till he was struggling along at a snail's pace. 'Tut, tut, Master Aaron. Try and keep up,' she grumbled, turning round and standing with her hands on her hips.

'How much further?' he wailed, coming to a standstill yet again.

'Oh lawks. I suppose I'll have to carry the bag. Here, give it to me.' She strode back and yanked up the bag. 'Now you've no excuse not to keep up,' she said sternly, and struck out for the city.

They walked down the long road between the fields and orchards of grazing sheep and cows and goats and horses running free until, after an hour, the sweet-smelling fields gave way to the stench, smoke and smells of city streets and houses and hovels. The noise of the capital began to gather and roar like a distant wave and they could no longer walk a straight path, but had to dodge and swerve and battle with a sea of people.

They arrived at the house in St Martin's Lane. Aaron looked up, awe-struck. He had never been into a real city house before. They didn't enter by the front door; Martha took him down a side alley and knocked on a door for the servants and hawkers. It was opened by a cheerful-looking youth who, grinning all over, laughed teasingly at Martha and said, 'Cor, Mattie, you look like a prize-winning beetroot!'

Aaron couldn't conceal a grin at this insolent remark, for it was true, Martha was as red in the face as anyone could be. Serves her right, he thought uncharitably, for having made me walk so fast.

'You cheeky little monkey, Timothy Parfitt,' she snapped, pretending to be cross and cuffing him round the head. 'Here!' She tossed the bag to him. 'Take this up to the attic and show Master Dangerfield where he's to sleep. You're sharing with him,' she told Aaron, jerking her head in the direction of young Timothy, who still stood grinning. 'Timothy Parfitt. Rogue and villain if ever there was one,' she pronounced. 'Go on. Get out of my sight, the two of you. Bring him back down when he's put away his clothes and he can have his tea.'

'Are you one of Mr Burney's pupils?' asked Aaron as he puffed up three flights of stairs till they reached the rafters in the roof.

'The devil, no!' Tim laughed. 'I'm footman, manservant, groom and Jack-of-all-trades. Mr Fetch-and-Carry, that's me. Now it looks as if I'm a nurse too.'

Aaron flinched at that last remark and dropped his head.

'Oi!' Timothy led him into a small room where even Aaron had to duck so as not to bump his head on the beams. It had a slanting attic window and two beds, one in each corner; proper iron bedsteads, with mattress and pillow. 'Put your turnip head there.' Timothy threw Aaron's bag on to the bed in the farthest corner from the slanting attic window. 'You don't wet the bed or nothink, do ya?' he demanded.

'No,' replied Aaron.

'And you don't snore?'

'No.'

'And you don't go yelling in your sleep or walking about?'

'No.'

'Good,' said Timothy, slapping him on the back. 'Neither do I,' and they both burst out laughing.

Aaron didn't meet Mr Burney till the next day. He had risen early, before dawn, when Timothy had to get up. When Aaron asked what he should do and where he should go, Timothy said, 'Just do as I do, ha'pence, and you'll soon learn.'

All morning, Aaron shadowed Timothy, fetching fuel for the kitchen fire, washing out the stable yard, raking out the hay, checking the horses, feeding the chickens and geese. Then, with loud instructions from Mrs Leatherhide the cook echoing in his ears, Aaron accompanied Timothy to Spitalfields to get a side of beef. Never had he felt so free. He just did exactly what Timothy did; and when Timothy strode all cocky through the city streets, dodging in and out of the horses and carriages and sedans and hawkers and sellers, whistling his head off, calling out to people he knew, and acting as if he owned half of London, Aaron did the same.

'Got another Coram boy, have yer?' someone yelled out at the sight of Aaron, so conspicuous in his red and brown.

Timothy quipped back: 'Apples and custard.'

'What did you mean, apples and custard?' asked Aaron curiously.

'Sharp as mustard, of course, ha'pence,' came back Timothy quick as anything. But Aaron wasn't sure if that was the truth.

It was four o'clock when he was summoned to go to Mr Burney's music room.

'Quick, wash your hands and face, straighten your jacket, tie this handkerchief round your neck. Come on, look smartish, lad.' Mrs Mount the housekeeper had come to check him before his audience with the master. Then she took him up the narrow, dark servants' stairs which led through a side door into an elegant hallway. Brass sconces gleamed from their wall brackets, finely woven carpets lay on polished wooden floors. Large oil paintings seemed to invite him to step into strange landscapes with beautiful people. Then he heard the sound of a harpsichord coming through a thick oak door. Mrs Mount gave a sharp but polite rap on the door. The music stopped. A voice called out.

'Enter!'

Aaron took one step into the room and the door closed behind him. The man who got up from the harpsichord was the man he had seen briefly in the chapel when Aaron had sung for Mr Handel. Aaron was puzzled. This was not Mr Burney, was it? No, Ashbrook, that's what Mr Handel had called him. The man frowned and scrutinised Aaron with deep, dark eyes, and Aaron felt strangely nervous, as if his very soul was being examined.

Then, from the far end of the room, another gentleman rose from the depths of a high-winged chair. Aaron stood just inside the door, looking as if at any minute he might bolt.

'Come in, boy. Don't be shy,' said the other man. 'I'm Mr Burney and this is Mr Ashbrook.' He strode over and examined the boy. 'So, this is Mr Handel's songbird, is it? Speak your name, boy.'

'Aaron, sir. Aaron Dangerfield.' Aaron dropped his head and gave a respectful bow.

'His benefactor's name,' explained Mr Burney to Mr Ashbrook, and Aaron bowed to him too. 'Well, my boy, you come to me with a strong recommendation. We are most intrigued to hear you. What shall you sing, Master Dangerfield?' asked Mr Burney encouragingly, as Aaron still stood stiff and shy. 'What is your favourite song?'

'I have many favourites, sir. Shall I sing the one about the swan? Mercy taught me.'

'Mercy?'

'Mercy Bligh, I expect,' explained Mr Ashbrook. 'Thomas Ledbury told me about her. She is a musical child, twelve years old now, but blind. She sings in the choir and plays the organ for prayers.'

'What swan song did she teach you?' asked Mr Burney with a smile as he went to sit at the harpsichord.

'This one, sir,' and Aaron sang the first phrase.

Mr Burney raised his eyebrows approvingly. 'Oh *that* one.'

Mr Ashbrook walked to the far end of the room and stood in the alcove of the window, gazing out with his arms folded, his face grave and thoughtful.

Mr Burney played some opening chords, and Aaron came in:

> *'The silver swan, who living had no note,*
> *When death approached, unlocked her silent throat.*
> *Leaning her breast against the reedy shore,*
> *Thus sang her first and last, then sang no more.*
> *Farewell all joys! O Death, come close mine eyes;*
> *More geese than swans now live, more fools than wise.'*

His voice had sounded well in that room, Aaron knew. He had sung as well as ever he could. He was sure that Mr Ledbury would have been satisfied with him, Mr Handel too. Aaron thought they might also be pleased and praise him. But Mr Ashbrook said not a word and didn't look pleased, though neither did he look displeased. He seemed dazed; lost in his own thoughts. Mr Burney sat silently too.

Aaron looked down at his toes. Already that journey to Spitalfields had scuffed up the tips of his boots. Had he been at Coram, he would never have been allowed into a drawing-room with his boots in that condition. He could hear a street seller outside singing her wares. He wondered how Toby was and when he would see him. He hoped that Mish was not in a state, bawling for him. Perhaps if Mr Burney didn't like his voice, he would send him back to Coram, then he would be with Mish again.

'Well!' The word came out like a small explosion and at last Mr Burney looked up. 'Come here, boy.'

Aaron approached nervously.

'Sing with me. Let's see how high you can go and how low.' He played a note in the middle range and Aaron sang it. Then step by step he went down the range and Aaron followed five notes down till his voice sounded like a grunt. Then Mr Burney took him up again, up, up, up, sixteen notes higher from where he had started. And still, Aaron's voice rang out as pure as a silver bell.

'Mr Handel was right, Alexander. He has a voice all right.'

Mr Burney gave him some ear tests. He played a note and asked him to sing four notes above or two notes down. Aaron did it perfectly. Mr Burney played two notes together and asked him to sing first the lower note, then the higher one. Again he sang perfectly. Even when he had to sing the middle note of three, he could.

After a few more exercises to test his memory and ability to extemporise, Mr Burney addressed Aaron seriously. 'You have been apprenticed to me and put into my care, not just to learn music but to serve me and my colleague, Mr Ashbrook. To begin with, all it will amount to is taking manuscripts to and from the publisher and delivering scores to those who may be performing our music. But you must learn to read and write music so well that you can be a copyist and make a best copy of our draft scores so that they are legible for publishers and performers. If you do not reach our standards, I will be forced to put you into another trade. So learn your lessons well, and you will not only be serving me, but serving your own interests, too. Mr Ashbrook will teach you how to play the harpsichord and violin. It is good to be able to play a number of instruments if you are to make music your profession.'

'Thank you, sir, I will, sir,' exclaimed Aaron, his face breaking into the biggest grin of his life.

'Oh, and by the way, you will continue to rehearse with Mr Ledbury *Messiah* for the benefit concert. Mr Handel has asked for you to sing one of the solos.'

Aaron looked very pleased. Already he could look forward to going back and seeing Mish.

'Well, Mr Ashbrook,' said Mr Burney, getting to his feet with a flick of his coat-tails and walking over to talk to the silent young man, who continued to stare out of the window. 'I think we have a goodly piece of material in our hands. I commend him to you. Let's see if we can make a musician out of him. I think you have a pupil here who will be a pleasure to teach. Do you not agree?' He paused patiently, waiting for a response.

Alexander Ashbrook looked at the boy, remembering himself as he had been at that age. He was filled with such a conflict of feelings: of regret for the past, the loss of family and home, the sacrifice of his status and inheritance – and for what? The bright young face before him was like his own mirror image; looking as eager as he had at that age. For a moment, he was that boy: keen, brimming with the love of music, and so confident about what he could do in the future. And then he knew why, all over again, why he had made the sacrifice. He had no choice.

'Do you think you and he will get on together?' asked Mr Burney, wondering at Ashbrook's hesitation. 'Do you see any reason why not?'

'No, sir. No reason at all.' The mists of doubt and sadness cleared and Alexander Ashbrook felt comforted. His face broke out into a warm and enthusiastic smile. 'I think young Master Dangerfield and I will get on like a house on fire.'

Chapter Twenty-one

⋆

A face from the past

Meshak was being dead. He lay like a fallen giant, his great body crushing the late summer grasses, the buttercups and daisies. He hadn't been dead for years. Not since he had run away with that precious little bundle and arrived at the Coram Hospital had he needed to be dead. All these years in the safety of Coram, living near his beloved angel, were like being in paradise. The only sounds of babies and children that he now heard were of them being cared for and nurtured, not beaten and abused, not starved and enslaved, not having their little mouths stuffed with earth and their eyes blinded with rain. He had forgotten those dark, deep, dripping woods; the digging and burying of squealing bundles. Till now. Now, since Aaron had gone, his dreams and demons came back. Everywhere he looked, he saw tiny hands and fingers clawing at the sky, he heard wailing voices and choking cries. Every ditch was lined with bones, every molehill he saw was a grave, every curve in the bough of a tree was the outline of an infant body, and even the water gushing in the stream sounded like heart-broken mothers, pleading for their babies. It all came back with such terrifying intensity that the only way he could escape the visions and sounds was to be dead.

And so he lay as dead as could be, all day, and the pollen from flowers coated his skin and leaves drifted down and settled on his brow, and little ants and spiders explored his clothes while he soared among the angels, chasing Aaron across the sky, dodging stars and meteors, catching glimpses of Melissa's face among the clouds. Their laughter resonated through the universe.

'Mish, Mish!'

A voice came into his ears like a strain of music, and it pulled his mind back to consciousness and, as though he were a kite on a string, he felt himself being pulled down, down, down, back to earth.

'Mish, wake up! It's me.'

Mish opened his eyes. 'Angel!' A broad grin spread across his face. He clasped his dear boy, his angel, and held him skyward in flight, propped on his outstretched arms above his head, and swooped him about.

And then they jumped to their feet and held hands, jumping around and chortling with joy at being back together again. And when they had calmed down, Aaron told Mish everything he had been doing since he was apprenticed to Mr Burney. How he was learning everything he could learn about music: to write it, copy it, play it, sing it.

'Mish! I'm coming back to Coram to sing in *Messiah*. Mr Handel asked for me. They're doing a special performance at Christmas for the benefactors and patrons. And then we're going on a tour, giving concerts all round the place to raise money, and I'm going too. Mr Ledbury asked if I could and Mr Burney said yes. Isn't that wonderful, Mish?'

Mish nodded and repeated, 'Wonderful, wonderful.' Anything that made his little angel so happy must be wonderful.

They wandered about over the Coram estate; through the orchards, and over to the pig sties and cow sheds, the chicken coops and sheep barns. Then, when the chapel clock struck three, Aaron said, 'I must go now, Mish. I promised to go on the stroke of three. But I'll be back next week and every week until Christmas,' and he flung his arms round his waist. 'And you will come and hear me, won't you, Mish? You must hear me sing my solo. Promise?'

Mish picked him up and hugged him till he gasped for air. 'Promise, promise, promise!' And then Aaron went running towards the school. When he got to the gate and was climbing over, he waved a last goodbye. Mish waved and waved, rooted to the ground, his eye fixed on the beloved boy. When he was out of sight, Mish walked after him to the back of the chapel, from where he could hear the children practising their hymns with Mr Ledbury. Their voices floated out, mixing with the swallows and house martins, the thrushes and blackbirds, who set up their own chorus in competition, as if their territory was under threat.

When the choir practice was over, Aaron returned to Mr Burney's. On these occasions, he was accompanied by either Martha Baines or Timothy Parfitt. He much preferred it to be Timothy, not because he had anything against Martha, for all her brusque manners and blunt no-nonsense speech, but she never wandered off the beaten track. Whereas Timothy was like a bird freed from a cage out in the streets of London. He would hurry along, often putting Aaron on his shoulders to move quicker, so he could have a drink of beer or stop to wander among market stalls. Most of all, he was always on the lookout for where the singer, Nancy Dawson, was performing. He was in love with Nancy Dawson. 'She's a beauuuuutiful person, is Nancy. With a beauuuuutiful voice like as what you ain't never heard, my lad.' She was often performing at Covent Garden or Drury Lane and, sometimes, Timothy pretended to be a coachman and joined the coach drivers up in the gods where they had free seats while they waited for their gentlemen.

'Are you going to marry Nancy Dawson?' asked Aaron curiously.

'Don't be daft. She wouldn't even look at the likes of me. She goes with gentlemen and milords, she does. But I can dream.'

Whenever Timothy was preoccupied watching his beloved Nancy, Aaron tried to see Toby. Although poor Toby hated being in the employ of Mr Gaddarn, he had one piece of good fortune: Mrs Bellamy the cook. She was fond of Toby, and when she caught Aaron trying to sneak in to visit him, instead of chasing him away with a thrashing, she allowed them to go down to the market or along the Strand on the pretext of an errand, so that they had some time together.

Today, Mrs Bellamy was in a fluster. There was to be a big party that night, and the kitchen was run off its feet trying to prepare for it. Toby had been at work since dawn, polishing. He polished the oak floors and the wooden panels and the long curving banisters, and he polished all the side tables and the dining table and every bit of arm and leg of every wooden chair, and when he had done with polishing wood, he was put to work polishing all the silver: the knives, forks and spoons; all the tableware – the silver candlesticks and the salt and pepper pots and the vinegar bottles and the mustard dishes and the tureens. Toby thought his arm would drop off, what with all the polishing he had to do.

But when he had finished, Mrs Bellamy said, 'Right, lad. Take an hour off.' She liked young solemn Master Dangerfield, who turned up so faithfully from time to time to see his friend. 'But mind you're back by seven o'clock. You've got to put on your clothes and turban and all those jewels. You don't want a walloping from the master, now, do you?'

'Thank you, thank you, Mrs B,' cried Toby joyfully, flinging his arms round her neck and slapping a big kiss on her cheek, and the boys ran out into the street.

There wasn't much time today to drift around the market or gawp at the street entertainers as they sometimes did. Instead, they went down to the river to look at the boats, the barges and sloops, the skiffs and huge trading vessels. They loved watching the loading and unloading of goods, or seeing the boats tilted to one side as they lay stranded on the mudflats after the tide had gone out.

'Look!' Aaron pointed to a line of Africans – men, women and children – all manacled and chained together, shuffling towards a gangplank and up on to a ship called the *Swallow*.

'Do you ever think that could be you?' asked Aaron quietly.

Toby made no answer.

'Does he still beat you, that Mr Gaddarn?'

'He beats all of us. I 'ate 'im.'

Aaron was shocked by the coldness in Toby's voice.

'What about you, then? Mr Burney. Does 'e beat you?'

'Oh never! He doesn't believe in it. Nor Mr Ashbrook. But Martha's got a sharp hand. I like him, Mr Ashbrook. He's good. When I grow up, I want to be like him. He plays the harpsichord.

I want to do that too, and he's a composer. Mr Burney says he's one of the finest musicians in England. Mr Handel found him, too, and gave him a job playing with his orchestra. Now he's teaching me, and he lets me watch him rehearsing.'

'When you're rich and famous, don't forget Toby, will ya!' Toby nudged his friend in the ribs.

'When I'm rich and famous,' declared Aaron, 'I'll buy a big, big house, and have lots of servants and horses and dogs. And you and me, we'll ride round in carriages like kings, won't we? And we'll have many musical parties, and we won't invite Mr Gaddarn.'

They went down to the water's edge and flipped stones across the surface of the water and thought about the future. Then the bells of St Paul's boomed and, like reverberating echoes, the other clocks all over the city began chiming seven o'clock.

'Quick! We must go. Run. I'll get such a walloping,' gasped Toby. 'Shall I see you soon?' he called as he fled.

'Yes, yes! Soon!' answered Aaron, and he too dashed away towards Drury Lane, crossing the busy streets, almost being run over by a coach, and sworn at by the irate coachman who had to calm his rearing horse. He needn't have worried. When he climbed the narrow stairs up to the gods, there was Timothy totally enthralled as he watched Nancy Dawson, a mere speck far away on that stage, dancing like an elf, tumbling like an acrobat, and singing so lustily that her voice carried all over the theatre as if there were six of her all rolled into one.

'Come on, Timothy, come! It's gone seven. We'll be for the stick if we don't go now,' and he had to drag on Timothy's jacket till he nearly pulled it off his back to get him away, and as they burst out of the theatre and stumbled home as fast as they could, Timothy, tiddly with too much gin, sang loudly:

> '*Of all the girls in Town*
> *The Black, the Fair, the Red and Brown,*
> *That dance and prance it up and down*
> *There's none like NANCY DAWSON.*'

Meanwhile, Alexander Ashbrook was hurrying with scores, taking exactly the same route, but instead of going to Drury Lane, he was going to Mr Gaddarn's house. A runner had come over to the Burneys at the last minute, beseeching a first violin and music director to take control of the evening's music, as the hired man had fallen ill: *Mr Gaddarn beseeches Mr Ashbrook, if he be free, willing and able, to come over to his residence tonight and save his party by taking over the orchestra.*

Alexander Ashbrook had not long stopped directing salon music, which had held his body and soul together since leaving home, so he was not above taking the job – especially as the money was so good. He still thought of Melissa and their dream of being together. As he hurried along, he might well have noticed Aaron and Timothy scuttling home, but London at that time of day was like an extension of Bedlam itself, and though they were barely a yard apart in the same street, they didn't see each other.

Alexander arrived at Mr Gaddarn's house for the first time and knocked on the door at the tradesmen's entrance down a side alley. He was curious. He had never met him, but Mr Gaddarn was the sort of man about whom gossip abounded. Yet very little of substance seemed to be known about him. He had bought his fashionable house about seven years ago, but from where he had come, no one seemed quite to know. Some said he was a new mill owner from the Midlands, others said no, he came from the North and owned ships. Though he spoke with a courtly accent, sharper ears detected a West Country burr. One fact was clear, he had enormous wealth. Had he plantations in Virginia and the West Indies? Had he dabbled in speculative property schemes? Was he a great gambler both at the tables and on the Stock Exchange? Had he lost a fortune with the South Sea bubble, but made it all again in the slave trade? But if there was an undercurrent of unsavouriness about Mr Gaddarn, it was also undeniable that he more than made up for it by his good works. He was a benefactor and supporter of a good many charities, and his huge donations to the Coram Hospital were well known. He went to great lengths to be better known for his good works than for his business dealings, and was working hard to get his knighthood.

Alexander was let in by a young liveried servant and shown to the drawing-room which ran the length of the first floor. About half a dozen musicians wigged and dressed in Sherwood green-and-gold livery were idly unpacking their instruments or flopping around, smoking pipes. They looked ill at ease without their leader, so they were relieved when Alexander entered. He was warmly greeted, for many of the musicians knew him and respected him. Quickly, Alexander took control and, in the short time before the guests started to arrive, he had organised them and selected the programme.

Alexander played and conducted the music from the harpsichord, and he angled himself so that he could see both his players and the guests. Soon the guests were rolling up in their carriages and sedans. The band performed suitable 'entry' music: delicate minuets and sarabandes, and extracts from the popular operas of the day; music suitable for introductions to be made, while the first trays of sweetmeats and delicacies were passed round. Footmen and maids scurried to and fro, some with candlesticks to light the way into the house, others to take charge of the fine velvet cloaks and feathered hats.

And there was Toby, Aaron's friend, all bedecked in his full princely regalia. His turquoise silken turban was wrapped round his head and strung with baubles and beads, his long, flowing, multicoloured, embroidered gown was split in front to show billowing turquoise pantaloons and gold-stitched slippers with points that curved upwards like tongues. He darted in and out with silver platters of sweetmeats and savouries. He made sure he flashed his bright black eyes, and gave a fixed, wide, toothy smile – just as he had been instructed to do. Once, when the child flinched with pain because a gentleman gave him a sharp kick for bumping into him, Alexander winked at him sympathetically.

Mr Gaddarn himself, in a specially fashionable wig all tightly curled and swept up at the front, wore a silken jacket and velvet waistcoat, breeches, black stockings and leather shoes with huge silver buckles. With what flamboyance he greeted his guests, effusively swooping low over the ladies' hands, and graciously bowing with sweeping hand before the fine gentlemen. Alexander kept catching glimpses of him from a distance but he never quite saw his face until, halfway through the evening, a group of ladies had flopped on to a row of chairs and grabbed at Toby, drawing him on to their laps. They pinched his cheeks and stroked his hair, they opened his mouth to see the pinkness of his tongue and popped sweets inside whether he wanted them or not. How they cooed and clucked over him, passing him between themselves as if he were a favoured pet.

'What a dear little creature! And could you ever imagine any human being so black? Why, he's as black as pitch,' and one of the ladies pressed her white powdered face against his, and they all laughed at the contrast.

'Oh, Mr Gaddarn,' another of the ladies chimed in in a bright piercing voice which lulled the conversation, 'What will become of this darling little man when he is no longer huggable and too big to sit on our laps?'

'Ooh, I say, he'll never be too big to sit on mine,' giggled another, sending a ripple of bawdy laughter across the salon.

'Why, madam,' Mr Gaddarn's voice was acid. 'If the day comes when I cannot make use of him here, I can always ship him to Virginia.'

Alexander turned in disgust at those words and looked directly into Mr Gaddarn's face.

It was only a split second before Mr Gaddarn turned away, but the glimpse was like an arrow, sharp with recognition.

As he waved his players into a lively polka, Alexander knew with certainty. 'I've seen that man before.'

Chapter Twenty-two

✫

Discovery

The drink flowed, the evening became more raucous. People danced with abandon, and those who weren't dancing withdrew to the billiard room to smoke, play billiards or gamble at cards.

Toby was at last forgotten. His head was aching. Every bone in his body was aching. The room tipped and swayed with dizziness. Exhausted, he slipped away into a side room at the back of the house which he knew his master only used to conduct business, and he surely would not be conducting business tonight. It was called the map room and it had intrigued him the few times he had been in it. In one corner was a vast globe on a table. It put the whole world under his fingertips and, with a tap, he could make it revolve and, like a god, see all the oceans and deserts and continents whirl by.

On one snatched occasion, when he had been sent there to polish the silver ornaments, he had found Africa. With his finger he had traced a route by sea; the route he must have taken in one of those great masted ships he had so often seen berthed on the Thames. He knew he had been carried inside his mother's belly across the ocean called the Atlantic, passing the coast of Spain and on round to the shores of England. At some point on that voyage, he had been born.

He had only heard about Africa from old Benjamin, who had described the Atlantic as the 'Great Ocean of Darkness' because of the way their people had been kidnapped in their thousands, snatched from their homes and villages and dragged, screaming, on to the ships. They were crammed deep down in the skyless, airless, dark-as-hell holds, row on row. They were so tightly packed that for the weeks and weeks it took for the ships to arrive at their destination, people could hardly move a muscle or breathe. Many died, so many – of disease or cruel treatment or just from a broken heart. Their bones littered the ocean bed, their souls howled soundlessly in that heaving, lonely waste, too far out for even the gulls to reach. And those who hadn't died wished they had, preferring to be dead rather than enslaved.

A low light glowed from the embers of a fire in the grate. The globe gleamed, casting a huge round shadow on the wall. Toby trailed his fingers across its surface with just enough force to make it spin slowly, and then he sank on to a windowseat behind a heavy oak carved screen. A great window overlooked the river, but Toby was too tired to do more than glance at the beachcombers' fires burning on the shore, and the spangle of lights hanging from so many yardarms all along the banks, and the frenzy of activity on the docks as ships were made ready for the next high tide. He curled up on the cushions which lined the windowseat and within a minute fell into a feverish sleep.

'Well, gentlemen, I think I can do business with you.'

The voice of his master broke into his dream.

Toby awoke, instinctively silent. Only his eyes opened. He did not move any other muscle. He heard his master welcome in three, maybe four more men. He could not be sure, lying there behind the screen. The light from a three-armed candlestick brightened the room and caused the shadows to swirl up and down the walls until it was placed on the central table. He heard the men seating themselves, lighting up pipes and pouring drinks.

Toby groaned inwardly to think he was trapped for possibly an hour or two while they discussed shipping, property and other speculations. But then he heard the word 'Coram'.

'I can take possession of four boys and three girls by the end of the month,' Mr Gaddarn said.

'Just three girls? Can you not procure a few more? Six, at least, would make it much more worth my while, and yours too.'

'Six would be risky,' said Mr Gaddarn. 'The Coram authorities are very particular about their children and like to keep records of their whereabouts and progress. I have told them that I have found positions for three girls in Virginia. I have a contact in Virginia who has been able to forge documents for me before, giving false addresses. He is even able to send a letter or two with information on the well-being of any Coram child, supposedly in their care, and credible descriptions of their lives in the service of good Virginian families. To do this for two or three girls is just about within the bounds of plausibility, but I fear six girls would arouse suspicion.'

'I would say it's a simple case of their appearing to be split up. Two can be thought to go to Virginia but one or two, let us say, can go to Boston. I have contacts there who could write similar letters, and the rest can go to India. It will take time to arrange letters, but I have a ship departing for India in two days and can send my request. In fact, we can build up a little store of letters from any number of places, so that the true destination of the children can be obscured.'

'That might work,' agreed Mr Gaddarn, his voice less hesitant. 'Very well, I agree to six girls, but let me say this: if I have one shred of doubt about the enterprise, any sense whatsoever that the whole thing is going sour, then I reserve my right to change the plan in any way I see fit, and if I think it safe to only take one girl, then one girl it will be. However, I agree to try and obtain six Coram girls. And what is to be their destination?'

'They will be shipped to Turkey and collected by our

middleman, Abdul Fazir. It is through him that the transactions are conducted. Many of his clients live in obscure desert kingdoms throughout North Africa. He may keep the best girls for the harems of Istanbul – and their price is higher.'

'What is the present going rate for white girls?' asked a third voice.

'One hundred pounds apiece if they be virgins,' came the reply.

'I want three hundred, minimum,' announced Mr Gaddarn.

There was an intake of breath. 'That's a lot of money.'

'Tell your sheikhs and middlemen, the Coram girls will not only be pure as the day they were born, but free of disease and educated as well. Not just riff-raff. I can obtain as many young girls as you like from the streets of London, but I can't guarantee them. I'll guarantee Coram girls. Boys too. I want no less than three hundred pounds a head for them. If any of them is found to be diseased or imperfect in mind or body, they can have their money back. So mind you bargain the best possible price. This is a risky enterprise,' said Mr Gaddarn, 'and it costs me much in the amount of patronage I have to bestow to remain in their good offices. It has cost me even more to build up my name and reputation.'

'Be assured, we are all of us interested in getting the best possible rate – and you, dear Mr Gaddarn, are of exceedingly high value to us. We will not do anything that undermines your status in society.'

Mr Gaddarn cleared his throat with gratification.

'As for the boys, I will pay you for the three and offer them to Sheikh Khalir. If he doesn't want them or will not offer me a good enough price, I can always sell them on to the navy or other enterprises though, of course, you will have to take a lower rate.'

'Agreed,' said Mr Gaddarn in a satisfied voice. 'When I have the children, I will send you word.'

'Pray, where do you keep them so that they do not have attention drawn to them?'

'Why, here, sir,' chuckled Mr Gaddarn. 'In this very room, so to speak, sir. Let me show you.'

Toby lay rigid behind the screen, terrified by what he had heard. What was he showing them? What did he mean? That there was a room within a room? He longed to look, but didn't dare, praying that his legs wouldn't cramp or his nose tickle. For by now his throat was so sore it hurt to swallow, but he was sure they would cut his throat if they discovered him. So he lay still as can be. The tobacco from their pipes had created a murky fog in the room. From where he lay, he could see the smoke drifting across the ceiling in faint grey wisps. He listened, hoping that his ears could be as good as his eyes, just like Mercy's. He heard them get up from the table. He heard them walk to the far corner of the room. The furthest away from the chimney breast, Toby decided. That was the corner where the globe stood.

'Help me lift this,' said Mr Gaddarn. Did he mean the table on which the globe stood? He heard a slight grunt and a sigh as the table was raised and then set down again. Then he heard the sound of something sliding, as a drawer would slide, wood on wood. 'Hold up the light!'

'Well, well, well! There's no end to your talents, Mr Gaddarn!' declared a voice.

'Good heavens,' exclaimed the second. The shadows in the room swung, and Toby knew the candlestick was being held aloft so that they could see something more clearly.

'This passage leads to a chamber in which I can keep up to ten children. There is a further passage on the far side of the room which becomes a tunnel and leads underground, opening up on the docks. Thus the children can be taken aboard ship without too much exposure to prying eyes.'

'I imagine it has its uses for goods coming the other way, eh what?' a man suggested, seeing it was ideal for smuggling contraband.

Toby heard the panels close. He heard the table lifted back into place and saw the candlestick swing its shadows over the centre of the room.

'Well, gentlemen, here's till we meet again. I have a ship returning from India within the month. It is going to stop on the Guinea coast to pick up a further cargo of slaves – I am hoping for at least three hundred destined for Honduras.'

'Perhaps I can make use of your chamber from time to time,' came another voice. 'I have quite a lucrative business in human cargo which sometimes requires discretion.' There was a clink of glasses, further formal exchanges and pleasantries, then the door to the map room was opened and all four men left, taking the light with them.

In darkness once more, Toby continued to lie utterly still. He wanted to be sure no one would return. He peered round the screen. The room was empty. The fire was almost out. Stiffly, he slid off the windowseat and emerged into the room. Part of him wanted to escape, to have nothing to do with it and to have no knowledge of it, but another voice in his brain said, No. See for yourself. What you have heard will be important.

He moved over to the mantelpiece. There was a jar of tapers. He took one and held the end of it to a last glowing coal. By the light of that single yellow flame, the room gleamed into visibility. He looked at the table on which the globe stood. Was he right? Was that the corner the men had gone to? Yes. As he moved closer, he could see the imprints on the rug. The table had not been put back exactly as before. So Toby held the taper up and looked at the panels. He could see nothing different about one from the others. He tapped gently. This one was solid, this one was solid. He continued tapping each one till, suddenly, tap, tap,

tap . . . this panel rang hollow. Excitedly, he pressed the palm of his hand to the panel and pushed it sideways. He couldn't believe the ease and silence with which it just slid open. The single taper was barely enough to expose more than the start of a narrow passageway with a closed door at the end of it. That must be the door to the room. He wanted to go inside, but then he was too terrified. The taper was low and the thought of being trapped in there horrified him. Not this time, he thought. He pushed the panel back and put out the taper. He listened at the door. Pray God, no one would see him leave.

He opened the door a crack. He could neither see nor hear anyone. Just snoring coming from Mr Gaddarn's friends, many of whom had drunk themselves into oblivion and, instead of going home, had draped themselves across the sofas and armchairs with wigs awry, or sprawled across the floor. Glasses were up-ended, pipe ash covered the rugs and the air was stale with the smell of bodies, alcohol and tobacco. Most of the candles had burnt themselves out and no one had come in to replace them.

Toby hurried to the servants' stairs and went down to the kitchen. Mrs Bellamy was still sitting in her winged chair by the fire, at the ready to receive orders but sound asleep. Her cap was at a tilt, her mouth was open. As no one had dismissed him from his duties, he flopped down on the rug at her feet and, like a dog, curled up in front of the grate. His head was burning up to a fever.

Through the railings of the basement window, he looked up at the square of night sky. Everything he had seen and heard was locked in the compartments of his mind, and his thoughts were on a treadmill, going round and round and round; questions without answers; fears without hope. What should I do? Who shall I tell? How can I save the Coram children? Who will believe me?

Too exhausted to sleep, he stared with blank, dry eyes at the last star slowly fading, as grey dawn came creeping across the city.

Chapter Twenty-three

☆

Child slaves

Aaron was feeling guilty. He hadn't been to see Toby for at least two months. But life had become so full, so busy. When he wasn't running on errands to publishers and opera houses for Mr Burney, he was learning notation and harmony and how to play the harpsichord with Mr Ashbrook. Up and down, up and down the keyboard he went, perfecting his scales and arpeggios. And he was also learning how to play the violin. He wanted to play all the instruments, he had told Mr Ashbrook excitedly: the violin, the horn, the bassoon. And then he would compose, and write wonderful music for them all, just as Mr Ashbrook did – and Mr Handel.

On top of that, Aaron had been practising for the benefit concert. Mr Ledbury had come over one evening with a message from Mr Handel, asking Aaron to sing the solo 'How Beautiful Are the Feet of Men', and now, once a week, Aaron went to the Coram Hospital for choir practice with Mr Ledbury. Thus, he could see Mish and his old friends.

These days, Mr Ashbrook was in a frenzy of activity. He had composed an opera which was to be performed at the Theatre Royal, and Aaron had been kept fully occupied copying out the parts for rehearsals. This was Mr Ashbrook's most important work yet, and Aaron frequently went with him to rehearsals. Aaron's quill and inks and manuscript paper were always ready to copy parts. He had developed a good hand now – and nearly burst with pride when Mr Burney reckoned he was as good a copyist as any in London, a judgement with which Mr Ashbrook heartily concurred.

Sometimes Mr Ledbury arrived to listen to the opera rehearsals. He said it was the most important thing that had happened to Mr Ashbrook. Aaron saw the smouldering excitement in his teacher, who seemed to find it so hard to smile or be light-hearted – except when his friend Mr Ledbury was there to listen or help. Then, Aaron could hardly believe it was the same man. It seemed they had known each other since childhood and, when they were together, they became like boys again, with Mr Ledbury cracking his jokes, just as he did with the Coram children, and Mr Ashbrook trying not to smile, yet suddenly laughing uncontrollably. Aaron would feel a sudden rush of happiness, at times thinking that he couldn't imagine feeling any happier on this earth, unless it was to discover his mother and father.

Then one night, he had a dream so vivid it made him wake up with anxiety. Toby was calling him, he was crying and howling. His face came before him as clear as if he were in the room itself, dripping with water from head to foot as though he had nearly drowned.

But it was Aaron who cried out loud, for Timothy groaned from the other bed, and muttered in the darkness, 'Shut up, ha'pence.'

'Timmy?' Aaron whispered. 'Are you going to see Nancy Dawson soon?'

'Might do,' grunted Timothy. 'If they send me to the Covent Garden market.'

'Can I go with you?'

'If I haven't strangled you first for waking me up,' snarled Timothy, and rolled over fiercely, defying any more talk.

Two days later, after lunch, Timothy breathed in his ear, 'I'm a-going to Covent Garden later, ha'pence! Do you want to come?'

'Oh yes! If I can get permission,' beamed Aaron. For several days, Aaron had worked extra hard, so he hoped his request wouldn't be refused.

Aaron now no longer wore the distinctive Coram uniform. Instead he wore Mr Burney's colours of Oxford blue and white. He was also given a neat brown wig to wear when he went out, 'As befits a member of my household,' said Mr Burney, who also provided him with a broad hat and cockade to go on it. So that's how he looked that afternoon, striding along after Timothy. Their mission? To buy vegetables. Their intention? Timothy to get into Drury Lane and watch his beloved Nancy, and Aaron to run over to Mr Gaddarn's house to see Toby.

Aaron rang the bell pull outside the door of the tradesmen's entrance. After a while, it was opened by a grubby-looking girl of about ten. Aaron stared at her with growing recognition. 'Margery, is that you?' She was a Coram girl.

'Aaron Dangerfield!' Her thin little face broke into a huge smile. 'I wouldn't 'av recognised you – looking like that. Why, you're a proper gent, ain't ya?'

'No, Margery, not a gent. This is servant's livery. All the servants wear this in the Burney household.'

'They do?' She looked wistful.

'Don't they dress you proper here?' he asked, not able to conceal the shock at seeing her so ill-clothed, with no shoes on her feet, no smock to cover her, and only a ragged mop of a thing on her head. 'Where's Mrs Bellamy?'

'She got kicked out. Dismissed. They said she wasn't doing her job properly.'

'Mrs Bellamy kicked out?' Aaron was shocked. 'Where's Toby?' He felt a stab of anxiety as his dream came forcibly back into his mind. 'Is he all right?'

'He got ill. Had a fever. We thought he was a goner. Mr Gaddarn wouldn't call a doctor.' Her voice dropped. 'Mean beggar. He was in bed for three weeks, was Toby. It was Mrs Bellamy what saved him. She kept all of us at it, sponging him day and night to keep the fever down. She neglected her household duties. That's why they got rid of her. Now there's a Mrs Whittaker to replace her. She's 'orrible. Hard with her hand and with her tongue.'

'I've only got a short time, Margery. Can I see Toby? Where is he?'

'You're in luck, Aaron. He's out in the courtyard, and Mrs W's got a day off to see her sister. Miss Tangley, her assistant, is sleeping off her lunch-time gin, so make the most of it.'

He followed her along a passage to another door, which opened up into a yard and backed on to the Thames shore. There was Toby, propped up against the wall, a large piece of hessian before him with all the dining-room silver, which he was polishing intently.

'Toby!' Aaron ran joyfully up to his friend.

Toby struggled to his feet and the tears just poured down his cheeks. 'I thought you was not never coming to see me again!' he blubbed.

'I'm sorry, Toby. Sorry, sorry, sorry. I've been so busy, what with learning and everything.' He flung his arms round him reassuringly, but he was shocked. Toby had become so thin and, like Margery, was all bedraggled. He no longer wore his Coram uniform, but just a dirty white shirt, a rough waistcoat and a pair of worn, patched breeches. He had no wig on his head and no shoes on his feet.

'What's happened? You look like a beggar,' exclaimed Aaron, shocked.

'The only time I look like a prince is at Mr Gaddarn's parties. Just for 'is fine friends. For the rest, 'e treats us like dirt and won't spend a 'alfpenny more than 'e 'as to. But look at you, Aaron. You done all right for yourself,' he said admiringly.

'Yeh, well. I'm lucky. Mr Burney is a decent gentleman.'

'Listen, Aaron, I've something of importance to tell yer.' Toby began to shake and Aaron thought he would fall. He began crying again. 'It's all my fault. I should have saved 'em.'

'What?' Aaron put an arm round Toby's quivering shoulders.

'Them Coram girls and boys what 'e sent away to be slaves.'

'What?' Aaron looked at his friend's wild face and wondered if his illness had made him deranged.

'I was going to stop it, but I fell ill. I wanted to tell someone but who would believe me? I wanted to tell yer. Aaron will know what to do, I thought. But I got the fever.' Toby saw Aaron's disbelieving face. 'See? You don't believe me. You think Mr Gaddarn's a great man, don't yer?'

Aaron shook his head helplessly.

'I can show yer. Come on, I can show yer.' Toby grabbed

Aaron's arm and took him through a back gate which opened on to a track which ran along the shore to the docks.

The tide was out and the mudflats glistened dark and sinister. Debris left by the outgoing tide left a long trail along the water's edge. Sometimes knee deep in the mud, straggles of children and old people combed the shore, scrutinising each and every item, picking up anything which might be of conceivable use, and tucking it into a shawl or ragged bundle.

Toby led Aaron along till they reached a slimy green wall which was the start of the docking area for the sloops, ketches and ocean-going cutters. 'Look!' He pointed.

'What?' asked Aaron, not sure what he was meant to be looking at.

'That gate.' It was a double gate with spikes, covering an entry into the wall – a tunnel of some sort.

'The gate? What about it?'

Then Toby told him. He was distraught. He begged him to do something. 'Did you see Margery? She should have gone, but she got my sickness and was too ill. They wouldn't take 'er. 'E's selling Coram children for slaves – and lots of others too. They pick 'em up off the street. Boys and girls.'

The two boys walked up to the gate and Aaron peered through the spikes into the dripping darkness. A terrible stench oozed out of it. He could hardly believe that such a tunnel could lead all the way into the very heart of Mr Gaddarn's house; into his own study.

'When the tide's up, see, they can get a skiff and just row down the tunnel and out into the river to a waiting sloop,' explained Toby. 'Now d'you believe me?'

'I believe you, Toby. I believe you,' Aaron whispered.

'I knew 'e was a bad'un. I always knew it,' muttered Toby bitterly.

Aaron glanced up at the sun. He had to remember the time. 'I've got to go.' Gently he led Toby back. 'Don't run away or anything like that. I'm going to the hospital tomorrow for a practice with Mr Ledbury. I'll be back soon, Toby. I promise. We'll find a way, honest we will.'

He hated leaving his poor, sad, pathetic friend, but Aaron knew he must run all the way to meet up with Timothy Parfitt at Drury Lane.

'What's up with you, ha'pence? You look like you've lost a sovereign,' quipped Timothy when he saw Aaron's face as they hurried away from Covent Garden.

Aaron was just about to tell him all about it, when a voice hailed them from across the street. 'Tim! How've you been, old chap?' And in no time at all, Tim was hooked by the elbow and marched off into a tavern by one of his pals. Tim shrugged at Aaron and, before he was yanked inside, shouted, 'Get on back, ha'pence. I won't be long in following.'

Chapter Twenty-four

★

Messiah

'Gentlemen are desired to come without swords and the ladies without hoops.'

This announcement was made by the authorities because of the overwhelming interest in the performance of *Messiah*, which Handel was going to conduct in the somewhat limited space of the Coram chapel.

There was a crowd of coaches queuing up to drop off their passengers at the doors of the Coram Hospital. The people poured into the chapel till soon every seat on the ground floor and all along the gallery was crammed. People of distinction, who had not bought a ticket, loudly expected to pay on the spot and be admitted, so that others, who had tickets, were sent away protesting. Mr Handel had to announce that he would give a second performance on a later date for those who had been disappointed.

The wealthy patrons and benefactors took their seats near the front. Aaron glimpsed Mr Burney and Mr Ashbrook on one side and, on the other, with a jolt of his heart he saw Mr Gaddarn. Could Toby be right? Again, he was filled with doubt. Mr Gaddarn beamed so genially at everyone and patted the heads of little Coram boys, who were showing people to their places, while the remaining Coram children and all the staff of the hospital packed themselves in wherever they could.

How he wished Toby was here. There was so much he wanted to ask him.

Aaron's eyes swept over them all, but he was searching for Mish. Where was he? He had promised to come. If only he had had time to find him and bring him to the chapel, but Mr Handel had kept them in all morning, practising hard, for he was a tireless perfectionist.

Aaron stood with the Coram choir. He was dressed, as all the choir boys were, in his Coram uniform with the white cassock over the top. Before them was the scarlet-jacketed orchestra: violins, violas, cellos, double basses, bassoons, horns and trumpets, and timpani. Mr Handel sat at the harpsichord with Mr Ashbrook to assist him. Any moment now, the concert would start.

A voice whispered in his ear. 'Are you all right, young Aaron?' It was Mr Ledbury, who had noted his wandering eyes and was anxious that he should be focused and ready to sing.

'I can't see Mish.' Aaron was agitated. 'I did so want him to hear me sing – and he promised.'

'Of course he's here. Probably up in the gallery – it's impossible to see everyone. Now, be calm, concentrate; otherwise he won't hear you at your best.'

Mr Handel's hand came down and swept up again in a rhythmic arc and the orchestra began to play the grave overture. Never till that day had Aaron been so close to the players. He felt the vibrations of the strings, and the bassoons shivering through his bones, and the plucked beat of the harpsichord and the rattle of the timpani. The overture ended; there was a pause and then the beautiful introduction to the first tenor recitative began: 'Comfort ye . . .' his voice pleaded so tenderly, and Aaron forgot everything except the music. When the tenor had sung 'Every valley shall be exalted,' Mr Handel's gaze fixed commandingly on the choir, preparing them for their first anthem: 'And the Glory of the Lord'.

Aaron sang as he had never sung before and, suddenly, he knew again that there was nothing else in life that he wanted to be except a musician. He saw Mr Ashbrook's expression. No longer was it the frowning look of someone constantly turned in on himself; his head was thrown back and his face glowing with pleasure, and suddenly Aaron liked him better than he had ever done before.

The music moved on. As his solo came nearer and nearer, Aaron's heart beat faster with nervous excitement. He swallowed hard and rubbed his sweating hands against his sides. Again, his eyes darted round the chapel. Where was Mish? It was time. He looked at Mr Handel. Mr Handel looked straight back at him, forbidding him to lose his concentration. They were playing the larghetto bars which introduced him – one and two and one and two: 'How beautiful are the feet of men, that bring the gospel of peace . . .' His voice soared out among the rafters and round the pillars and up into the gallery; it was as pure as crystal water spouting from a rock. He glanced at Mr Ashbrook, who never praised him, and saw tears rolling down his cheeks. He came to the end. There was a hushed silence as the reverberations of his voice hung in the air. People looked at each other, nodded and smiled at the beauty of it. As the last echo died away, no one stirred, no one so much as breathed.

Then a single pair of hands began clapping furiously. 'Well done, my angel. That was truly well done!'

All heads turned in outrage and consternation. Mr Handel rapped the lectern for attention. Aaron's hand flew to his mouth in horror. 'Oh, Mish, Mish!' he groaned with embarrassment.

From his seat in the chapel, Alexander too turned to see who had caused such a disturbance. He only got a glimpse of the giant red-haired fellow right up in the gallery, being hustled away, but it was enough. Instant recall struck him like a thunderbolt. Meshak Gardiner.

Mr Handel rapped the lectern yet again and glared around. He waved his baton and, obediently, the choir entered briskly with, 'Their sound is gone out . . .' but it was several bars in before the indignant whispers and rustling of the audience subsided.

Alexander's mind was in turmoil. Now he knew where he had seen Mr Gaddarn before. After the concert, with the 'Amen' chorus ringing in his ears, he took his leave of Mr Burney, saying he would catch him up, and struggled through the excited crowd to find Thomas.

'But, Alexander, that's not possible.' Thomas shook his head. 'Otis Gardiner is dead. Executed at Stroud. I saw him hang. It's not possible.'

Later, the two friends sat in a tavern together.

'What do you mean, executed?' Alexander shook his head disbelievingly. 'It is the man, I tell you.'

'Otis Gardiner was hanged at the crossroads outside Stroud – soon after you left Ashbrook. I saw it with my own eyes. I saw him up there on the gallows. I saw him swing. Thousands of people came to watch. It was the biggest event of the year.'

'Why? What was his crime?' Alexander was astonished by the news.

So Thomas told him what he knew. It involved so many people – some of wealth and influence. It was murmured that even the high sheriff himself could have been implicated in the crimes. Everyone had heard of Otis Gardiner's arrest. The crimes of which he had been accused were splashed and talked of all round the county of Gloucestershire and beyond. First, a dog had been heard howling piteously for days somewhere on the Ashbrook estate, and when a search of the woods was made, they found a dead dog tied to a tree. Then down by the lake they found a bloody shawl and, nearby, the half-buried remains of several babies.

'In Ashbrook?' whispered Alexander, horrified.

'I'm afraid so.' Thomas patted his arm with concern, wondering whether to continue, but Alexander waved him on.

'Many poor women and girls came forward to say that the babies were theirs, and they had paid Otis Gardiner good sums of money to deliver their unfortunate infants to the Coram Hospital. It was a rowdy and menacing crowd which attended the trial, I can tell you. They'd have strung him up on the nearest tree if they could have got their hands on him.

'He was accused of murder, extortion, fraud and blackmail. He had persuaded ignorant young women that he would safely carry their illegitimate infants to Coram, where they would be cared for and educated. They had paid him everything he asked for. Where he treated the poorer classes callously, he used all his charms to persuade higher-born women to give him their babies. Then he blackmailed them. Every time he called in their district, he made them pay both for his silence and for the supposed upkeep of their infants. If any woman objected, he threatened her with exposure and disgrace. Many were the daughters of gentlemen of influence and reputation, for whom exposure would have brought public humiliation.

'But Otis did not act alone. He was in the pay of many churchmen and parish officers keen to rid themselves of their liability to provide for all persons, legitimate and illegitimate, within their boundaries. They reckoned that it was worth their while to pay off Otis, rather than be forced to provide for bastard children and their disgraced and often penniless mothers. No one asked questions. No one cared what he did with the babies or if they lived or died – just so long as they weren't a burden on their own parish rates. Otis got away with it until a young gentlewoman, Miss Price, the ward of Mr Theodore Claymore had entrusted her child to him. Throwing all concerns for her respectability and reputation to the winds, she had denounced him when he tried to blackmail her, and also implicated a gentleman connected to your own family, who fell under great suspicion for being part of the racket – Admiral Bailey. The admiral sat on the committee for the Ashbrook orphanage.'

Alexander was horrified. 'Oh God! Don't say my own family was implicated in this?'

'No, no! Not your family – at least – not directly. But Admiral

Bailey was found to have paid Otis large sums of money to shift the destitute out of the Ashbrook parish boundaries; he was also aware of the violence and murder associated with these acts. You can imagine how grievously this affected Lady Ashbrook. I had hoped you would never hear of this. I vowed at your request never to speak of your family, I know.'

Alexander dropped his head on to his arms with an agonised groan. 'And what of the admiral – my God– ' he gripped the hilt of his sword, 'he should die too for bringing such evil to my family.'

'Admiral Bailey was charged with conspiracy, but . . . We all know what money and influence can do. The admiral managed to persuade the law officers that he had nothing to do with any crimes, and that he had only lawfully paid money to Otis to return women who were about to give birth back to their own parishes. He proclaimed himself a guardian of the interests of his parish, for which he knew the parishioners thanked him most heartily. He escaped prosecution – rumours said – for a hefty price.'

'Then he still needs punishing!' exclaimed Alexander, leaping to his feet, drawing his sword.

'No need, my dear fellow.' Thomas restrained his friend and pressed him to be seated again. 'The man is dead – of apoplexy. It was God's justice.'

'And my mother, Lady Ashbrook? What of her?'

'Lady Ashbrook was not implicated in the slightest way – not one word, not even a whisper besmirched her reputation.'

'Thank God!' Alexander fell into silence. He clasped his hands under his chin and frowned. Finally, he looked up at Thomas and shook his head. 'But Meshak! What is Meshak doing here at Coram? You saw him, didn't you?'

'No, I wasn't in a position to see up in the gallery, but I've heard young Aaron talk about his friend, *Mish*,' murmured Thomas thoughtfully. 'No one knows what happened to Meshak. He is widely believed to be dead, for no one had ever seen him parted from his dog, and we know the dog is dead. Mish. Meshak. Is it the same person?'

'How strange. A man you say is dead, I'm sure is alive, and someone called Mish could perhaps be Meshak? Could that man's own son be here at Coram?' Alexander raised a face full of questions and doubt. 'We must find out more, Thomas, we must.'

'Tomorrow we leave for Ashbrook,' said Thomas. 'I will make further enquiries about Otis Gardiner. But, I tell you, I saw a man hang on the gallows; a man I believe was Otis, who *looked* like Otis – though I admit I was at quite a distance . . .'

'And I saw a man in a drawing-room,' said Alexander, 'so close I could have touched him. A man who calls himself *Mr Philip Gaddarn*, but who I would swear is Mr Otis Gardiner.'

Chapter Twenty-five

✫

There came six boys

Melissa sat at the virginals in Waterside cottage. The silence was unnatural. The silence and absence of children.

Today was their child's birthday – on this day eight years ago she had given birth to their baby, and not one day had passed when Melissa hadn't thought of her son. Alexander's son. She had imagined each stage of his development: now he would be crawling, now sitting, now taking his first steps, now speaking his first words. If the baby had lived they would have been celebrating today with a service of thanksgiving at the church, followed by a party for everyone on the estate, with feasting and dancing.

Waterside was no longer the play cottage of their childhood. Alice and Edward had long since stopped coming to it. Edward had been sent to Eton, and Alice spent most of her time up at the house being tutored in music, dancing, fencing and sewing tapestry. She was being prepared to enter society.

These days, Melissa saw less of Isobel, who was a young lady of means and status. She was now expected to play her part in society and was constantly being invited out, whether it be to take tea with other young ladies or attend balls and soirées, where her parents fervently hoped she would meet a suitable husband. But whenever she could, Isobel joined Melissa at Waterside, where they would drink tea together and talk – talk about the one subject forbidden everywhere else: Alexander and the baby.

Melissa longed to confide in her mother: she had been present at the birth; held her grandchild; looked into its face . . . Melissa felt a rage rising up inside her. Why wouldn't her mother talk to her about it? Tell her how she felt then, what she felt now? But when she tried to question her, Mrs Milcote would turn pale and start crying. 'Hush, child, hush!' was all she would whisper in frantic undertones, as if the walls themselves had ears. 'It could have been the end of us. Never speak of it again.'

'But I need you to talk to me!' Melissa had stormed. 'Why can't we share this burden together? It was my baby. Your grandchild. We are both grieving, but you won't allow me to help you and you won't help me.' But it was no use. Every time Melissa tried to share her anguish with her mother, Mrs Milcote would claim to have a headache and retire to her bed.

Melissa felt trapped in the past; trapped in that day she gave birth. Everything was unresolved. After her baby was born, they took it away. They told her it was a boy, and that he was stillborn.

She never even saw her own child, alive or dead. What was he like? Who did he resemble? If only she could have held his body; kissed his face; cuddled him and whispered a prayer over him. Where was he taken? Where was he buried?

Isobel had looked like a ghost. She didn't speak for days afterwards and then, when she did, she couldn't say either. She had hardly seen the baby. Tabitha had delivered it, Isobel had only briefly held it, then Mrs Lynch had snatched it from her and rushed outside, followed by Mrs Milcote. They had never seen the baby again.

No one answered any of Melissa's questions and her mother only said, 'Your baby was mercifully dead. Now, for your own sake, forget it.'

Yet though Mrs Milcote would not talk to her daughter, Melissa often had the feeling that her mother talked to Mrs Lynch. If she happened to come into the room their conversation would cease abruptly; her mother would look guilty and Mrs Lynch would look in command.

Then Thomas had come to tell them that he had found Alexander; that he was living in London; that he was a composer and performer with a growing reputation; that he sought a reconciliation. He brought a letter for Melissa – the first she had been permitted to read, for all of Alexander's other letters had been destroyed before they were opened.

How she held it, smelt it, pressed it to her cheek and cried, before she even dared to break the seal and read its contents. Then, when she did, the words had danced on the page, and she had to read it over and over again before she could feel reassured that it was truly from Alexander and that he still cared for her. He wrote:

> *I said I would write to you and I did, but I know my letters were not given you. I said I would return when I was successful and ask you to marry me. For five years, I struggled in poverty and had to go abroad to earn a living. When I returned, so many years had passed, how could I assume that you had waited or would feel the same about me any more? We were children when I left, though I hear from Thomas that you have not married. But at last, during the last two years, my efforts are bearing fruit, and I have come to have quite a reputation for myself. My first opera is to be performed at the Theatre Royal. My feelings for you are the same. I long to come home to Ashbrook and pray that Thomas, as my intermediary, can soften my father's heart and get his permission for me to return.*

Melissa had wanted to tell her mother, ask her advice. Should she reply? Could she keep from him the secret that she had had his baby? Or should she have nothing further to do with him? But, in the end, she didn't confide in her mother. She couldn't trust her mother not to pass it all on to Mrs Lynch, and Melissa had come to despise and loathe Mrs Lynch who, she felt, had come between her and her mother. There was some kind of bond between the two of them: something sinister which excluded her. So she sent back a simple reply with Thomas, feeling guilty that she had not told her mother about it.

> *Dear Sir,*
> *The best news in all these years is to hear you are alive and well and thriving so. My heart overflows. Thomas says he is doing his best to be an intermediary between you and your father, and is confident that in the near future you will be welcome at Ashbrook. We all pray for it.*
>
> *Thomas will apprise you of everyone's well-being here, so suffice it for me to tell you that I am well and convey to you my most sincere good wishes, and hope that we may soon be graced by your presence which has been so sorely missed.*
>
> *I am, as ever, your true friend,*
> *Melissa*

Mrs Milcote's role as governess was over. She had feared that she and Melissa might now be asked to leave and so be forced to look for a situation elsewhere, and she was relieved and grateful when Lady Ashbrook asked her to be in charge of the orphanage. She had agreed gladly. Melissa, too, had a rôle helping the children to read and write.

Lady Ashbrook had heard of the Coram Hospital, and wanted her orphanage to be modelled on it and known, too, for its care and management of children combined with tenderness and compassion.

So Melissa worked alongside her mother, and though they never talked about her lost baby, at least she could do something for other lost and abandoned children by teaching them.

The only time Melissa smiled or laughed out loud was when she worked with the children: teaching them, playing with them and caring for them when they were ill. Some said she was like one driven by some private vocation. Even when infectious diseases such as measles, smallpox, diphtheria or typhus swept through the orphanage, it was Melissa who went in day and night to care for the sick and comfort the dying.

Lady Ashbrook, having failed to persuade Melissa to stay away for the sake of her own health, suggested that she sleep at Waterside, so as to avoid bringing any infection into the house. Until then, the cottage had held only the most bitter memories. But now it had become her refuge. Though it had been the scene of her greatest distress, it was also the place which held her dearest memories of Alexander, and while her quarantine was over a long time ago, Melissa still came to the cottage almost every day to play the virginals and find some peace for her tormented soul.

But today, she was happy. Thomas was coming. Dear Thomas, and he would give her another letter from Alexander. And this time, he was bringing with him a group of Coram boys from his choir in London.

It had been Isobel's idea. When Isobel had heard about the benefit concerts they gave in London on behalf of the hospital, she had said to her mother, Lady Ashbrook, 'Why, we should do the same! Thomas has told us so much about the work at the Coram Hospital. Just think how important it will be for us to receive Coram children, so that people can see what it is you are trying to achieve with your orphans. And,' she cunningly said to her doubting father, Sir William, 'imagine! We could be the first people in Gloucestershire, indeed the first people in the whole of England outside London, to hear music from Mr Handel's *Messiah*.' Even Sir William, though unmusical, had heard of George Frederic Handel.

Lady Ashbrook agreed with enthusiasm and soon persuaded her reluctant husband. Invitations were sent out. The Coram boys would sing anthems from Mr Handel's oratorio in the chapel on the estate in three days' time. Thomas had been sure that this would be a prelude to Alexander finally being forgiven by his father.

When Melissa told her mother about the visit, Mrs Milcote had turned pale and looked ill. Melissa was so alarmed that, after she had helped her mother to lie down, she went to fetch Mrs Lynch because she didn't know who else to call. As she shut the bedchamber door behind her, Melissa heard her mother burst out crying. 'Time does not make the burden any easier.' Then the wailing was stifled and the voices lowered so that they were inaudible.

No, time did not make the burden any easier. Melissa bowed over the keys of the virginals, trying to concentrate. Her fingers ran over and over the keys in her efforts to master a particular passage in a sonata by Scarlatti. The light from the window was briefly obscured. A shadow glanced in the reflections of the polished wood, and a blackbird flew away. She looked up, but all she saw was an empty space. Yet the space quivered as if a presence had only just slid from view the instant her eye fell upon it.

She got up and went to the open doorway. Outside, a sheen of pale green moss and lichens clung to the branches. Autumn leaves dropped from the raw wood. The only sound was the fretful blackbird chirping away in the cold air. She looked up the track which led into the woods of the Ashbrook estate.

There was a deep hush. She felt eyes in the tree-trunks looking at her and sensed living creatures hiding in the undergrowth. Overcome with unease, she stepped back into the doorway when, suddenly, there was Isobel hurrying along the path towards her.

'Melissa dear!' Isobel flung her arms round her friend. 'I know what you are suffering, today of all days. It is *his* birthday. Our little Alexander. Today, he would have been eight. Eight, and ready to step out of infancy, and we would have thanked God for him and beseeched Him to see our child safely into manhood. Come with me to the chapel. Let us say a prayer for his soul.'

It was the small Cotswold stone family chapel, set in a glade just beyond the rose gardens through a wooden lych gate. They walked up the grassy path and entered through the sharply arched Norman door. They did not step into gloom, but rather into a warm, light space, where the sun flowed like honey through the high stained-glass windows, bringing alive the faces of the angels and saints, splashing their colours down upon oak pews, and embroidered hassocks, and gold-stitched altar cloth.

They walked arm in arm down the centre aisle towards the front.

They knelt before the cross of Christ and solemnly prayed, pleading for the soul of that poor, innocent, unchristened child;

beseeching dear God to allow him into heaven, and please to not leave him till judgement day suspended in the pitiless purgatory between heaven and hell.

'Amen, amen!' The breathed words rose into the air, resonating.

The girls turned their heads to see who joined in their prayer, but at that moment the west door was suddenly opened wide and there, in the streaming sunlight, stood six little boys all dressed in brown serge breeches and jackets trimmed in red.

> *There come six boys on their knee*
> *When do they come?*
> *They come by night as well as by day*
> *To take thy maid, Melissa away.*
> *My daughter Melissa is yet too young,*
> *To stay away from her mam.*
> *Whether she's old or whether she's young,*
> *We'll take her as her am.*

'Thomas, is it you?' Isobel blinked into the bright sunlight at the taller shape who came into view behind the boys.

'We've just arrived, and came looking for you!' It *was* Thomas.

Melissa and Isobel ran joyfully down the aisle. Each clasped an arm and whirled him round and laughed to see his cheery, friendly face, and then became tearful. 'Welcome,

welcome! How good to see you again. Dear Thomas!'

'Meet my boys!' cried Thomas. Six little boys lined up with their caps clasped politely to their chests, their eyes cast shyly down. 'Meet Geoffrey, Ned, Stephen, Aaron, Benjamin and Matthew.'

There come six boys.

Meshak watched, anonymous and invisible, as all who serve can be invisible. No one looked into the face of the man who had sat on the roof of the coach, his back to the driver, a shotgun in hand ready to ward off highwaymen or vagabonds. Once they had entered the estate he had leapt, unseen, from his position on the coach and cut across up the bank and through the woods. He had only one thought on his mind, and that was to see his angel after all these years. And, yes – there she had been, just as he remembered her, playing the virginals, her auburn hair, which as a girl had hung round her neck in ringlets, was now plaited soberly back round her head in the fashion of a young woman, and tucked under her cap. He had stared at her through the window a long time before she had turned to see who blocked the light.

When Isobel came and the two of them walked to the chapel, Meshak watched them go. He had followed them to the chapel and, when they reached the altar rail and knelt there together, he crept in too, and lay flat on the ground between the pews, listening to their hushed prayers, staring up at an angel in one of the windows.

And now, there she was again, so joyful to see Thomas, and so sweet with the young boys, ruffling their hair and tickling their chins; among them her own boy, if she did but know it. His angel.

He might have wondered what Melissa would feel if she knew how near she was to her own child; that her son had bowed before her; that soon she would be putting a meal before him and giving him a glass of milk to drink. She would look into the boy's face and see her own mirror image and not know it. Meshak might have been touched with pity and imagined the happiness she would feel if she knew this was her own son. But he didn't think like that. He only thought how Aaron belonged to him. Melissa could never be his but he could always have her son; that was the only way he could own part of her.

He waited till they had all gone, Isobel, Melissa, Thomas, and the six Coram boys, walking in crocodile towards the house where they would stay for a few days. Then he came out of the chapel.

Why he went to the wood, he did not know. He entered among the tall crowding trees, hung with creepers furry with winter moss; the woods where he and his father had so often camped with their wagon. He must have known it would be full of ghosts, and that it would all start up as before. There in the dells, dark and deep, he blocked his ears from the sound of infants crying. They seemed to be everywhere. He saw the roots of trees bursting from out of the ground but, to Meshak, they looked like bones. The wood was a haunted place; he had forgotten how haunted, so full of eyes and fingers, soft-skulled heads and liquid mouths rooting and snuffling. And there was the lake, quivering with reflections, as if it still trapped in its liquid eye the time when he had dipped Melissa's baby into its cold waters and brought him to life.

He lay before the lake, flat on the ground, staring at his reflection. He looked at a stranger. 'You should tell her, Meshak, Mish, turnip head, carrot face. You should tell your angel and your angel's boy, you should you should,' said the face in the water.

'But then I'll lose my angel – lose them both – and then where will Mish go and what will Mish do?' He wept bitterly. He dipped in his arms up to his elbows, and angrily dashed water over his red hair, sending ripples scurrying across the surface.

'What will Meshak do then, poor thing?'

He clambered to his feet, all dripping, and ran from the wood. He ran until he came to the open pasture, where the cows grazed, where, as before, he flung himself down among their bulging milky bodies. He lay, feeling himself merge with the earth and the overhanging sky, and die in its blueness, and die until he found himself, once again, among the angels. But this time, he felt they shunned him and fled from him.

Chapter Twenty-six

✮

The Coram boy

Suddenly there was music again. Music back at Ashbrook. Everyone heard it, and everyone was reminded of Alexander. The servants murmured among themselves, cook wiped away a tear, Nanny went very quiet and withdrew to her parlour where, now that she was old, she was being allowed to live out her years. The harpsichord was restored to the drawing-room where, in the old days, there had been so much music. The Coram boys could be heard practising *Messiah*, and who could fail to remember young Alexander, when their pure treble voices echoed through the house? The boys would give their benefit concert in a few days' time but, meanwhile, they were to practise their music and enjoy the freedom of the estate.

It had been Thomas's idea. The evening before the concert, the family was gathered as usual in the drawing-room, and Thomas suggested that the Coram boys should give them their own private concert. It would be a rehearsal for them, though there was more to his plan than an after-dinner entertainment.

Thomas hoped that the sight of the young boys would remind Sir William of his son and soften his heart, and prepare the way for the reconciliation.

Canon Maybury had come on a visit and Sir William was at home, so everyone was present. The boys sang several anthems and choruses from works by Handel, including extracts from *Messiah*, and it was true – everyone was reminded of the choir school in Gloucester, and Alexander as a boy, whose face seemed to hover among them.

Then Thomas singled out Aaron. 'Come, boy! Let them hear you sing! This is the lad Mr Handel discovered and insisted be trained as a musician,' Thomas told them. 'For not only has he a voice as pure as any you will have ever heard, but he has been apprenticed to Mr Charles Burney, who will make a fine musician of him. He shows remarkable talent for his age.' Thomas sat at the keyboard. 'Well, lad, what shall you sing?'

' "The Silver Swan"?' whispered Aaron in his ear.

Thomas nodded enthusiastically, and began to play the introduction. Aaron sang:

> 'The silver Swan, who living had no note,
> When death approached, unlocked her silent throat.'

When it was over there was a stunned silence. Lady Ashbrook

wept into her handkerchief, Sir William cleared his throat and got up out of his chair to pace the room, and the canon whispered, 'Good Lord!'

No one needed to say it. The boy was like their own Alexander used to be, and the song he had sung was the last song they had heard Alexander sing.

Sitting in a far corner, Mrs Milcote had turned ashen. 'Melissa, be so good as to accompany me to my chamber. I'm feeling unwell,' she muttered.

Isobel looked at Thomas, her face distraught. 'Was this well done?' she asked.

'Yes, if it brings Alexander home,' replied Thomas quietly.

The evening broke up early; the candles were extinguished, and soon everyone had retired to their own quarters.

Mrs Milcote was dreaming. A boy came to the edge of her bed. He was covered in blood and earth, and leaves hung in his hair. He held out his hands and opened his mouth as if he sang. But no sound came from his throat, just worms coiling out and birds which flew in and out of the blue-green skies of his eye sockets. And he looked and looked at her.

She awoke with a shriek, her heart practically leaping from her chest with terror. But there was nothing. The phantom had gone. She listened. Had Melissa heard her cry? No, no one stirred. By her bedside, the candle was very low. She took a taper and lit another. She went over to her dressing-table and opened a drawer. Inside was a small silver box. When she opened the lid, there lay a curl of auburn hair. Pulling a gown round her shoulders, she let herself out of her bedchamber and, like a sleepwalker, made her way to the schoolroom where the Coram boys were sleeping. She had to see him again, the boy who sang 'The Silver Swan', the boy whose voice sounded so like Alexander and who had sung the song he had always liked to sing.

She reached the schoolroom, where they had laid mattresses on the floor for the boys to sleep, and quietly opened the door. One low candle spluttered into the wax. Soon it would be daylight. She moved from one sleeping boy to the next, bending over each one and holding the lamp to his face to recognise him better.

She came to Aaron. This was he. She knelt down. Was it her fancy that she saw a strong resemblance to Alexander? The large brow and deep-set eyes, the full lips and firm-set chin; and his hair – were they not the same auburn curls as Melissa's? She set down the candle and took out the silver box from which she withdrew the lock of hair. She placed it on the pillow next to his head. She rocked to and fro on her heels in silent grief. Such a boy could be a child of Melissa and Alexander. This could be that babe. Oh, if only it were. But no, her boy – her dearest grandson – was dead. They had found the shawl in the woods, all covered in blood. Otis Gardiner had admitted killing all the babies he had collected that day from the district – and even he was long dead, hanged from the gallows at the crossroads and left to rot as an example.

But she could see what her boy might have been if only he had lived. She gazed upon Aaron. How had she lived till now with such guilt? Was she not as much a murderer as Otis? She stretched out a hand, pleading, as if somehow this boy could forgive her. He stirred. Perhaps the light from her candle penetrated his eyelids. Hastily, she drew back, and left the room.

Before she returned to her bed, she went to the adjoining chamber where Melissa slept. If only she could ask her forgiveness. But how could she bear to see the horror in her daughter's eyes? And yet, and yet . . . How long could she continue to live with this secret burden? Must she go to her grave with such a sin upon her soul? Must she die without the forgiveness of her daughter? A sob escaped from her throat. Melissa's eyes flew open. She sat up in alarm. 'Mother?'

Melissa quickly took the candle from her mother's shaking hand and set it down. Then, with a compassion transcending any knowledge, she put her arms round her and drew her into her bed, and Mrs Milcote told her everything.

Chapter Twenty-seven

☆

Recognition

The benefit concert was held in the parish church in the village. Everyone came. Even the chapel in the Coram Hospital had not overflowed as much as this one did. Not just the Ashbrook household and their estate workers, or their neighbours near and far, but the wealthy, the influential and well-connected: the sheriff, the magistrate, the bishop, the archdeacon, the parish officers, all came to see the Coram boys.

Dressed in white ruffed cassocks over their brown and red uniform, they looked like a row of cherubs, one boy hardly distinguishable from the next.

Thomas sat at a harpsichord at the front of the choir with the six boys standing in a semi-circle nearby, where he could see them and conduct them in.

The Ashbrook family sat in the front pews, so close, so intent, their hearts and minds full as they thought beyond this day to the day when Alexander would return.

As Thomas waited for everyone to settle into their seats, his eyes moved over each of their faces. Sir William, positioned between his wife and Isobel, instead of looking severe and implacable, had an expression Thomas had never seen before, and he wondered if Alexander had ever seen it either. He looked chastened, humble, as if somehow he had discovered that he loved his children – for he held Isobel's hand and, every now and then, reached out to pat young Alice and murmur to his wife how he wished that Edward was here, too.

But Thomas knew that it was Alexander above all who filled their thoughts. That morning, after breakfast, Sir William had requested Thomas to come to his study. As if to emphasise the informal nature of their meeting and to put Thomas at ease, he was not wearing his wig, but a soft green turban, and instead of his formal brocade coat he wore a long, flowing, silk jacket. At last, all his antagonism and anger and outrage against his oldest son had melted away like snow in fire.

'Tell me,' he said in a quiet subdued voice. 'Are you in touch with Alexander?'

'I am, sir,' answered Thomas.

'And is he well?' The simplicity of the question belied the depth of feeling in his voice.

'He is well, sir, and much regarded in the music circles of London. Indeed, he has been summoned to Court on a number of occasions to give concerts. He is also to have his first opera performed at the Theatre Royal. This will surely establish him as one of our foremost musicians.'

There was a pause. Sir William sighed. He shook his head, and Thomas wondered if he had said the wrong thing. Finally, Sir William spoke again. 'Do not misunderstand me, I am not interested in whether my son is wealthy or famous, has succeeded or failed since he left this house. I am only interested in whether or not he will return here and be reconciled with us.' He smiled gently. 'If it was your purpose to bring about a change of heart in me; if it was your purpose, in bringing these boys and letting young Aaron sing that particular song to open my eyes, then, by heaven, you achieved it. No, no . . .' He waved a hand when Thomas looked as if he were going to apologise. 'You were right. I have not only inflicted great pain and distress on my wife and children, but on myself. I did not truly know till now how much I loved my son and miss him. And now that I have allowed some honesty with myself, I want to remedy the situation as speedily as possible. So I ask you in all humility if you would kindly deliver this letter to Alexander along with your personal plea on my behalf, that he return to Ashbrook as soon as possible – not to be its future master – if that is not his desire – but to be reunited with his grieving family, who all this time were not allowed even to enquire whether he was alive or dead.' Sir William held up a white document, folded and sealed with the family crest.

Thomas took the letter and tucked it deep into the breast pocket of his coat and promised to deliver it safely.

As he scanned their faces now in church, there was a mystery. Something he couldn't define. It was not with Sir William or Lady Ashbrook, who seemed so close and reconciled, as if their first born was already at their side. It was with Isobel, Melissa and Mrs Milcote. They seemed to glance at each other and yet avoid each other's eye, as if they shared some common anxiety which both united and divided them.

An expectant hush descended on the congregation. Thomas pulled his thoughts back to the music. He looked encouragingly at the boys, then began to play the opening chords to bring in their first anthem: 'Come unto me, all ye that labour'.

Though Melissa and her mother sat side by side, the closeness of the night before was gone. Only the darkness was left of a night which was part of an endless space, a huge void which would separate them for ever. All Melissa could think of was the betrayal. She couldn't bear to look at the circle of six boys before her. Each boy's face was suddenly the face of her own child. Her baby had been alive. That's what her mother had told her in that dawn of tears, with their arms wrapped round each other. But her own mother had handed the baby to a murderer . . . her baby had been alive, could have been alive . . . but was surely dead. They found the bodies in the wood; pathetic, little babies all betrayed, like her own.

Mrs Milcote sat next to her, still and expressionless as a statue. Her eyes fixed hard upon the boy they called Aaron. Ever since he had sung 'The Silver Swan', ever since she had looked at him asleep and held the lock of her grandson's hair against his, she had become obsessed. If only she had gone herself to give the baby into Otis's keeping. If only she had seen what happened. If he had been taken to Coram as had been planned, then a boy such as this could so easily be her grandson.

The visit was over. Mrs Milcote and Melissa stood apart from the family, who crowded round Thomas and the Coram boys, wishing them a safe journey and to hurry back soon, with Alexander.

'God speed, Thomas,' whispered Isobel, taking his hand. 'God speed and return as soon as possible. Bring him back to us.' Then she had gone and joined Melissa to link an arm through hers.

Six young boys clambered into the coach, while the grooms controlled the four chestnut horses, which Sir William had ordered to be harnessed so that they could return to London as quickly as possible. With bags and baggage stored, the driver took up the reins and Thomas clambered up next to him. Finally one last man, who had been scurrying round checking the provisions, examining the coach wheels, helping the boys up, now himself took up his position at the back of the coach with shotgun in hand, in case of attack by the many bands of vagabonds who roamed the highways. There was a final cheer. The six boys waved and yelled, 'Goodbye.' The coachman flicked the horses with his whip, and the coach lurched forward.

At that moment, the guard looked up, his face raised and clearly visible as the carriage pulled away. The crunch of hooves on the gravel and the voices yelling farewell almost drowned out a short fierce shriek.

'Meshak!'

The coach gathered speed down the long avenue, winding away, soon to be out of sight.

Mrs Milcote, who had been standing apart from the others at the top of the steps in front of the house, shrieked again. 'Meshak?' She stumbled and fell down the steps, picked herself up and ran as if she might try to catch up with the coach and leap aboard.

'That's Meshak Gardiner! Stop, oh stop! What happened to the child? For pity's sake, what happened to the child? Come back!'

The coach wound away down the avenue with Mrs Milcote stumbling and shrieking like a madwoman. As it passed through the gates, she came to an abrupt stop like a rabbit felled by a catapult. A terrible, long, despairing cry rang through the air. Then Mrs Milcote collapsed to her knees and sprawled face down, motionless.

* * *

'Why did that woman scream like that?' Aaron asked Meshak as the carriage turned out of the Ashbrook estate.

'I don't rightly know, my angel,' muttered Meshak, agitated.

'What did she mean when she asked what happened to the child. What child, Mish?'

'It's a mystery to me, my little love.'

Aaron frowned. 'Did you see? Did you see? That woman fell. Do you think she was hurt? Did she call your name? Shouldn't we go back?'

'No, not mine! She was just sorry to see us go, that's all. She probably tripped. Her daughter was there soon enough.'

'How do you know that was her daughter?'

'Enough of that, you brat! For pity's sake, will you shut that mouth of yours and stop your prattling.' Terror and anger charged through Meshak. He stared at his little angel and saw his face crumple with disbelief, for never ever in his life had Mish used a harsh word to him.

The boy recoiled as if he had been burnt and scrambled away like some poor animal to join Thomas and the other boys. Mish wanted to call him back, but he was overcome with confusion and fear. All he could see was Mrs Milcote. Before the coach had turned the corner, she had looked into his face and recognised him; even at that distance, their eyes had met and he was sure she knew the truth. Any moment now, they would come after them and take away his little angel.

Mish clutched the shotgun in his arms. Somehow, they must get away. He had saved his boy once before, so he would save him again. Aaron was his – his own angel; they could never be parted.

> '*They come by night as well as by day,*
> *To take your little child away.*
> *My little child is yet too young,*
> *To stay away from his mam.*
> *Whether he's old or whether he's young,*
> *We'll take him as he am.*'

Mish sang the song obsessively as the coach came on to the London Road and headed east for the capital. The weather was dry and the going good. They easily went through marsh and mire, covering the miles, but Meshak sat facing the rear, his eyes never leaving the road behind. The coachman reckoned they could get as far as Lechlade before resting the horses. Meshak willed it, and further too. Only when they were back in London would he feel safe again.

In childish revenge for Meshak's ill temper, Aaron stuck close to Thomas and the other boys when they stopped at the inn, and ignored Meshak. He tucked into his bowl of broth and gobbled up his bread. But Meshak didn't seem to notice. He saw to the horses and did not try to make amends. All the time, he checked the road to see if anyone had followed.

Two hours later, they were all aboard once more, heading for Wantage. Thomas hoped to get beyond Wantage to the Vale of the White Horse before they stopped for the night and, if the weather stayed fair, they could get to London by nightfall the next day. He was so keen to deliver the letter to Alexander. But by mid-afternoon the weather changed and the rain came hurtling down. Within the hour, it had turned the roads to rivers of mud.

Thomas and the boys squeezed themselves inside the coach, while Meshak endeavoured to cover their baggage with a sail cloth.

The horses slithered and slipped, the wheels ground in the ruts, and it was obvious that they could not go much further. They didn't want to risk losing a wheel, not out here in this god-forsaken wild place. The coach driver yelled to Meshak to get down and take the lead horse by the bridle, and walk with it until they reached some kind of shelter.

Half an hour later, as if by a miracle, they came across a small inn, The Cross Hands, just beyond a crossroads. The boys and Meshak could sleep in the barn, the coachman in the saloon by the fire and there was one bedchamber free for Thomas upstairs.

But first, they all crowded into the kitchen to stand, steaming, before a roaring fire.

It rained all night, and was still raining the next morning. Thomas gazed up at the sky. The clouds were shifting and patches of blue were visible to the south-west. From out of the stables, a man emerged, wrapped in a sealskin cloak, a leather hat pulled low over his head. He said he was Matthew Parks, dispatched by Sir William Ashbrook. He had arrived at nightfall last night, having ridden hard, even through the dreadful weather, to catch up with the Ashbrook coach. Seeing the unharnessed carriage in the stables, he had entered the inn.

Everyone looked up. What would bring a man riding hard through the wind and rain all the way from Ashbrook to catch up with them? 'Nothing is amiss at Ashbrook, I hope?' said the coachman.

'I'm looking for a Meshak Gardiner, one of your grooms, I think.'

The coachman looked bemused. 'This is one of my lads, Jacob Turner. My other one, Mish, he's somewhere. Seeing to the horses or the boys. I haven't yet seen him.'

Matthew Parks strode out of a back door which led directly into the stable yard. The barn was at the far end of the slimy yard running with mud and manure and animal droppings. Chickens scuttled round his feet and the dogs barked furiously as he strode up to the barn door and pulled it open. 'Mish? Come out!'

'Mish ain't here, sir,' came a chorus of boys' voices.

'We ain't seen 'im.'

'Not since we woke up.'

Five boys tumbled out into the drizzly yard and stood there, not knowing whether to tuck in their shirts or shield their faces from the rain. Thomas came out to see what was going on. 'Where's Aaron?' he asked, counting five boys.

'Dunno. He ain't here neither.'

'Probably with Mish.'

''E's always with Mish.'

Mish. Meshak. Thomas looked astounded. Could that be the man? Was Alexander right? He had never bothered to look into his face – or even noted the colour of his hair under the brown straggly wig he wore when on duty. But where were they? 'Why? Why do you want him? What has he done?'

'Can't truly say I know, sir,' said Matthew Parks. 'But Mrs Milcote wanted to tell him something. She ran after the coach as it pulled away. Reckon you didn't know that, or heard her shouting?'

Thomas shook his head.

'The lady then fell down dead, sir. Dead as dead can be. God rest her soul, but she had been calling for Meshak Gardiner.

Reckon he's your man, Mish. Sir William is concerned that this particular person should return with me to answer questions. He could be tried as an accomplice to murders for which his father, Otis Gardiner, was hanged.'

'Otis Gardiner!' Suddenly, Thomas felt as though he was in the middle of a tightly closing net. Alexander was sure he had seen Otis. Now Mrs Milcote had cried that she had seen Meshak. And Mrs Milcote was dead. He was overwhelmed with a great fear. Where was Meshak and where was Aaron?

Chapter Twenty-eight

☆

On the run

'Where are we going? Why do we have to go? Mr Ledbury will wonder where we are. Why can't we tell Mr Ledbury?'

As Mish urged Aaron deep into the woods, Aaron kept asking these questions.

'Because a man came,' answered Mish. 'He wanted to take you away. I saw him. I know. You don't want to leave Mish, do you? If he'd have got you, he would have taken you away from your Mish for ever.'

'What man, Mish? I never saw a man.'

'I did. He came late in the night.'

'In all that rain?'

'Yeah – in all that rain. Him and his horse, looking like they'd been pulled out of the river, they did. So wet they wouldn't let him indoors, but gave him the other barn with cows.'

'But how did you know he wanted me?'

' 'Cos he was an Ashbrook man, little angel. I heard him ask if we were the ones who had come from Ashbrook. He mentioned my name. And then I knew. He had come for you.'

'Why do you think they want me, if it's you he asked for?' That was the main question to which Aaron wanted an answer, but on getting no clear response hadn't the energy to ask again – or perhaps he felt Mish didn't know. At any rate, he just thought it but didn't ask it any more, as Mish dragged him on and on through the dripping undergrowth and drenched grass and over flooded streams.

Aaron had always trusted Mish and never feared him, so though he didn't understand why they were running away, he tried to keep up to the best of his ability.

They seemed to have been in the forest for hours. They drank water at odd streams which they crossed and they chewed on wild garlic leaves to stave off the hunger but Mish could see that Aaron was done in, so he yanked the boy up on to his shoulders and kept going.

'I'm hungry, Mish,' wailed Aaron, resting his head on the top of Mish's head.

'Yes, my angel. Soon, soon, I'll get you food, don't you fret.'

Deep into the forest, they saw and smelt smoke. Must be a dwelling nearby. Mish plonked Aaron down back on his feet and they followed a fork in the track, not speaking, and always poised, ready to run. It was a rough and tumble dwelling, patched together, unwattled, with stones, planks and dried branches. Animal skins were spread over a tin roof and held down with stones and branches. A few hens and chickens clucked quietly in the grass and they could see a ramshackle lean-to, where stood a single cow, mournfully flapping her ears. Mish held up a hand and motioned to Aaron to stay out of sight. Then, tentatively, he sauntered forward, his eyes scanning the area for any sight of the owner. He peeped in through the open door. A fire was freshly lit, and a tin can of water boiled from a spit. He circled the hovel, but saw no one, so quickly he entered, put the jug under the cow and began to tug on her teats. Pure white milk spurted out. He opened his mouth and milked some straight down his throat then, feeling restored, filled up the rest of the jug and quickly returned to Aaron.

With something in their bellies, it gave them the strength to carry on through the forest.

'Where are we going, Mish?' asked Aaron, not for the first time.

'Back to London, my angel. Back to London.'

'How do you know the way?'

'Mish knows. Don't you worry.'

'Shall I go back to Mr Burney's house? It's where I'd like to go,' said Aaron anxiously.

'Maybe, maybe. We'll have to see.'

'Mr Burney is a good man, Mish. He wouldn't hurt me. Nor Mr Ashbrook . . . Funny he has the same name as the house . . . do you think he's from those parts?' pondered Aaron.

Mish grunted, but his mouth stayed clamped shut.

The sun was now dropping down into the west. Aaron was gripped again with hunger and fatigue. 'When are we going to be there?' he wailed. 'I'm hungry.'

'Last bit, my angel. Last bit. Mish knows.'

They were still deep in the forest so Aaron couldn't understand how this could be the 'last bit'! They were nowhere near London and, since the hovel, they hadn't seen another dwelling in the past two hours and not a single other human being. Ahead, the trees seemed as tall, the branches as spreading, the creepers as tangled, and the grass deep and as wet, for not much sun had penetrated throughout the day.

Aaron's head was down as he dragged along behind Mish, when Mish suddenly cried, 'Look, angel! Look!'

Aaron looked and blinked in disbelief. Something bright red slid silently by beyond the trees.

Mish laughed. He ran back to the boy and lifted him up on to his shoulders, and then trotted off with renewed energy. Now he saw a stretch of shining water, and another sail slid by. ''Tis the river, dear angel. 'Tis the river – just as I knew it would be. Goes all the way to London, angel. All the way to the city.'

Chapter Twenty-nine

☆

Everything is time

Melissa was dressed in black. Her rich auburn hair was gathered underneath a full black hat from which hung a black veil around her shoulders. She wore a modest woollen black jacket over a thin, high-necked muslin blouse and high-waisted, hooped black linen skirt, and she carried a black cloak on her arm ready to go outside.

It was the day of her mother's funeral. She wandered round the east wing of the house, where she and her mother had lived. She took a corridor which led away from her living quarters towards the schoolroom and nursery. It was a long time since she had taken that route.

At the end of a corridor, she glimpsed herself in the large oak-framed oval mirror. She drew closer, fascinated with her own image. 'Who am I? A mother without a child, a child without a mother.' She stared at her face, which was no longer a child's, but already bore the marks of anxiety, unhappiness and grief. Where was the joy? she asked herself. Would she ever again

experience the joy of that childhood before Alexander went away
– before, before?

Over her shoulder, she saw another face looking into the
mirror. Her heart jolted. She had thought herself alone. She
stared in confusion. It was the Coram boy – the boy who had sung
'The Silver Swan'. She turned, wondering what he was doing
here. But no, it wasn't a boy, at least not a living boy. It was a
painting. She was looking at the portrait of Alexander as a young
chorister at Gloucester Cathedral, wearing his choirboy's cassock.
She looked back into the mirror where his eyes seemed to stare
into her eyes. She remembered her mother screaming as she ran
after the coach. She had screamed Meshak's name – but – was it
that boy who had triggered such a reaction? The boy who looked
so much like Alexander?

'Melissa!'

Isobel came hurrying towards her. 'Melissa, dearest. It's time.'

Time. Everything is time. Past time. Time passing so fast
that she was hardly ever aware of a present. 'Time?' she asked in
a daze.

'The hearse is here. We are waiting for you to accompany the
coffin to the chapel.' Isobel put her arm round her friend. 'Sweet
Melissa. Do not despair. We are your family. We have always been
your family – but never more so than now. Will you come now?
With me?'

'Isobel.' Melissa held her friend back for a moment and turned her to the portrait. 'Look.'

'It is Alexander. Papa had the painting moved here from where it had hung in the ante-room. He couldn't bear to look at it.'

'Does the face remind you of anyone?' asked Melissa.

'I see no one, except our own Alexander,' replied Isobel softly. 'I'm sure he will come soon. Thomas will have delivered the letter by now, for sure. But if there was any other resemblance, it would only be of your own lost child, Alexander's own son. He would surely have looked like this boy in the painting.'

'Yes,' murmured Melissa. 'I thought so too.'

'Miss Isobel! Miss Melissa.' Mrs Lynch stood there, looking at them, her hands folded over her black skirt, her eyes glittering – like a snake – or so Melissa thought, as she stared back. Whatever power Mrs Lynch had had over Mrs Milcote was now dead along with her mother, but Melissa wondered if Mrs Lynch thought she could transfer that power to enthrall her? Did she wonder how much Mrs Milcote had told her daughter? The two of them looked deep into the other's eyes. Mrs Lynch's were narrowed and watchful, like a predator gathering itself to pounce. Melissa knew that her expression was defiant.

'Sir William and my lady await you. It is time.'

'We're coming, we're coming this instant.' Isobel took

Melissa's arm and walked her swiftly away, down the stairs to the front door.

The coffin stood on a trestle in the hall. It was covered in lilies. Sir William and Lady Ashbrook, hearing their voices, came out of the ante-room. Each embraced her.

'Have you prepared yourself, my dear?' asked Sir William kindly.

Melissa nodded. Then he waved a hand to the butler, which was the signal for the coffin carriers to be admitted. Six men, in tall black top hats entered and, three on each side, lifted the coffin on to their shoulders. They carried it out of the house to the two black horses with black plumes waiting patiently to pull the hearse on its carriage to the chapel.

It was a simple ceremony. Only members of the family and workers from the estate gathered as the congregation, and a row of orphans from the Ashbrook orphanage, the girls with black ribbons in their hair and the boys with black armbands.

The choir sang, 'The Lord is my Shepherd, I shall not want, He taketh me down to the green pastures, he leadeth me beside the still waters . . .' and Melissa sobbed quietly and remembered how, only a few days ago, she and Isobel had knelt in the same chapel and prayed for her lost baby. When the service was over, they filed into the graveyard and stood before the open grave. Melissa tossed her lilies on to the lowered coffin and cried, 'Oh, Mama, forgive me. It was all my fault.'

In the sunlight, slanting down through the yew trees and the huge old chestnut, a figure stood watching. He hadn't changed so much that they didn't recognise him even after eight years. Isobel saw him first. He was taller, broader; his face had lost its boy's sheen and was more chiselled, shadowed. She didn't cry out but just walked swiftly over to him and, throwing her arms round his neck, wept on his shoulder.

This was not the homecoming Sir William had dreamt of. Not like the father who prepared the feast to welcome home his prodigal son. Instead, it was as if fate had swept him back to their door. But the joy was as great. Nothing mattered. The past meant nothing. Alexander was back.

The next day, it was in the play cottage they gathered, Alexander, Isobel and Melissa. Sombre in their black clothes; sombre with the thought of what they must talk about. Mrs Milcote's death had released the truth. But there was not just one truth, because there was not one person there who knew the whole of it. So each told what they knew.

Melissa had had a baby, Alexander's baby. Tabitha had delivered the baby, and very soon after had been dismissed by Mrs Lynch. Mrs Lynch and Mrs Milcote had taken the baby from the cottage that night, telling Melissa and Isobel that the baby was dead, though it was alive. The night before she died, Mrs

Milcote told Melissa that her baby had been alive when she gave it to Mrs Lynch. She had told her a lie for the best. She had thought Melissa would forget the child quicker if she believed it to be dead. Mrs Lynch had handed the baby to Otis Gardiner, who had been given a goodly sum of money to take it to the Coram Hospital.

'Meshak was there,' whispered Melissa. 'My mother said Meshak was there, waiting outside the cottage that night.'

Barely a week later, the gamekeeper on the Ashbrook estate had come across a bloodied shawl and then discovered some graves in the woods in which a number of infants were buried. The shawl was the one Melissa's baby had been wrapped in, so Mrs Milcote and Mrs Lynch had assumed he was dead too.

'My mother told me that Mrs Lynch used her power over her to coerce money out of her – even after they both believed the baby was dead, even after Otis was arrested, tried and executed. She threatened to tell Sir William if she did not continue paying. My mother was certain that we would have both been thrown out of Ashbrook into destitution if Sir William had found out about the baby.'

'Meshak should have stood trial too along with Otis,' said Alexander, 'but he disappeared and was never found. Now Meshak has disappeared again and has abducted a Coram boy called Aaron Dangerfield. Thomas is looking for them at this moment.'

There was a long silence as everyone thought of the boy.

'We have one main question.' Alexander spoke softly and held Melissa's hand with the utmost tenderness. He knew he must speak out loud the one question everyone was asking. 'If Otis isn't dead and is now living as Mr Philip Gaddarn, and if the man who Mrs Milcote saw on the coach was Meshak, then . . .' and this was the most difficult thing to put into words . . . 'is it possible that . . .' Alexander paused. 'God knows, there has already been too much distress. Isn't this too fantastical?'

'Say it,' said Isobel.

'Say it, Alex,' Melissa said calmly.

Alexander looked into Melissa's eyes. 'Is the Coram boy, Aaron Dangerfield, our son?'

Chapter Thirty

☆

'Save him, sir!'

Mr Philip Gaddarn prowled among his guests like a prize Bengal tiger. He should have been pleased with himself. He had just made another fortune speculating in the South Seas, and one of his clippers had come in from India laden with spices, materials and many precious stones, which would fetch him huge sums among the jewellery houses of London.

Furthermore, he was expecting a batch of Coram girls, ostensibly for positions with good families in New England and Virginia, but who were in fact destined for the harems of North Africa and Arabia. A ship was leaving for Marseilles in two days.

But for the moment, all he could think of was Meshak. Since the boy had run away from him, he had hoped he was either dead or somewhere in the Midlands in obscurity – or even in the madhouse. He had tried to find him; asked along the drovers' roads; informed Mrs Peebles and Mrs Lynch if they should hear any news of him that he was to be told, though what he would have done, he wasn't sure. The higher he rose through society, the more he was convinced he would kill him rather than lose all he had achieved.

So it had been a shock to see him in the Coram chapel, clapping like an idiot after one of the boys had finished singing. Mr Gaddarn had suddenly felt a terrifying void open up under his feet. A dizzy surge of fear and fury had swept over him. His whole livelihood, position in society – indeed his life – suddenly seemed like some hideous joke. How could his future be in the hands of a simpleton, an idiot, a washed-up piece of useless humanity whom he should have disposed of at birth, but hadn't, for some strange reason he had never been able to understand in himself. He had sat through the rest of the concert till his heart, racing uncontrollably, had calmed down. He needed to think. With the greatest difficulty, he resisted his urge to interrogate one of the governors to find out how Meshak came to be there.

But after a day or two, on the pretext of negotiating for a further group of Coram girls ready for employment, he asked discreetly about the mad fellow who had caused such a rumpus.

'Oh, that's just Mish. A bit of a simpleton, and harmless,' explained one of the governers. 'It was he who brought the boy to Coram – we always assumed it was his son, though he never claimed him as such. But he dotes on the boy, so we must excuse his excess of enthusiasm, don't you think?'

'Mish?' queried Mr Gaddarn. 'Is that his name? Nothing else?'

'No. The lad was too simple to tell us more of himself. Just Mish.'

Mr Gaddarn returned to the hospital a few weeks later and wandered round the back and into the orchard as if he were on an inspection. He enquired after Mish.

'We ain't seen 'im a long while now. Did a runner with one of the boys. Angel, he called him.'

And that was all anyone knew. Mish and the boy 'angel', otherwise known as Aaron Dangerfield, had simply vanished on their way back from a visit to Gloucestershire.

Once again, Mr Gaddarn felt the ground heave under his feet, ready to crack open and swallow him up. He wanted to believe that Meshak was of no danger to him but it was unfinished business and, until he knew where he was, he felt threatened to the quick. He must get the lad back in his power or dispose of him.

He sent out spies to the city of Gloucester, to Mrs Peebles – if there was any gossip or innuendo, she would know about it. Of course, like everyone else, she thought he had been hung on the gallows years ago. So the spies were warned to be utterly discreet. In due course, they came back with the information that Mish had been with the party of Coram boys who had given a benefit concert on the Ashbrook estate, and that it had been on the way back to London that Mish had absconded with one of the boys. The Ashbrook family had been sufficiently concerned to send out a search party to help the Coram teacher, Thomas Ledbury, look for them, but no trace had been found of them. Mrs Lynch had disappeared mysteriously, as well.

Mr Gaddarn put a hand to his throat when he heard the name Ashbrook, remembering it was round his neck the noose should have been tightened, and not that of some poor wretched thief who had gone to the gallows in his place. Even then, the Otis Gardiner of those days had enough power to blackmail the local magistrate. How much more power did he have now as Mr Gaddarn? No, he persuaded himself. He shouldn't need to worry. How could a poor simpleton like Meshak be any threat to him?

He kicked Toby, his little black boy, his drawing-room pet. The child was asleep again. Perhaps it was time to get rid of him. He'd got tired of his mournful face. At least when he first came into the household, he knew how to smile and show his teeth and respond prettily to the ladies. But now, the child had got thin and surly, and seemed more intent on escaping notice than attracting it. There's nothing worse than a sulky servant. No, he would put him on the next slaver and be done with him. Coram boys had too high expectations. He had warned the governors many times not to give them too much education. They got above themselves. Here was proof. But those bleeding-heart benefactors seemed intent on giving those useless foundlings more and more.

His way had been best, and he knew many a parish thought the same, if only they weren't so hypocritical.

He gave Toby another kick. 'Get out there, boy, and earn your fine clothes,' he sneered.

Toby woke with a jerk. It was two in the morning by the clock in the hall. He had been up since dawn and was exhausted. Mr Gaddarn was right. Toby could no longer hide the loathing he felt for this household. But he felt hopeless and abandoned. Aaron hadn't come back as he had promised. It was a month now since he had seen him. One load of Coram children had already been shipped away into slavery. Toby was too frightened to tell anyone. Once, when he had accompanied Mrs Whittaker on a shopping expedition, he had caught sight of Timothy.

'Oi, please sir, it's me, Toby. Aaron's friend. Where is he? I badly needs to know. Tell him Toby needs him.'

'Aaron ain't here, boy. He's gone missing. No one knows where he is, poor devil.'

Then Mrs Whittaker had seen him and yelled to him to get over and help her.

'If he comes back, I'll say Toby was asking for him.'

'Thanks, sir,' cried Toby.

'Come here, my little black puppy!' Large, white hands, all powdered and ringed, grabbed him and he found himself plonked on to the lap of a large bosomy lady. She forced her fingers into his mouth and fed him a marshmallow. Toby was sure he would be sick. But Mr Gaddarn was watching, and he had no choice but to beam at her and show his white teeth.

A footman entered and caught Mr Gaddarn's eye at the far end of the salon. Such an action would have to mean some serious business, otherwise Mr Gaddarn was never to be called out of one of his parties. Mr Gaddarn made his way casually, nodding at his guests, kissing the fluttering fingers of his ladies, and reached his servant. Words were exchanged. Mr Gaddarn's face changed. Several expressions raced across his face: surprise, anxiety, fury. He turned on his heel and left the party.

The lady on whose lap Toby sat got bored with him and tipped him off. He slid away behind a screen and then, with swift movements, moved from behind the screen to behind a sofa to behind the keyboard, then out through the door to hide behind a tall chest in the hall. He was just in time to see a bedraggled Aaron, his hand held tightly by the strangest tallest, reddest, scruffiest fellow, who Toby hardly recognised as Mish!

'Aaron!' Toby had to stifle his cry by stuffing a fist into his mouth, for suddenly there was Mr Gaddarn and a servant, hustling them away through the entrance hall to the back of the house.

'Da! Da!' spluttered Mish.

'Get that lunatic out of here!' Mr Gaddarn's voice was deadly. 'Put him in the map room – the boy too. Lock the door and guard it. I'll see to you when my guests have gone. But don't move a muscle or my man will kill you.' The words weren't shouted in anger, but hissed almost under his breath with icy coldness. Then Mr Gaddarn swept back to the drawing-room. The perfect host once more, he adjusted his wig, licked a finger across his eyebrows, acquired a smile and re-entered the room.

The map room. Aaron and Mish were in the map room. Toby felt a shudder of fear. Up until now, he had felt too weak from illness, too scared, too dumbstruck to have any idea who he could tell about Mr Gaddarn. But now that his best, most beloved friend, Aaron, was locked up there with dear old Mish, he knew he must act.

He was wide awake now. He went back into the drawing-room and, picking up a silver platter, began circulating among the guests, simpering up to the fine, fan-fluttering ladies. If Mr Gaddarn could pretend, so could he.

Already most of the guests had eaten and drunk too much. Some had hailed their carriages or ordered their sedans to carry them home. Others were already unconscious, sprawled across the sofas and chairs to sleep off their excess till morning. But though Mr Gaddarn constantly had a goblet of wine in his hand, Toby knew he hardly touched it, and that his master was deadly sober. Mr Gaddarn moved among his guests, his eyes hooded and watchful, like a swordsman having to watch his front and his back.

When, at last, everyone was too tired or drunk to notice him, Toby slipped away as if to go to his bed, down in the kitchen. The fire in the grate flickered low. Mrs Whittaker was in her parlour, the housemaids and menservants were up in their garret rooms, Miss Tangley was fast asleep in front of the cooking range, her arms clasped round the cat.

Toby's bed mat was on the other side of the range, but he didn't go to it. Lighting a taper, he went through the kitchen into the pantry. There was a door in the pantry which led down some steps to a wine cellar. But Toby knew there was a hatch in the cellar which opened to the street above, through which deliveries of wine could be made. He held up the taper.

It was a heavy wooden hatch door. He stuck the taper in an empty bottle. He knew he would need both hands to slide the bolt open. Sure enough, his first try didn't even budge it. He tried again, wriggling the bolt up and down. With every movement, it grated noisily. Anyone might hear; Miss Tangley or the nightwatchman and his dog. Dear Lord, if he was caught, it would be the end of him. His fingers shook with terror. But he must persevere – whatever the cost. So he wriggled the bolt up and down, up and down, at the same time forcing with all his strength.

Wham! The bolt suddenly shot back.

Toby was sure the whole house must have heard, the whole city. He expected the dogs to start barking and the night-watchman to come running. He paused, his heart beating fit to burst. Then without waiting further, he pushed open the hatch, heaved himself out, closed it again, and set off running through the city towards St Martin's Lane and the home of Mr Charles Burney.

Dawn was breaking when he arrived at Mr Burney's door. The housemaid was already up, pumping water. She was alarmed when Toby came staggering towards her, panting and coughing with the exertion. 'Mr Burney!' He gasped. 'I must see Mr Burney. It's about Aaron.'

Hearing the name Aaron was sufficient. She dropped her pails and went in running, calling for Mrs Mount, the house-keeper.

Within minutes Toby found himself in the music room standing before not just Mr Burney in dressing-gown and night cap, but Thomas Ledbury too.

'Why, Toby!' Thomas strode forward and put a kindly arm on the boy's shoulder.

It was the first kind act he had received since leaving Coram, and he collapsed at his feet, weeping. 'Save 'im, sir, save Aaron – and Mish. 'E's got 'em, sir. He'll send 'em to be slaves just like all the others.'

Chapter Thirty-one

☆

The river flows to
the sea

'Don't be dead, Mish, not now, please don't be dead,' begged Aaron, kneeling beside a prostrate Mish. Mish lay flat on his back with eyes wide open. By the light of one candle, as he stared into those unseeing eyes, Aaron seemed to see all kinds of reflections flitting across his liquid eyeballs: shapes with fluttering wings and outstretched hands and fingers trailing like forest creepers.

They had been on the move for weeks, travelling on all kinds of barges and boats, heading down river for London. And when no vessel would take them by water, they moved back to the road, cadging lifts from passing tinkers or just simply walking, walking, walking.

They had lived rough and wild, trapping hares or rabbits for food, stealing the odd chicken, and milking a cow whenever they could avoid the farm dogs and get close enough. But there had been days when their stomachs had been empty, days when Aaron was so weak that Mish had had to carry him.

At first when Aaron had said, 'Where are we going, Mish?' Mish had replied vaguely, 'Somewhere safe, little angel. Somewhere where they won't take you away. You wouldn't want that, would you, my angel?'

'No Mish, no!' Aaron reassured him. 'You and me will always be together.'

But as they got nearer and nearer to London, Mish began to say, 'I have a da, little angel.'

'A father, Mish? You never told me,' Aaron exclaimed with surprise. 'You're making it up.'

'No, angel. As truthful as this is my own hand, and if I cut it, as this be my own blood, I have a da. And your da is meant to protect you, isn't he, angel? Just as I protect you?'

'Then shall us go to him, Mish? I'm so tired, and I ain't feeling too good.'

'Yes, angel. We shall go to my da.'

And so they did. But Aaron thought he should have realised Mish had made it all up. There they were, standing before one of the grandest houses in London – the house where Toby worked. Poor Mish, his mind all in a muddle. How could he think that Mr Philip Gaddarn was his father just because Toby lived there?

'Not here, Mish,' Aaron had pleaded. 'This is the house of Mr Gaddarn, don't go here.'

'This is where he lives, angel, you'll see.'

A powerful manservant grabbed Mish as they approached the door. But Mish had suddenly straightened up to his full giant height. 'I've a message for your master,' he said. 'Tell him, Meshak is here.'

Another manservant was summoned and sent into the salon to deliver the message. After a while, Mr Gaddarn appeared in the doorway. It only needed a glance to know. He was stunned. He and a manservant marched Mish and Aaron down an alley to the servants' entrance. They were taken into the house and led to a room at the back. They were pushed in and the heavy oak door was shut behind them. Aaron heard the key turned in the lock. They were prisoners.

One single candle cast a shadowy yellow light across the room. Aaron looked around him with amazement. They were not in a cellar, but some library. How strange that they should be locked up in so fine a room, with carpets and velvet chairs; with cabinets, and bookcases and fine oak-panelled walls. And in the corner a huge globe which glistened in its own dark universe.

They listened and waited. An hour passed, then two, but no one came to them.

Meshak lay on the floor. He lay on his back like a felled giant, his body stretched across the room. For a while his eyes travelled round the ornamental ceiling: the unlit chandelier which hung like a crown above his head, and the rows of maps hanging from the picture rail, maps of routes across Europe, Africa and Asia. He began to drift, leaving his great clumsy body spread-eagled there and rising, rising through the ceiling, up, up into the night sky. The city glimmered like a great dragon beneath him. He thought he heard Aaron call to him.

'Are you leaving me, Mish? Don't leave me!'

But Mish's eyes rolled up into his skull, leaving only the whites showing.

Aaron curled up into the velvet chair, trying to understand. Questions churned round his brain. Why had Mish brought them here? Mr Gaddarn? Toby? He put his ear to the door, but heard no sound. Where was Toby? He returned to the chair. From an inside pocket, he pulled out the silver locket which had come with him to the Coram Hospital. He opened it up and gazed at two locks of hair. One which had always been inside the locket – his mother's hair, they said – and the other which he had found lying mysteriously on his pillow at Ashbrook House and which looked as if it came from the same head. He wondered at them both, and smoothed his little finger over the shining hair, as if by doing so, he soothed the terror in his heart.

The candle smouldered. Aaron closed the locket and

returned it to his pocket. Feeling pacified a little, he dozed off.

'Angel, I hear the sea.'

'Good, you're awake!' cried Aaron, waking up too. 'Don't go dead again, will you? I'm always scared when you go dead, 'cos I think you'll never come back.'

'Why do I hear the sea, angel? I hear the water lapping and the gulls crying.'

'You're still dreaming, Mish. There ain't no sea.'

'I'm scared of sea.'

'Don't be scared, Mish. We're in a house – not a boat no more.'

'You listen. Listen.' Mish pulled Aaron down on the floor beside him and pressed his ear down.

'Why, Mish! I do believe you are right,' cried Aaron.

It was true. He too could hear water lapping, and the faint sounds of screeching gulls. He got to his knees and looked around the room. Then he realised with a deep fear, this was the room Toby had told him about. The room with a tunnel which led to the docks and the ships. The room through which Mr Gaddarn sent children into slavery.

The last of the candle spluttered down into the wax. They had been in the room for hours now. Surely it was daylight. He went behind the wooden screen to the window, but the shutters were tightly locked together so that not one speck of light could enter, and as soon as he realised it, the candle went out.

Now it was Aaron who felt dead. In pitch darkness, he stumbled across the room to Mish and lay down beside him. 'I reckon I'm dead along with you, Mish,' he mumbled, taking Mish's big raw hand in his. 'I reckon we're both dead.'

Aaron drifted in and out of dreams. Hand in hand, he and Mish were flying out across the land. Forests and rivers crawled beneath them and, above them, the stars whirled in a blizzard of sparkling shafts of light, white feathers and angels' wings, and the treble voices of cherubs and choristers sang silver, piercing, pure sounds with harp and trumpets, cymbals and drum.

Then there came, falling through the sky, plunging, hurtling, a dark figure, like Satan being cast out of heaven. His vast shape gobbled up the light and obliterated the land beneath, and his howls of rage and fury deafened the heavenly singing.

The door opened. A yellow light illumined the room. Aaron opened his eyes. The door closed again, but only after it had admitted the devil himself, who loomed over them. 'Get up!' The voice was deadly.

Aaron rolled over on to his knees, still clutching Mish's hand. He stared up at Mr Philip Gaddarn. The wavering light hollowed out his face and eyes, stripping it down to the bone so that it was like looking into a skull. Mr Gaddarn lashed out with his boot and kicked Mish in the head. Mish let out a long whistling breath.

'Mish, Mish!' Aaron rolled across his chest and held his face. 'Mish, wake up.'

Mish opened his eyes. 'Angel?'

Another kick brought him struggling to his feet. 'Da, is it you, Da?'

'I'm not your da,' said Mr Gaddarn. His voice was low and deadly.

But Mish didn't hear him. He crawled over and clasped Mr Gaddarn's boots. 'Forgive me, Da, for running away. I had to. You see, I couldn't kill my angel's child. So I took him, see. Took him to Coram like they wanted. I didn't tell you, because I thought you'd take him away from me. And then when I seed you come to Coram – such a fine gentleman in your coach and horses – I hid away from you so you wouldn't find out about my angel's child. I'm sorry, Da. Sorry, sorry, sorry. But you'll help us now, won't you? You being such a fine gentleman and all. They know, you see. They know, and they'll come and take him.'

'Who knows?' Mr Gaddarn's voice was chill as ice.

'Them at Ashbrook. We was all taken there, see, to sing and the like. And little angel, he's so like his da, and they recognised him, so I ran away again.'

Aaron slowly released Mish's hand. What was he saying? His brain seemed to break up in a maelstrom of thoughts and questions and fears and confusion.

'Get up,' said Mr Gaddarn.

Mish got to his feet. He turned and held out his hand to Aaron. Aaron took it again, standing on wobbly legs. He felt dizzy. They hadn't had food or drink for hours.

Mr Gaddarn set down the candle and went to a far corner of the room. He shifted a table away from the wall and rapped one of the panels. The panels parted to reveal a passage. Then he whirled round, gripped Mish by the scruff of the neck and thrust him into it, pushing Aaron in after him.

There was a strange, musty, dank smell and the sounds of slurping and lapping. They went into another inner room, which smelt of humans in distress. Mr Gaddarn opened another door, and they found themselves staring into what seemed like oblivion, had not Mr Gaddarn's candle reflected on water. There was a boat moored. 'Get in,' he ordered.

The boat tipped violently as Mish put his weight into it, first one foot then the other. Aaron came after, clambering over the wooden seats to be close to Mish. Mr Gaddarn then took up position in the stern, holding up a flare, while his man undid a rope, got into the boat and took up a pair of oars.

It was a dark, low tunnel. They often had to bow their heads right down. Dark-green evil-smelling slime and moss clung to the bricked tunnel roof, and rats scuttled and swam all around, their high-pitched squeaks echoing eerily. After a short time, a bright pinprick of light came into view, and grew larger as the boat got closer and closer to the end of the tunnel. Then suddenly they were out with the wheeling gulls and the hubbub of the docks, the schooners and ketches and sloops and barges, all nudging and edging around each other. They rowed to the end of one of the docks, right under the prow of a huge sailing ship. Aaron saw the name painted beneath its soaring figurehead: the *Lucky Nancy*. Little boys and men swarmed all over it and up and down the rigging as they prepared it for the long voyage across the Atlantic to America. The tide was up and they would set sail any moment now.

Meshak and Aaron were shoved out of the boat on to the pier, ducking their heads as great sacks and crates of goods swung across from the docks on to the ship. A steady line of slaves, with neck irons and leg irons and all shackled to a long chain held by an overseer, trooped miserably up a gangplank on to the ship. Mr Gaddarn hailed the master.

'Buckley! I have two more for you. Can I send them on board?'

'Don't want to go to sea,' Meshak began to stammer. 'Don't like the sea, Da. Can't us stay with you? Don't like the sea.'

'Shut up,' snarled Mr Gaddarn.

'Where are we going?' Aaron too began to panic. 'You're not sending me to sea, are you? I'm not going,' and he tried to make a break for it, but Mr Gaddarn caught his arm, swung him round and slung him into a pile of sacks.

'You just stay there if you want to keep a hide on your back!' And he looked at him with such loathing, his fists clenched and his face bursting red with anger, that Aaron thought he would just crush him like an insect.

'Don't you hurt my angel!' protested Mish, rushing forward. But in response to a nod of his head, Mr Gaddarn's man got out a sword and held it at Mish's chest, and then with a mighty shove sent him down on to the sacks on top of Aaron. 'Wait there!' he commanded. And the man with the sword stood over them both, with its point aimed, ready to strike whoever attempted to move.

'Aaron, Aaron!' A high, piercing voice rang out above the scream of the gulls. 'Aaron, are you here?'

Aaron recognised Toby's voice. Mr Gaddarn and his man didn't respond, as they had not heard the boy called by name. Then suddenly there was Toby, hurtling down the quayside, followed by Alexander and Thomas.

The burst of joy Aaron felt at seeing Toby gave way to horror, as Mr Gaddarn swung round in a fury, drawing his sword and motioning to his man to be prepared to fight.

Toby went rashly on, running straight over to his friend. But Alexander and Thomas stopped. They looked around, realising that they were in enemy territory. These were Mr Gaddarn's kind: slavers and smugglers; men and boys who had been brutalised by a life at sea, by murder and piracy, and who would as easily kill for a jacket off a man's back as a pouch full of gold coins.

Captain Buckley, watching from the deck, clicked his fingers and already a number of sailors came sliding down the ropes, landing on the dock. 'Go on, get 'em, get 'em, fine bloody gentlemen,' they chanted.

Alexander and Thomas drew their swords and stood back to back as they were encircled. It was obvious that they were out-numbered and sure of defeat. Aaron saw Alexander looking at him. If looks alone were weapons, Alexander would have defeated all the demons of the world. If looks alone were words, he would have said, 'I am your father. Forgive me for what has happened to you.'

With his eyes still on Aaron, Alexander yelled, 'We know who you are, Mr Philip Gaddarn, or should I say, Otis Gardiner? Even if you kill us here, you're done for. Exposed. Everyone in London knows now who you are and what you've done. So why don't you hand over the boys? If you let them free, I'll speak in your defence. It might mean transportation rather than the gallows – which is what you deserve – but let the boys go.'

Meshak got to his feet. All he could see was Alexander Ashbrook, and all he could think of was that Alexander was going to take his angel away. 'Oh no, no, no!' he bellowed like a madman. He grabbed Aaron and held him tightly.

'That's my son, you have there!' pleaded Alexander. 'In the name of God, let him go.'

A gentleman you were born, a gentleman you are and a gentleman you will be.

Aaron heard Mother Catbrain's words echoing in his head.

'He's not your son, he's my angel,' howled Meshak. 'Mine!'

Alexander took a step forward, his sword still at the ready. Meshak, with Aaron still tightly gripped under one arm and Toby clinging like a limpet to his coat-tails, charged through Mr Gaddarn's men and lunged at him. With one swinging blow across the head with his giant hand, he knocked Alexander unconscious to the ground.

'No, Mish, no!' Aaron's screams ripped through the air; the sails quivered, the seagulls added to his screams as he struggled desperately in Mish's arms. 'Not him, Mish. Not my father. Not Mr Ashbrook!'

At the sound of that name, Mr Gaddarn lifted his sword in the most calculating and pitiless manner. So this was Alexander Ashbrook, the one who could destroy everything. He lunged. As the sword came down, Thomas threw himself over his friend. Without even a cry, he took the brunt of the murderous thrust.

Aaron gave a howl of despair.

Now Otis Gardiner faced Meshak. 'My son!' he snarled. He was filled with a deep, raw resentment. This blithering simpleton, with one brat clutched to his chest and that wretched black pup, Toby, hanging on to his coat, he should kill him right now. Meshak had always held him back. Look what he had achieved in the seven years without him. Ever since he had been born, the boy had been a burden. This idiot son threatened his very existence and all the fortune and status he had achieved.

Kill him and be done, he's barely human anyway, a voice goaded inside him. Once again, Otis lifted his sword. He stared into those silly, wide, blue eyes, bubbling with tears like the big booby he had always been.

'Don't hurt my angel, please, Da!' blubbed Meshak.

'Take them, Buckley. Take them away!' Otis Gardiner swung his sword aside. 'Get them out of my sight!' he roared like a madman to the captain of the *Lucky Nancy*. 'Take this one to America,' he pointed at Meshak, 'but do what you like with the other two. Sell them or throw them overboard, I don't care. Just see those brats never come back to these shores.'

The anchor was being raised. Six men rushed at them with nets and ropes and, one by one, each was overpowered like a wild animal. Meshak would have fought them to the death, but Aaron shuddered in his arms. With all the tenderness of a mother, he stroked the boy's head and murmured over him. Quietly, like a resigned beast accepting defeat, Meshak allowed himself to be herded up the plank with Aaron hanging like an unstrung puppet over one shoulder and Toby slung under his arm.

How quickly the dock emptied. Philip Gaddarn vanished just as Otis Gardiner had. No one so much as paused near the bodies of the two young men, whose life blood flooded out across the flagstones.

The bosun's whistle pierced shrilly and the brass bell on the mast head clanged incessantly. 'Away, away! All aboard!' they shouted. With its anchor loosed, the ship took the current. The wind blew into the sails of the *Lucky Nancy* and soon she was moving down river to the open sea.

They sat in the darkness of the hold where they had been thrown.

'I'm afraid of the sea, little angel,' moaned Mish.

They heard the slash of the whips, the clank of chains but, worst of all, the long, low, endless moaning, like a wind which never ceased, rippling up and down the ship, and up and down, up and down; a moan from three hundred slaves, lying crammed, side by side, some barely living, some dreaming, some dying; a moan that would go on and on with the pitching and creaking of the ship.

Toby sat rigid, his arms round his knees, listening, as if the whole of his kinsmen, the whole of Africa, cried out.

It was as though they had been forgotten or didn't exist; nobody cared.

They sat down there in the hold, unchained, unguarded. After all, why should anyone bother? They were almost out of the Thames estuary now and into the ocean.

'I'm afraid of the sea,' Mish was muttering over and over.

Aaron didn't reply. He didn't speak. Couldn't speak. Not while he felt the kind of pain which those slaves must feel, ripped from their kin and country, being carried further and further away from everything they knew. And now he was being taken from his father. Alexander Ashbrook was his father.

'Alexander Ashbrook is my father.' He repeated it over and over again.

Only later did the other thoughts creep into his mind. Why hadn't Mish told him he had a father and a mother? A living mother, living now: the one person he hadn't dared to dream of because he was sure she was dead. But Meshak had now admitted she was alive, though he refused to say who she was or where. The pain of the knowledge, the excitement of knowing, tore at his guts, pitching his emotions like the waves of the sea. Now in this moment of discovery, his father might be dying, even dead. The sight of Alexander lying on the quay with Thomas sprawled like a shield across his chest was branded on his mind.

'I'm afraid of the sea,' Mish said again.

'Yes, Mish.' Aaron's voice was hard.

'I only did it 'cos I love you, my angel.'

'Yes, Mish.'

'You do forgive me, don't you, angel?' Mish pleaded.

Aaron hesitated. He was saved from answering by Toby yelling excitedly. 'I can see light. Look!' They saw slivers of light through the hatch above them. Toby crawled across to Aaron. 'We can climb the sacks.' And he set off climbing them.

Aaron followed. He was weak with hunger and fatigue, but he began to crawl after Toby.

'Don't leave me, little angel,' begged Mish, reaching for Aaron. But Aaron pulled away and continued his climb, following Toby, scrambling and gasping over the sacks, boxes and crates, higher and higher still.

'Where are you going?' Mish got to his feet, swaying and stumbling as he tried to follow.

Toby reached the top and stretched. He could almost reach the opening with his fingers. Fighting for every last bit of strength, Aaron reached him. Toby climbed on Aaron's shoulders and pushed. The hatch opened. He heaved himself out and then helped Aaron.

'I'm afraid of the sea, little angel,' Mish's voice repeated, over and over in the darkness below.

'You stay there, Mish,' Toby reassured him. 'You'll be safe there.'

Mish looked up and saw his beloved boy poised in the square of light above his head. 'Come back, angel,' he whispered. But it was his last sight of Aaron before the hatch came down and plunged Meshak into hell.

The boys crept to the side of the ship and peered over the edge. They could still see the low, marshy land and, all around them, little boats bobbed; fishing-boats and trading boats hung on to the tails of the west wind as they passed the Isle of Sheppey and headed for the mouth of the estuary and the North Sea beyond. A fishing smack was close enough for them to see the men assembling their nets, ready to cast overboard. The coast was fading through the mist.

'We are crossing the ocean of endless darkness,' whispered Toby. 'They'll sell us as slaves.'

Voices were shouting at them. A sailor on the yardarm had spotted them. More sailors came lurching towards them along the deck. They had chains and neck clamps in their hands. Toby began to shiver with dread. 'They'll put me in chains; they'll make me a slave. No, no! I won't not never be a slave, Aaron. Not never,' and before Aaron could stop him, Toby had climbed on to the ship's rail. Below him, the sea heaved and tossed, green and white.

'No, Toby. No!' cried Aaron, trying to hold him back, but suddenly the sailors were on to them, jeering and shouting.

'He don't want to be a slave, eh, lads!' roared one.

'You don't have to be,' laughed another, and simply swiped him off the side.

Aaron stared in horror as Toby's body plummeted down to the green, green ocean. It hit the surface with barely a splash and disappeared.

Aaron didn't think or cry out or look about him as a sailor's hand reached out to grab him; he just tipped himself over the side.

'Angel! Angel! My child! Come back to me!'

The cry mingled with the screech of gulls.

The fishermen looked up from their nets, then quickly went for their oars.

Chapter Thirty-two

☆

The crying wood

A low stone wall bordered the chapel graveyard. Three sad young people, dressed in mourning, stopped before one grave. A newly sculpted angel knelt at prayer, with clasped stone hands and eyes raised to heaven. The inscription read:

> Here lies Margaret Milcote
> widow of Henry Robert Milcote
> 1712–1751
>
> Fortune gave her a precious daughter,
> But life's troubles were too much.
> Burdened down she closed her eyes,
> And left her child for Paradise.

The 'precious daughter', Melissa, went forward with her husband, Alexander, their hands clasped. He still moved slowly from his injuries. He kissed her then released her hand, and she knelt down at the headstone and placed a small posy of flowers on the grave. No one spoke. Isobel went to the other side of the grave and also placed a posy.

After a while, Alexander turned to go. Melissa did not follow. He moved on through the deep grass to another grave, down by the far stone wall, beneath a small rowan tree. They let him go ahead to be by himself. He still found the pain unbearable. The inscription said it all:

> *Thomas Ledbury, 1730–1751*
> *Son of Frederick, a carpenter, deceased, and Jane, his wife.*
> *No bird sang sweeter, no friend was truer,*
> *no man was ever more missed.*
> *Rest in Peace.*

Should there be another grave? Ah, my son!

He followed the path through the woods, the path which led to the play cottage. Each step rippled with memory. Sometimes tinkling laughter rang out, as if the ghosts of their childhood still hung around, listening to another of Thomas's stories. When he felt brave enough, Alexander would enter Waterside and play the virginals. Here – here was where everything had been decided, everything that would happen. He heard his own unbroken voice singing, 'Remember me, remember me,' and he remembered

Aaron, and it sometimes seemed that he was his own son and that somehow they had fused into one person.

In his mind's eye, like an ever-recurring dream, he would visualise the birth of his son and stare at the spot where he had been handed over into the charge of Otis Gardiner. He would hear the juddering, shuddering cry of a doomed infant and feel Melissa's broken heart, and he would strike his head with horror, weeping uselessly, 'If only . . . if only . . .'

Today, he carried on quickly as if to escape from the crying voices mingling with the piercing trill of the skylark; past the cottage until the woods gave way to pastures. He leant on the stile and looked across to the Ashbrook orphanage. His eyes followed the fields hazy with barley; across the meadow where slender horses cast long-legged shadows as they moved, sleek and slow, cropping at the sweet grass. He gazed tenderly on his mother, Lady Ashbrook, shepherding her orphans, who clustered round her, clutching her skirts as if she were their own mother. Thank God for her, thank God for Captain Coram, who had saved so many little children. Yet just to see them brought a shudder too, for the shadow of Otis Gardiner still lingered and encircled the world like a menacing whirlwind whose terror had never been harnessed and who had never been caught to face justice.

A tinker's dog scampered and barked. He heard the creak of

wooden wheels grind to a stop and boys' voices drifting up from the track beyond the trees.

'Thanks for the ride, mister!'

Then an old voice chivvied his weary nag onwards. 'Oi up, Nell!' and the creaking wagon continued on its way.

Alexander heard a panting and a whistling of breath sucked up between teeth. He caught sight of caps and clothes, of hands and bare feet climbing through the long grasses. The sounds came nearer and nearer. He heard low voices, young voices, gasping and mumbling.

Two boys emerged from the undergrowth and came to the stile. One white. One black.

Alexander's heart stopped beating. Everything ceased; even the birds in their flight seemed suddenly suspended. The children of the crying woods faded away.

One boy, the white boy, came forward slowly and stood before him.

'Mr Ashbrook,' said Aaron. 'I think I'm your son.'

Weep no more my own dear darling
Take your baby on your knee;
Weep no more for a gallant sailor
He'll come home and be with thee.

Epilogue

He wasn't really surprised the first time he saw a child. It was not one of the local children, not a living child, but one of them – one of those poor souls – a child of the woods, green complexioned, as the grey-green bark of the trees.

At first it had stared at him like a wild animal, its startled eyes round and liquid gold; its hair like the brambles from which it had emerged. Unprepared and horrified, he had backed away after that first encounter and fled, not going back for weeks and weeks. But then he was overwhelmed by a compulsion to return, and he began to see others. Some were old enough to walk; most were newborn babies, unchristened, condemned to purgatory; cradled in the mossy earth, shaped into the angles of twigs and branches, moulded into the curves, protuberances and twisting torsos of stubby trees.

'Why didn't you save me?' accused a child with silent gaze.

'I wish I had,' wept the old man. 'I saved some of you, but I couldn't save you all – not that night – not on my own. Please forgive me.'

Sometimes he felt as if they did forgive him. He felt their cold lips brushing his cheek with chill kisses. But other times, when they wound their thin little arms round his neck, he felt they would smother him and choke him to death in their despair.

With nothing much else to do, he had taken to walking five or six miles a day, leaving his earth-floored, rough, stone cottage on the edge of the village, and climbing up and up to the high fields at the top of the escarpment, from where he could see the drovers' road winding out of Gloucester to meet the Cotswold Way.

He used to vary his route, keeping to the tracks which took him to neighbouring villages or farmsteads, where he could get a sip of ale with the locals. Drooling simpleton that he was, they tolerated him and took many of his stories for senile fantasies. There were not many people left from the past who knew what had happened to him and could believe him when he told them about life in the Americas, working on sugar and cotton plantations, and sailing on the slave ships. Not many of them had ever been much beyond Gloucester, let alone over the ocean – so even if the stories were made up, they were interesting enough to earn him a mug of ale.

He found himself returning obsessively to one particular place. Following a small off-shoot of the drovers' road, he stayed with it an hour or two until it dwindled into a rut – a wrinkle in the forehead of the hillside, just broad enough for a mule. It wriggled along a steep incline, briefly exposed to the sharp winds which thrust upwards from the plains below, then it escaped from sight into the copse. The wood was no more than scrub – wild and uncoppiced – choking with brambles, hazel and dog rose, and riven with badger setts and ancient molehills. It was fit for nothing except wild rabbits to dig burrows and their predators, the foxes, to scoop dens beneath tree-trunks or into overhanging banks.

He had his favourite spot. Favourite? No – again, it was a compulsion which made him go there. There had been a time when he had been able to push the terrible memories to the back of his mind, and he could just stand gazing through the cluster of ash trees, thin as harp strings, which swayed and sang as if plucked by invisible fingers. He could admire the blue haze of the Welsh hills, and the mighty sweep of the River Severn, bristling with vessels of every description. He could wonder at the city of Gloucester, rosy-bricked, honey-stoned and black and white half-timbered, clambering, clustering, genuflecting around the massive beige stone cathedral, which looked as if, rather than being built from the base up, it had been placed whole by some giant's hand from above. 'Ah, how beautiful!' he never failed to exclaim, always impressed by its powerful grace and beauty; how it never looked the same from one day to the next – one hour to the next – the way the shadows of clouds raced across its face; dull, bright, sun, rain, the endless variety of seasons.

In the far distance below, he could see a pedlar and his cart plodding slowly, ant-like, with four or five mules in tow, their saddlebags stuffed with pots and pans and tools and novelties to sell – not just in the city, but all round the district in the villages and isolated hamlets and big estates. For sure he would call in at Ashbrook, just as his father, Otis Gardiner, had done all those years ago – a pots man – only he hadn't just sold pots: Otis Gardiner had had another line of business in those days. Just as before, when he looked down at the mule train, he glimpsed a boy sitting at the back of the wagon, swinging his legs – just as he used to do.

But, increasingly, he no longer looked at the view. Increasingly, memories rushed in and thrust him back into the past with such clarity that he relived those events over and over again. Some of them took place in this wood, and he never did know when he would see the children, hear their thin voices or feel their icy fingers.

Locals called it the crying wood, because they said they often heard the sounds of infants crying. Parents tried to stop their children going there. They knew what had happened, albeit a long time ago. But eventually they stopped worrying, for no harm ever befell their living children. If all they heard was the sound of crying, then let that in itself be a warning not to go there. It succeeded, except in the blackberrying and hazelnut season, when the children would plunge in and fill their willow baskets.

But if he walked round a ridge to a promontory, he could see Ashbrook House. He often saw *them*. That's why he braved the crying wood. He called them his angels: Melissa and Aaron, and Toby. Thank God, thank God. He had found a way to come back; across that dreadful ocean of darkness. But he would have returned from the dead, just to see them again.

He was tired today. Fixing his eyes on the gardens below, he slowly sank to the ground beneath a tree and leant back against the trunk, still staring. With the image of his beloved angels imprinted in his brain, he tipped his head, his eyes turning upwards, up through the branches and twigs and the canopy of foliage through which he could see a dense blue sky. The blue darkened to black as his eyes rolled back into his head. The stars and planets swirled into motion. There was such a fluttering and scattering, such a swishing of wings and trailing feathers; and the air was filled with singing choirs and shooting stars; and there was his mother, with fingers silver-tipped, reaching out to clasp his hand.

'Can I be dead now?' he asked her. 'Is it time?'

'Yes,' she smiled. 'Yes, yes, yes. It is time.'

Love doth have a rose garland,
The lilies perform a dance,
They have been purified within;
They step ahead, forward advance,
At love's most high demand.

Love's splendour is, as I shall tell,
The lilies bend, they stand quite still,
Love wishes to rise high;
The lilies float in ecstasy,
Who may praise love enow?

Love doth stand, love doth go,
Love doth sing, love doth spring,
Love rests in those he loveth,
Love doth sleep, love doth wake,
How can one comprehend it?